Don't lose it again

Three friends, Daniel, Ruth and Arthur, have survived the Second World War and are determined, in their different ways, to play a part in preventing such a catastrophe from ever happening again.

Almost by accident Arthur wins a seat in Parliament in the 1945 General Election. To Daniel's great satisfaction the Army assigns him a job preparing for the peace-keeping rôle of the new United Nations Organization. Ruth, who was a teacher of German before the War, has an idea for a novel that will remind people of a different Germany that existed before the years of the Kaiser and Hitler.

Daniel and Ruth also have unfinished business from 1939, when they had postponed their plans to marry; and each is uncertain about whether to reveal a wartime secret to the other. Arthur is impatient to start a family with his Spanish refugee wife, Margarita.

However, as in the years before 1939, it is public events in distant places that determine how their private lives develop; and the action moves between London, New York, Switzerland and Paris in ways that they couldn't have predicted.

Don't lose it again

Derek Walker

Eileen

With all good wishes

Derek Walker

27.08.2014

ISBN 978-0-9561569-2-1

Typesetting and design by Christine Price

Published 2014 by Derek Walker,
Dorset Square, London NW1

Distribution at www.lulu.com

ABOUT THE AUTHOR

DEREK WALKER grew up in Northern Ireland and was educated at Portadown College. He graduated at the London School of Economics, majoring in International Relations, and since then he has continued to live in London. For ten years he worked as a journalist, latterly as Deputy Editor of the *British Weekly*. In 1966 he became Education Officer of the newly-formed Voluntary Committee on Overseas Aid and Development. When VCOAD was dissolved in 1977 he became Director of the Centre for World Development Education (later renamed Worldaware) which took over its educational work. For ten years he chaired the European Development Education Curriculum Network (EDECN). In 1997 he was appointed OBE. Since retiring from Worldaware he has published seven novels (see end pages).

CHAPTER ONE: 8TH May, 1945 - RUTH

The District Line train was full of people who were actually talking to each other in happy, excited voices when Ruth and Rebecca boarded it at Putney Bridge station. They managed to find enough space for their hands to clutch the central pole as the carriage jolted into motion.

"I can't remember when I last saw so many people travelling into town at this time of the day," said Ruth.

"Maybe, like us, they all waited at home to hear Mr Churchill on the wireless, and when that was over they set out to join in the celebrations," Rebecca observed.

"I hope they listened to what he said about this being just 'a brief period of rejoicing'. We've been given two days off, but after that it really is going to be back to – what did he call them? – 'toils and efforts that lie ahead'," said Ruth.

"Of course you are right about that, but we need to have the rejoicing, too. I think you English are not very good at that, but now is the time to do it and forget about everything else, just for a few hours."

Ruth looked at the unfamiliar smile on the usually serious face of her Jewish refugee friend and squeezed her arm. "You're absolutely right. If we can't be happy today we never will be; so let's enjoy it while we can. I hope we're going to be able to see Margarita when we get to Embankment. I asked her to wait for us just outside the Villiers Street entrance, but with so many people around it might not be easy for her; and she's not very tall."

"But I am, and I expect I'll be able to pick her out," said Rebecca. "It was very unselfish of her to volunteer to go into work this morning. She really seems to love her job."

"She does; but I wonder how much longer it's going to last, now," said Ruth. "I should think the BBC Monitoring Service will soon start cutting back on its Spanish language activities. They'll probably be spending all their resources on South-East Asia."

"Poor Margarita must have mixed feelings about today's celebrations," said Rebecca. "Her country is the one that hasn't got rid of its fascist dictator. Franco was very cunning, wasn't he, to keep Spain out of the war even when Hitler seemed to be winning?"

"Margarita was always hoping he would get involved, even though she knew it would make things more difficult for the Allies," Ruth replied. "But maybe when the new United Nations organization has been properly

1

set up it will be able to do something about isolating him and squeezing him out."

"You've known Margarita since the time she came here as a refugee, haven't you?" asked Rebecca.

"Yes. That was in 1938, after her father had been killed by the fascists. There was a little group of us in those days who were friends, and one of the group was active in an organization that was helping Spanish refugees. He met her and introduced her to the rest of us. I remember we all went for a walk together through Regent's Park. That was when Arthur, her husband, met her. I think it really was love at first sight."

"She's very beautiful," said Rebecca. "She's always talking about Arthur. I think she must miss him a lot. Maybe he'll soon be back in England, even if he has to stay awhile longer in the Army."

"Unfortunately he seems to have been so good at his job the Army might want to keep him in Germany," said Ruth. "Organizing supplies and transport is going to go on being important for quite a long time, I would think."

"They must think well of him," Rebecca agreed. "Margarita was so proud when he was given the medal – and when he was promoted to Lieutenant-Colonel. I've never met him. I think his last leave was before D-Day. I hope he will soon come back to Margarita, though I expect you and I will have to find somewhere else to live when he does."

"I suppose it's possible they might want to have him back soon in his previous job at the Ministry of Supply," said Ruth. "He had a lot of trouble persuading them to let him leave it and join the Army. It was only after Dunkirk that he managed to get permission. Now they'll have all kinds of new problems to deal with and they might want to have his expert help."

At Victoria so many more people crowded into the train that further conversation became impossible; but the pressure was eased at St James's Park, when half the carriage emptied on to the platform, on their way, no doubt, to Buckingham Palace.

"Was the man you write to in the Army one of that group of friends before the War?" Rebecca asked when they were able to resume their conversation.

"He was," she replied. "He and Arthur were both postgraduate students at the London School of Economics when I first met them. In fact, Arthur went back there to do research and teaching after he got his PhD, but then he was very quickly seconded to the new Ministry of

Supply." For some reason she found herself reluctant to talk about Daniel, even though she had been thinking about him all morning, and daring to hope that it might not be very long now before she saw him again.

"I know we're only going two more stations," she went on, noticing that there were now some empty seats, "but let's sit down. It could be hours before we have another chance to get off our feet."

They sat down as the train began to move, and Rebecca picked up a copy of the *Daily Mirror* that someone had left on her seat. Looking at the back page, more than half of which was covered by a photograph looking down on a tightly-packed crowd of excited people crammed into Piccadilly Circus, with a few taxis and buses marooned in their midst, she exclaimed, "I don't think I'd want to get caught up in the middle of something like that. If there were so many people on the streets last night what is it going to be like today?"

"Don't worry," said Ruth. "We must take care not to get too far away from an exit route. It's a funny thing, but the last time I was in a crowd of people celebrating it was on the night that Mr Chamberlain came back from Munich and told us we could go home and sleep quietly in our beds because there was going to be peace in our time. I was with Daniel in Downing Street and the Prime Minister spoke to us from a first floor window. The crowd went wild with delight."

And then she remembered what had happened next – how she and Daniel had extricated themselves from the crowd and had gone down the steps to Horse Guards Parade and there, for the very first time, had exchanged a passionate kiss. But that was a memory that she didn't want to share.

Rebecca was scanning the newspaper. "It says here that Pastor Niemöller was liberated from a prison camp yesterday."

"That's brilliant," said Ruth. "I thought he must have been killed years ago. My father met him once. He was so brave, speaking out publicly against Hitler – even though it didn't do any good. Oh, that's a really powerful cartoon, isn't it?" She looked at the drawing, occupying almost a complete page, which depicted a wounded soldier standing on the rubble of a ruined building and holding out to the reader a laurel wreath bearing a label, 'Victory and peace in Europe'. Underneath the caption said, 'Here you are – don't lose it again'.

"Yes. It's good to remind people that today is only the beginning, not the end," Rebecca replied. "Have you thought yet about what you're going to do now?"

"I haven't, really," she replied. "It depends on things that I don't know about yet. I'm sure the Foreign Office won't be keeping me on much longer. They aren't going to need all the extra translating, and I expect they'll have to start saving money very soon. I could go back to my old job, teaching German and French to little girls, but I'm not sure that I want to. What about you, now that there aren't going to be any more German broadcasts to monitor?"

"I don't know what I will do in… 'the long run', you say?... but just now I would like to find some work that will help the Jewish people who are still alive in Europe. When I read about those terrible camps that the soldiers found last week at Belsen and Buchenwald it made me realize just how lucky I am to be alive. If my father hadn't managed to get me out of Austria… I don't know… I suppose I would have ended my life somewhere like that. I feel I owe something to the ones who weren't so lucky, the ones who are still alive. I must do something to help them if I can. Life's too precious to waste doing things that make no difference to the world. There's a United Nations agency that was set up two or three years ago, called UNRRA, to help displaced people in Europe. Maybe I could get a job with it. They must need people who speak German, and I have a bit of Czech as well."

The train jolted to a halt at Westminster and soon the carriage was almost empty. "Do you hope that some of your family might still be alive?" Ruth asked, very tentatively.

"Sometimes I hope and sometimes – usually in the middle of the night – I tell myself that hoping will only make it worse when eventually I find out what has happened – if I ever do. The last letter I had from my mother was in September 1938. She tried to appear cheerful, but she mentioned that several people we knew had been taken away by the Nazis in the previous week. Since then I have never heard anything from my family."

"I'm sure it won't be long before there is an organization drawing together all the information about where people went and… what happened to them. Someone at the FO is bound to know what's happening. I must make some enquiries," said Ruth.

"Since tomorrow is also going to be a holiday maybe we should plan to do something 'normal'. If the weather continues to be sunny we could have a picnic, perhaps. Do you think Margarita would like to do that?" Rebecca asked.

"We should soon be able to find out, if she's managed to get to the station," said Ruth. "I was thinking I ought to visit another friend who

4

was in the little group I told you about. She's going to be specially sad just now, because her husband was killed in the War."

"Oh, yes. It must be so much sadder if everyone else is being happy because they know their husbands or their fathers are safe at last, and you know that it's too late for the one that you wanted to come back. When did he die?"

"It was just after last Christmas, in Greece. It's somehow ironic that he – his name was Freddie – was a conscientious objector and he was the only member of our little group of friends to be killed in the War. The story is a bit complicated, but he eventually joined the Friends' Ambulance. It's a Quaker organization that helps the victims of war but tries to remain neutral. He was driving an ambulance somewhere near Athens and Communist partisans fired a mortar bomb at it. I suppose they didn't believe that anybody could really be neutral. It's even more tragic because he and Nancy had a child."

"That is terrible," said Rebecca. "How old is the child?"

"Leo is about four. They called him after Tolstoy, who was one of Freddie's heroes. I think he identified with Tolstoy because he was from an aristocratic family himself and he'd revolted against the whole idea of privilege. By another strange irony he'd actually inherited the title not long before he was killed. He'd never expected to because he was the second son. There's an old expression used to describe his situation: 'the spare, not the heir'. But his brother, who was in the Grenadier Guards, was killed when they tried to break through to Arnhem last September. And then, in November, his father died of a heart attack. I suppose it could have been brought on by grief. He wasn't an old man – only in his fifties.

"So now Nancy's little boy is Viscount Newingham, and technically Nancy is the Dowager Viscountess. It's bizarre. She's still not met her mother-in-law, though she says that she's been in touch with her and wants to be reconciled – and, of course, to see her grandson. I really must go and see Nancy."

"Where does she live?"

"In a flat near Swiss Cottage. They rented it when they got married, just before the War. Luckily they'd kept it on when they went to Ireland just at the start of the War, and when they came back to have the baby they were able to move in again."

"It seems a strange decision, to have a baby right at the beginning of the War," said Rebecca.

"They didn't actually decide to have the baby. He was an accident. As you probably know, Ireland is a very Roman Catholic country and contraception is illegal over there. When the contraceptives that they'd taken with them were all used up they weren't able to buy any more, and… well, they'd not been very long married. Leo was the result.

"Nancy seems to be coping very well; but she's going to have to make some complicated decisions about the family estate, somewhere in Somerset, which now belongs to her son. I've been wondering if another member of our little group, called Roddy, might be able to help her. He took a law degree, but he's an actor now. At the moment I think he and his wife are in a concert party entertaining American airmen at the bases in Norfolk. I really must try to contact him."

"It must have been dreadful having a baby in London at that time," said Rebecca. "Wasn't it during the Blitz?"

"Luckily she was able to go and stay with my parents when the baby was due. She stayed there in the country for about a year afterwards, and then things got better in London and she came back with Leo to the flat."

"Your parents must be very kind people to let them stay for so long."

"They are kind people. My father is a Church of England rector, as you know; but that's no guarantee of kindness, of course. He's just a very kind man – and my mother, too. She said she enjoyed having a baby in the house again, though I can't think why."

The train arrived at Embankment station and they ascended the stairs to the entrance hall. "There's Margarita, just inside the door," said Rebecca.

Their friend greeted them enthusiastically. "I was afraid there might be so many people I wouldn't be able to see you," she said, "but it's not so very crowded here. While I was waiting I remembered that night when Arthur and I went to the Palace to see Mr Chamberlain and you and Daniel went to Downing Street and yet, in spite of all the crowds, we accidentally met you in the Mall."

"How amazing!" Ruth exclaimed. "Just a few minutes ago I was telling Rebecca about that evening. It all came back to me very vividly when we were looking at a newspaper photo of the crowd in Piccadilly Circus yesterday. It was one of those coincidences that you think aren't possible, but sometimes they do happen.

"Shall we try to see what's happening in Whitehall? If we go under the railway bridge we can cross Northumberland Avenue into Whitehall Place and Whitehall Court. That leads into Horse Guards Avenue, and off the end of it there's a sort of alleyway that runs behind the Banqueting House and into Whitehall. I sometimes use it as a short cut when I pop out of the office at lunchtime. If the crowd is too dense in Whitehall it will give us an escape route."

Following Ruth's recommended route they were very soon on the fringe of the huge crowd that was packed into Whitehall waiting for something – they weren't quite sure what – to happen. Once again Ruth remembered the night in 1938 when she and Daniel had made their way through the crowd into Downing Street by following close behind the rump of a police horse. If only Daniel could be here now; but if he was they'd have better things to do than standing around in a purposeless crowd – she hoped.

Margarita interrupted her thoughts. "What do you think is going to happen now?"

"I don't know," she replied. "The crowd doesn't seem to have any particular focus."

Two young men in American Air Force uniforms were standing in front of them. The taller of the two turned around and spoke to her. "You just got here, honey?" he asked.

She nodded and he continued, "You missed seeing Mr Churchill. A guy told us he was going to a thanksgiving service at the church down that-a-way. He sure looked happy with his cigar in his mouth, but it took a long time for his car to get through the crowd. I guess it'll be a while before he comes back this way again. Say, would you and your friends like to come and have a drink with me and my buddy, Nathan, if we can find some place that's open?"

"That's very kind of you," Ruth replied, "but there's something else I think we ought to be doing now – somebody we've got to visit. Enjoy the day. I hope you'll soon be able to go home." Smiling, she turned away and Margarita and Rebecca followed her. "Sorry for taking it on myself to make the decision," she said to them, "but I didn't think you'd want to spend the rest of the afternoon with a couple of Yanks, however nice they might turn out to be."

"Some things are best done quickly," Margarita agreed. "Were you thinking that maybe we should pay a visit to Nancy, if she's at home?"

"That's what I had in mind," she replied. "I've been telling Rebecca about her and Leo, and how she's trying to make up her mind about the whole family inheritance business. Today she must be feeling so lonely. Everybody else being happy is bound to remind her that for her there's not going to be any home-coming."

"Let's phone and see if she's at home," said Margarita. "There should be a phone box in Charing Cross station."

"Will it be all right if I come with you?" Rebecca asked, as they moved back along Whitehall Gardens. "I'd like to meet your friend, but if you think it would be better for her just to have people she knows I'll go somewhere else."

"No. Please come with us," said Ruth. "I think it would be good for her to meet someone new. And you probably understand even better than we do how she must be feeling. For both of you the end of the War isn't going to be the start of new... personal happiness, like it is for us."

"You didn't hear anything from Daniel this week, did you?" Margarita asked.

"No. His letters take some time to come through, not surprisingly. In his last one, that got to me last Friday, he said he expected to be on the move fairly soon. He was at Alexander's headquarters when he wrote it, and they'd just brought the German generals down from the north to sign the surrender document. But Daniel said he would be going up to Bologna the next day for a meeting with officers on the staff of the American General Truscott. Now that they're not so strict on censoring the letters he's been able to tell me that his main job these days is liaison with the Americans."

"Do you think he'll soon get some leave?" asked Margarita. "He's been away such a long time."

"He's certainly due for it. The last leave he had was in Palestine, nearly three years ago, after he was wounded in Egypt."

"When did you last see him, then?" Rebecca asked.

"On the day the War broke out. We had a few minutes together outside Marylebone Station before I took some evacuees from the school where I was teaching out to its new home in the country. About six months later, when he got embarkation leave before they sent him out to the Middle East, we had arranged to meet in London. He was going to be on his way back from visiting his family in Northern Ireland. But his train was delayed somewhere in the Midlands and we missed each other. I was working in the Foreign Office by then and I couldn't be late for my shift. So the last time I spoke to him was when he called me from a phone box in Euston Station. But at least I've had letters – lots of letters."

Ruth remembered the shoebox that she kept in her old bedroom in her parents' house. On every visit there she had deposited another batch of Daniel's letters in that box, so that if a bomb should demolish

Margarita's flat, where she was living in London, she wouldn't lose them all.

"Arthur actually met Daniel in Cairo," Margarita said to Rebecca. "It was after Daniel had been wounded in the first battle of El Alamein and was in a hospital there. Arthur had just been posted to General Montgomery's staff, and he only found out about Daniel being there because he saw his name on a list of recommendations for the Military Cross. The moment he saw Daniel's name he felt sick in his stomach, he told me, because at first he thought it was a recommendation for a posthumous award. When he realized it wasn't he was determined to track Daniel down, and he found him in the hospital."

"Daniel wrote to tell me about their meeting," said Ruth. "He was really thrilled to see Arthur, because he had no idea that he was in Egypt. By that time Daniel was convalescing. His wounds weren't very serious – or so he said. But unfortunately he didn't have a chance to see Arthur again, because he was sent off to a course at the Staff College in Haifa; and when that was over he was posted to General Alexander's staff. So he stayed in the Mediterranean, while Arthur came back to England with Montgomery, after the start of the Italian campaign, to prepare for the D-Day landings."

"Well, at least Daniel had a staff job; so I presume he didn't get into that kind danger ever again," sad Rebecca.

"Actually he did," said Ruth. "I was glad I didn't know about it until it was all over. It was after Anzio, in January last year, when the losses had been so heavy. There was a shortage of officers in front-line units, and Daniel volunteered to go back to his battalion. He was involved in the fighting around Monte Cassino, but he's never told me anything about it, except that he got a mention in dispatches. After that Alexander wanted him back again on the staff, to work on liaison with the Americans. And he was promoted to major – he said it was so that his American contacts would take him more seriously."

"I hope now they'll give him some leave," said Rebecca. "You must be longing to see him again."

"And I hope they don't think about sending him to the Pacific, if he's supposed to be good at working with the Americans," said Ruth.

"I so much want to meet both of them, now that I've heard so much about them," said Rebecca. "They've been away from you for such a long time. Surely they'll both soon be given some leave."

"Look! There's a phone box," Margarita exclaimed. "Has anyone got any pennies?"

CHAPTER TWO: 18th June, 1945 - ARTHUR

Even though their two 'lodgers', Ruth and Rebecca, were seated at the breakfast table, Arthur was unable to refrain from hugging Margarita around her hips when she approached with a rack of freshly-made toast. The night before, after twenty-six hours of continuous travel, he had had energy enough for only the briefest enjoyment of her welcoming body before falling into an exhausted sleep. Now he was ready and ravenous to enjoy once again those delights he had last experienced for only a few days some thirteen months ago, before departing for the beaches of Normandy.

"When did you make the decision to stand for Parliament?" Ruth asked him, as he began to butter a slice of toast – with margarine.

"Only when I was asked to, by Ronnie Harkness, a chap I work with at HQ. His family live in the constituency and they've always been prominent members of the Labour Party. He'd had a letter from his father telling him that the sitting Member had dropped dead with a heart attack the day before Mr Churchill announced there was going to be an election. And then the Tories adopted a serving officer in the RAF as their candidate. So his father asked him – I think only half seriously – if he knew of an officer who would make a suitable candidate for Labour; and Ronnie thought about me, I suppose because I'd discussed economic issues with him when I was showing him how to do the admin. I was surprised when he suggested it, because the idea had never occurred to me. As you know, Ruth, I was interested in politics before the War, but not as much as you were; and I'd never seriously thought about taking it up professionally. But then I had a thought – I'm never going to admit this to anyone else, so keep it to yourselves – I had a thought that this could be the quickest way to get out of the Army. They don't need me any more, but they might well put me to work on the whole boring business of demobilization. And I want to get back to Margarita just as quickly as I can."

He looked across the table at his wife and the glow in her large brown eyes told him everything that he needed to know.

"Has the constituency party already adopted you, then?" asked Ruth.

"No. I'm going to meet their selection committee this evening. But Ronnie tells me that it all happened so unexpectedly they don't have any other serious candidate. I'll just have to do my best to impress them. I'm completely out of touch with the details of party policy, but I read the newspaper reports of the Blackpool conference and I think I can remember enough to plagiarise one or two of the speeches. Aneurin Bevan was very strong on the need to apply modern science to our heavy industry if we're going to be competitive in the world. That's something I used to lecture about at the Polytechnic. But I wish I had Daniel's oratorical skill," he added, with a smile at Ruth.

"Which constituency is it?" she asked. "Margarita said it was somewhere in north London."

"The constituency is called Middlesex North-West," he replied.

"Well, that really is a coincidence!" she exclaimed. "You probably don't remember, but that was the constituency Daniel and I were working in for the by-election in November '38, when we were in the Fraternalist Party; and then our candidate, the fat man with lots of money, withdrew at the last moment when the Labour Party bribed him with a peerage in the New Year Honours."

"Yes, I do remember," said Arthur. "The seat had been a Tory marginal but Labour won it in that by-election by something like eighty votes. I think it's going to be a hard fight to keep it. Churchill's popularity is bound to sway a lot of the voters, so soon after VE-day – and how could you blame them for that?"

"I wouldn't be so sure about that," said Ruth. "He made a very silly speech on the wireless on Monday. You probably didn't hear it; but he talked about Labour needing to have some kind of Gestapo if it wanted to nationalize everything and then suppress the public discontent that was bound to follow. He's probably exhausted and wasn't thinking clearly. After all, he's an old man now. But people may not be so influenced by his personality any more. I'm sure you'll have a very good chance of holding the seat for Labour. And I'll come and canvass for you, if you'd like me to."

"And I'll come, too," said Rebecca. "We've got to make sure that you get out of the Army and come back to Margarita, haven't we?"

It was the first time he had really looked at Rebecca, although he had been aware of her presence. Margarita had told him about the Jewish refugee who had become such a good friend when they met at work, and about how she had taken her in after a V2 rocket had destroyed the place where she was living. Now he noted the hint of humour in Rebecca's dark eyes, and guessed that behind her long, pale face there was a highly intelligent brain.

"I shall be grateful for all the help I can get," he said, "if the constituency decides to take me on board. They say that Parliament's going to be dissolved next week, and then there'll be only about three weeks before an election. That doesn't leave much time for campaigning."

"It will be easier than a by-election," said Ruth. "The wireless and the newspapers will all be full of election news every day, and people are sure to turn out for meetings. Your main job will be to get around the constituency and show yourself, and let them know you have their interests at heart. But I think this time the voters are going to make up their minds on the policies more than on the personalities. Already I've been hearing a lot of people talking about how we mustn't go back to the bad old days, when lots of men were out of work and people couldn't afford to pay for a doctor when they got sick."

"Yesterday one of my colleagues, Dr Gombrich, said Hitler had given us a marvellous opportunity by getting rid of so many of the slums with his bombs. Now we could build somewhere better for people to live in the future – but we would need to get on with it pretty quickly," said Rebecca.

"Is your colleague also somebody who managed to get out of Germany in time?" Arthur asked.

"Yes, but he's actually from Vienna – the place that I come from. He was already in London working at the Warburg Institute before the Nazis invaded; so naturally he stayed on. Before he left Austria he published a wonderful book, a history of the world for children. It was one of my favourite books, even though I was starting university when I first read it. But I had to leave it behind when I came here, and it hasn't been published in English. I hope it will be one day. I said to him that he ought to translate it when I first met him, but he thought English children wouldn't be interested because it doesn't have very much in it about English history. He has a brilliant mind but I think he's too modest."

"Well, he's certainly right about the housing problem," said Arthur. "It's bound to be a big issue at the election, and if I'm standing it'll be near the top of my manifesto."

"If Rebecca and I were your constituents you'd get our votes," said Ruth. "We'll both be needing somewhere to live now."

"Oh, you know that you can stay here as long as you need to," Margarita exclaimed.

"That's very kind, but you and Arthur deserve to have your home to yourselves now, after you've been apart for such a long time," said Rebecca.

"Ruth, have you heard from Daniel recently? What are the chances of him getting some leave? He must be due for it," Arthur asked.

"Long overdue," Ruth replied. "He should be on his way by now; and at least I don't have to worry that he might meet a U-boat before he can get here. I had a letter from him yesterday and he said he was coming home, but he didn't know for how long. There's a possibility that he might be sent to the Far East, to relieve somebody on Lord Louis Mountbatten's staff. I don't like the sound of that. How long do you think the war out there is likely to go on for?"

"It's hard to say," Arthur replied. "The Japs seem to be pulling back everywhere, and the Yanks have pretty well wiped out their navy. But if what's been happening in Okinawa is anything to go by, their soldiers have been indoctrinated to go on fighting till they've all been killed. If that's how they continue to fight an invasion of Japan might take a couple of years before it's all over – and an awful lot of people will be killed. The Yanks lost five thousand sailors to kamikaze attacks in the Okinawa landings." The thought that winning a seat in Parliament would be the surest way to avoid getting involved in the Far East flashed through his mind, and he had to suppress a feeling of guilt.

"Daniel has been away for five years without a break," said Margarita. "They surely won't expect him to do any more."

"I certainly hope not," said Ruth. Arthur noticed that she seemed to have lost weight, but her hazel eyes still had that sparkle of energy and intelligence that had attracted him to her when first they met.

"I'm sure Daniel will feel the same," he said. "He'll not be up for any more volunteering. By the way, have you been in touch with Nancy recently?"

"We went to see her on VE-Day – all three of us," Ruth replied. "It's a tough time for her but luckily, because of little Leo, her thoughts are mainly about the future. He'll soon have to start school; and because of the teaching she's given him at home he's already able to read and write and do simple sums. He's a really bright kid. But she's determined that he doesn't get sucked into the upper class education system that Freddie hated so much, even though she could easily afford it. Freddie's will left everything that he'd just inherited to her, although the big house and the estate in Somerset are entailed in some way to Leo, with her as his trustee till he's twenty-one."

"And I suppose when he's twenty-one he'll also have a guaranteed seat in Parliament, if he wants to take it," said Arthur. "It's an extraordinary turn of events, when you remember how Freddie used to be so adamant that, because he was the younger son, he would not get caught up in the Establishment."

"If Labour is elected next month do you think the House of Lords will be abolished?" asked Rebecca. "If you're an MP would you vote for abolition?"

"I've never really thought much about it," Arthur replied. "If we do get elected then there'll be a lot of other things needing much more urgent attention. Of course, if the Lords tried to prevent a Labour government getting on with the job then it might have to get rid of them. I think I'd be in favour of replacing it with a different kind of Second Chamber – one made up of the kind of people who'd had a lot of experience in different walks of life, and not just in politics. But I'd be very surprised if anything like that happened in the next Parliament. There'll be far too much work to be done getting the country back to prosperity."

"I wonder if it mightn't be better in the long run if Labour didn't win this election," said Ruth. "Whatever government is elected things aren't suddenly going to get better. Everything's worn out and everybody's exhausted. It'll take years to sort out all the problems, and when they don't see quick improvements people are going to start blaming the government. Maybe it would be better if the Conservatives had the job of clearing up the mess, and then when people realized that they weren't up to doing it properly they'd be swept away in another election, and Labour would have the kind of majority that would enable it to make the changes that we really need."

"There's a lot of truth in what you say," said Arthur, "but I'd still rather get on with the job now and hope that people will be able to understand the difficulties the new government is facing, and be patient enough to give new methods time to work."

"What's really important is that Middlesex North-West should elect a Labour Member," said Rebecca. "We're all going to try to make that happen."

"If I'm not going to be late for work I'll have to leave in about five minutes," said Margarita, looking at the clock on top of the kitchen cupboard. "My shift ends at four o'clock, but you'll be needing some lunch before that."

"Don't worry," said Ruth. "This my Saturday off; so I'll make sure that Arthur gets some lunch – though it might not be as substantial as Army rations."

"I've got to be off to work, too," said Rebecca. "If I don't see you again before then, I hope the interview will go well for you this evening."

"By this time next week all three of us might be out of a job," said Ruth. "If we are we'll have plenty of time to help you with your election campaign. Margarita, would you like me to see if the butcher has anything reasonably edible that we could have for tomorrow's lunch? If I tell him we have a colonel to feed he might be willing to stretch the meat coupons a little bit."

Confronted with the complications of civilian life Arthur experienced a feeling of disorientation. "For just a few hours I'd like to pretend that everything is back to normal again," he said. "I'm going to search the wardrobe for my sports jacket and flannels, and hope they still fit me. And then I'm going to walk to Putney Bridge and look at the river. I expect that it, at least, will still be flowing in the same direction."

Margarita came round the table and kissed him on the cheek. "Don't get lost," she said. "I'll be back in good time to help you get ready for the meeting this evening."

CHAPTER THREE: 26th June, 1945 - DANIEL

"There have been a lot of 'days that will live in history' over the past couple of months," said Daniel, "but I wouldn't be surprised if today will be seen as the most significant of all in a hundred years' time – and yet I doubt if people tomorrow will take much notice of whatever is reported about it in the papers."

He was standing in the living-room of Arthur and Margarita's flat, a place he remembered only dimly from his last visit to it, almost exactly six years ago, when his friends had just begun to settle in after their wedding. Since Ruth was lodging with them he had come there as quickly as he could after arriving in London from Northern Ireland, where he had been visiting his family. To his delight he had found her alone, because Margarita and her other lodger, whom he had never met, were both at work.

"What's happening today, then?" she asked, closing the door behind her. "I didn't have time to read the papers this morning."

"The countries that have agreed to join the United Nations are all going to sign the document that officially brings it into existence – even though, of course, 'United Nations' is actually what the Alliance has been called for the past couple of years. Do you remember how much time we spent debating why the League of Nations wasn't working, back in the days when we were first… getting to know each other? Now the world's governments have been given a second chance to stop us from having any more big wars in the future. Let's hope they don't mess it up again this time."

"It's funny, but that's exactly what a big cartoon in the *Daily Mirror* said on VE-Day – not actually about the United Nations, but about what the world needed to be doing. When I saw it I thought about those discussions we used to have, and the things that we tried to do – and about that day when you decided the only thing left for you was to join the Territorials." She sat down in one of the two small armchairs that flanked the fireplace with its unlit gas fire.

"I'm glad you still remembered those days," he said. "So much has happened since then." When she'd opened the front door to him they had kissed each other on the cheek, almost as if they had been apart for only a couple of days. Now he felt uncertain about what to do next. So many times he had remembered the passionate embraces they enjoyed in those last few weeks before the outbreak of war. They had actually planned what would have been categorized by a lot of people as 'a dirty weekend' in Broadstairs, but the suddenness of his call-up had prevented them from getting away. Their five-year exchange of letters had been regular – or as regular as the exigencies of war would permit – and warmly affectionate, though always conscious of the censor's intruding eye. But in five years a great deal must have happened in Ruth's life about which he knew nothing, just as he himself had had some significant experiences which he had not wanted to recount in his letters to her.

"Too much for us ever to be able to catch up with it all," she said. "Do you remember what we talked about when we had our last proper conversation? It was outside Marylebone Station on the day the War began. I said that when it was all over we'd need to think again about what we were going to do, because everything was going to be different, and you agreed. And I think you quoted a bit of *Hamlet*, about the time being out of joint."

"I remember," he replied. Was she about to say that so much had changed they could never go back to where they were in those few wonderful weeks in the Autumn of 1939, he wondered, as he sat down in the armchair on the other side of the fireplace. Maybe she was going to tell him that now there was somebody else at the centre of her life. It would be surprising if, over those years, a lot of men hadn't tried to win her affections, and maybe some 'desk warrior' had succeeded, behind the filing-cabinets. And then he instantly reproached himself for allowing his fear to prompt a thought so maliciously unfair. "I think I was trying to be philosophical in the face of catastrophe," he added.

"The funny thing is," said Ruth, looking intently into his eyes, "that I don't feel as if anything really important has changed at all. Maybe it's because I've stayed in the same place and the changes have all been going on outside of me, if you understand what I mean. For you it must have been quite different, with new places and new people to deal with all the time."

Daniel felt a surge of excitement as hope was instantly revived. "That's true. Things were constantly changing and I had a lot of new experiences – some of them pretty awful. But the one thing that never changed was wanting to be back with you. There were a few times when I thought it was never going to happen, and those were not good times. And now," he said, standing up and moving across to kneel beside her chair, "what I want most of all is to know that we're going to be able to stay close to each other from this moment onward. I still want to make that dream we had come true – about having fun while we find things to do that we know are really worth doing."

Her serious face dissolved into a radiant smile and she bent forward to kiss his forehead. "Oh, we're right back where we used to be," she exclaimed. "There were so many times when I was hoping you were going to say something that I was thinking, and you said it. Do you remember that time after the Fraternalist Party meeting in Friends House? Everybody had applauded your rousing speech but I'd thought something was bothering you while you were speaking; and then you told me you'd realized you didn't actually believe in what you were saying."

"Of course I remember," he said, taking her right hand between his two hands and squeezing it gently. "That was the turning-point for both of us. You'd already started thinking in the same way, but you'd not wanted to let me down by admitting it. And it sometimes worked the other way round, didn't it? Do you remember that time in my room in Dorset Square when you surprised me by saying that you weren't in a hurry to get married but you wanted us to do everything that married people were allowed to do?"

"I've thought about it a thousand times," she replied, bending forward to kiss the top of his head, "and how Hitler frustrated our wonderful plan to spend a weekend in Broadstairs."

"Now that women have been doing nearly all the jobs that used to be reserved for men I can't believe we'll go back to the situation where you wouldn't be allowed to do a worthwhile job if we got married," said Daniel.

"Are you saying that we don't really need to start planning another Broadstairs because we could get married now and still be able to live in the way that we want to live?" she asked, and he saw that a smile was hovering around her lips.

"Yes, that's what I am saying. I want to marry you now and put an end to all the waiting. But I've got no right to ask you to do that. The future's just as uncertain now as it was in '39. I'm still in the Army and it's quite possible in the next few weeks they might send me off to the Far East. Nobody knows how long that show is going to last. The War isn't over, and even when it is I'm not going to have a job. Why would you want to marry me?"

"Because I love you," she replied, rising to her feet and tugging his hand so that he got up as well. She put her arms around his neck and very deliberately raised her mouth to be kissed. As their lips met he felt a surge of contentment, as if he had suddenly relaxed and left behind all the tension and uncertainty of five long years. And then the warmth and softness of her body in his arms reawakened the desire that he had subconsciously been holding in check. As his hands began to caress her contours through the thin material of her summer dress he detected a change in the rhythm of her breathing.

But then, with a gentle push against his chest, she extricated herself from his embrace, saying, "I want to. I do, but this isn't the place. I'll talk on the phone to Daddy about special licences and find out what we can do to speed things up."

She stepped back a pace and almost tripped over the armchair, recovering herself by clutching his sleeve. He put out his hand to steady her.

"You mean you want to get married now, before I have to go back to wherever they send me?" he asked, a mixture of surprise and pleasure making his voice sound strangulated.

"Why not? It would mean we could start to plan the future in whatever way we want to – even though we might not be able to do very much about it just now. And it would also save us having to waste time and money on a big, traditional kind of wedding that would be mainly for the benefit of other people – my college friends turning out to try and catch the bouquet and your pals bringing their swords to make us walk underneath them. And I won't have to go around begging for clothing coupons so that I can buy a proper wedding dress that I'll never wear again. And Mummy can still enjoy laying on a little wedding breakfast for a few intimate friends, but she won't have to struggle against the temptation to go on the black market to provide a bigger one for lots of hangers-on."

"You are amazing!" he exclaimed. "You've done it again – saying what I was thinking but not daring to suggest. I thought you might like to have a traditional wedding, with all the friends and relations turning out to gawp, and if you had I would have gone along with it to give you pleasure. But I've always believed it was a waste of money that could be better used in setting up a new home. How quickly do you think we can arrange it?"

"I don't know, but I'm sure Daddy will be able to tell us. He's done all kinds of weddings in his time. But you'll want to give your parents enough notice to arrange a journey over here if they'd like to come, won't you?"

"Yes, of course. And I hope my younger sister, Sarah, might be able to come too. She and I have always been great pals. I expect her hospital will give her time off. What about your sister? She's in nursing too, isn't she?"

"Penelope is with the FANY in Germany. When she last wrote – which she doesn't do very often – she was helping with some prisoners of war who'd just been released in pretty bad shape. I'm sure she'd be glad of a good excuse to put in for some leave. I'll ring Daddy this evening and maybe then we'll be able to start talking about a date. This time I'm not letting the Army send you off again before we… before we become 'one flesh', as the Prayer Book puts it." She sat down in the armchair, saying, "Now, tell me how things went on your visit home. I bet they were pleased to see you."

"Yes, they were," he replied, sitting down again in the opposite chair, "but with typical Ulster laconicism my brother, Mark, said, 'Good to see you again. When will you be going back?'"

Ruth laughed and said, "I'm looking forward to meeting these emotionally continent people that you've told me so much about. I don't really believe it. I'm sure they're every bit as friendly as people over here."

"Oh, they're friendlier. It's just that if you're not born among them you have to learn how to read the unexpressed emotion. One thing they hate is to be thought insincere. Even my mother, when she greeted me, just gave me a hug and said, 'It's been a long time, son. There were times when we thought we might never see you again. The Lord has been very good to us.' I was tempted to say I was shortly going to be visiting another family to whom the Lord had not been so good, even though I was sure their prayers had been no less fervent than hers – but I didn't. She taught me superstition but she also taught me to read and to reason, and I'd never want to question the things that comfort her."

"Who were the other family you were going to visit?" Ruth asked.

"The parents of one of the men in my platoon, back at the time of First Alamein. He was killed by the same shell that knocked me about a bit."

"Tell me what happened, please," she said, looking into his eyes with that serious expression which brought back memories of conversations he had almost forgotten. "You said very little about how you were wounded when you wrote to me from hospital – but I know they gave you the Military Cross for whatever it was."

"It was just the kind of thing that happens in battle all the time. It must have happened a thousand times that day to other people. My platoon was dug in on the crest of a tiny ridge – though 'dug' isn't exactly the right word because the ground was so hard we could only scrape out a bit of space to lie down in. By this time the Jerries were only a few hundred yards away and we were expecting them to rush our position, coming over the crest of another little ridge that must have been about fifty or sixty yards away.

"We'd been exchanging small arms fire and then a gun opened up on us. A shell exploded just behind and to the left of where I was lying. I'd just turned to my right to shout to the men along the line to hold their fire till they could see the enemy, and I felt the blast on my back, and the sting of what I thought was shrapnel. But I wasn't knocked out.

"When I looked to my left I saw that the machine-gunner who was next to me had taken a massive hit in the back – well, there wasn't very much of his back left; so I knew he must be dead. That was Corporal Henderson – John George to his friends – and it was his parents that I visited the day before yesterday."

"Do they live near to your family?"

"About a dozen miles away, close to Banbridge. My brother-in-law, Tom, gave me a lift, which was very good of him since petrol is so scarce; and my sister, Mary, and their two kids came along for the ride. Having the kids there stopped me brooding and getting myself worked up on the way."

"It must have been difficult meeting them," said Ruth. "On an occasion like that what is there to say?"

"I could only tell them that their son had died bravely, doing his duty. And that it had been a very important battle, even if people had later forgotten about it; for if we hadn't beaten Rommel back in those July days there would have been no Second Alamein and all the successes that followed on from that. And I told them that John George had been well liked and popular in the platoon – which he was – and that his death had been instantaneous – which I hope it was."

"Weren't you certain, then?"

"Pretty certain, but there was no time to check. I could see that the Jerries were trying to rush us and I had to get his gun firing. His Vickers was our only machine-gun. Amazingly it wasn't damaged, because his body had protected it. I couldn't move his body away from the gun because I knew I'd been hit and I had to conserve my strength, and he was a pretty big chap. So I had to kneel on top of him to fire the gun. The Vickers is mounted on a tripod and he'd already sighted it very accurately. I just traversed it from left to right and back again three, or maybe four times. It was like one of those old films about the Great War. I could see this line of figures – there must have been a full company – running down the slope, and then they started falling over like skittles in a bowling-alley. Of course, by that time my riflemen had begun to give them ten rounds rapid; so it wasn't just the Vickers that was knocking them over.

"And then the ammunition belt was empty and I stood up to find another one because the gun's loader had been knocked out by the same shell. He actually survived, though one his arms had gone. Anyhow, I passed out, presumably because I'd lost a lot of blood, and that was the end of the battle for me. I heard later that a troop of Matildas arrived soon after and put an end to any hope the Jerries might have had of breaking through in our sector."

"Matildas? Do you mean Australians?" asked Ruth.

Daniel laughed. "No. That was the name of one of the types of tank we were using in those days – slow but reliable. It was called after that duck in the cartoon."

"And what happened to you then?"

"I have only a pretty hazy memory of being taken back to the field dressing-station. Then they got me into an ambulance and the next clear memory I have is of a nice white bed in a Cairo hospital. The wounds weren't serious but I'd lost a lot of blood. Remind me, if I should forget, that I'm going to be a regular blood donor, wherever we may be living. They put somebody else's blood into me and it had me back on my feet in a few days, though the wounds took a bit longer to heal."

"I've been a blood donor since the start of the Blitz," said Ruth. "But how many wounds did you have?"

"Six – or seven if you count separately two that were joined up. But none of them went deep. What I didn't tell the Hendersons was that my wounds weren't caused by shrapnel. They were made by fragments of poor John George's backbone and couple of bits of his kit. The only scar that's visible is this one." He drew his forefinger along the scar on the left underside of his jaw. "The others are all in places where... where I hope you'll be seeing them before very long."

"I'm longing to see them," she said softly and then, in a louder voice, "Were you surprised when Arthur turned up at the hospital?"

"I could hardly believe it. I didn't even know he was in Egypt. Seeing his face was like stepping back into the past – into a completely different life. And of course he'd been talking to you and Margarita only a few weeks earlier, when he'd been on embarkation leave. He came to see me a second time but then, unfortunately, they sent me off to Haifa and we lost touch again."

Suddenly the image of that second meeting flashed into his memory – sitting under the date palm with Charlotte in her crisp white uniform with that expensive little watch suspended by a blue ribbon on the generous curve of her bosom, and seeing Arthur approaching across the hospital courtyard. "Did Arthur… did he say very much about me in his letters to Margarita?" he asked.

"Not nearly enough," she replied, with feigned indignation. "I felt quite frustrated to think that he had actually been talking to you and all he was able to tell us was that you seemed to be making a very good recovery. And then he went on about how you'd recalled that day in Regent's Park when we all went for a walk together and he first met Margarita. Oh, and he said that after the MC was announced you'd become quite a hero in the hospital, but you were being your usual modest self and saying you hadn't really done anything special. By the way, did you know that he's back in London now?"

"Here? So he's managed to get some leave. Where is he today?"

"Canvassing in his constituency." She smiled mischievously as she watched him working out the implications of what she had said.

"You mean he's standing for Parliament? Which constituency?"

"It's an incredible coincidence. You'll never guess."

"Not Barnsley, the place where he was born? That must be one of Labour's safest seats."

"No, not Barnsley. Middlesex North-West."

"The scene of our great débâcle? I should think that's one he ought to be able to win if the national trend doesn't go too strongly against Labour, with people voting for Churchill out of gratitude. Winston has tremendous powers of persuasion. I remember what a boost he gave to morale when he visited Egypt. It was just before I was sent off to Haifa and I didn't actually see him, but everybody was talking about him. One of the stories going around was that he'd said to a Sapper, who was working with no shirt on, that when he was at Omdurman in '98 the theory was that White men should never expose their skin to the African sun but, like a lot of other theories, that had been shown to be false. Anyhow, he could still swing the way this election goes. I'm surprised that the Labour Party wanted to have it so quickly."

"I've heard that Mr Attlee wasn't in favour of it," said Ruth, "but at the party conference in Blackpool there was an overwhelming vote to end the coalition now and not wait until the war with Japan is over. I read a lot of the speeches in the *Manchester Guardian*. One of the best was by an Army officer on leave who's going to be standing in the election, a Major Healey."

"I think I met him once," said Daniel. "He's a Sapper, and he was a beachmaster when we landed in Sicily. Did a good job by all accounts. But I didn't know that Arthur was planning to stand for Parliament."

"He wasn't; but when the candidate for Middlesex North-West died unexpectedly somebody connected with the constituency who was a colleague of Arthur's asked him if he'd take it on. The Tory candidate is a serving officer and they thought it would be a good idea to match him.

"I've done a bit of canvassing in the constituency and I think Arthur stands a very good chance of winning. Do you remember when we were doing our reconnaissance and walked up and down all those endless streets of semi-detacheds with neat little gardens in front of them?"

"I certainly do. I suppose it hasn't changed very much if there wasn't any bombing up there."

"The gardens have changed. A lot of them have been dug up to plant vegetables – you know, 'Dig for Victory'. And of course the railings around them have all disappeared."

"The railings? Why have they gone?"

"To be melted down for munitions, although I have heard rumours that a lot of them are still lying in scrapyards."

"I suppose that's inevitable in wartime," he said. "Decisions have to be made quickly, but if circumstances change they don't always get carried through and people just move on to deal with the next crisis. It can be wasteful, but the biggest waste of all would be to spend time worrying about yesterday's problem instead of getting on with solving today's. The historians can have fun writing about the mistakes – but only if they're on the winning side."

He heard the sound of a key in the front door. "That will be Rebecca," said Ruth. "She's always the first to arrive home on Tuesdays. I'm glad you're going to meet her. She's become a very good friend."

"And she will be the first person to hear that you and I are going to be married," said Daniel. He kissed her quickly on the lips before Rebecca came through the living-room door.

CHAPTER FOUR: 14th July, 1945 - RUTH

As the Underground train accelerated out of Victoria station Ruth thought she should say something reassuring to Rebecca. "It's a very pleasant room, with that big window letting in so much light. And I'm sure you'll get along very well with Dodie. As I told you, I lived with her in the hostel for a couple of years before the War and she was the kind of person that everyone liked. Daniel actually met her brother when he was at the staff college in Haifa. Robert's an officer in the Palestine Police."

"She said she works at the National Gallery. Was she involved with the lunchtime concerts, do you think?" asked Rebecca. "I managed to get to some of them and they were wonderful."

"Yes, I think she helped with the organizing, and with the fire-watching. That was her war work and she was allowed to stay with it. They had an awful lot of damage to the roof, but she says the pictures will be back quite soon from their underground hiding-place in Wales. But I shouldn't think the Gallery will be able to display very many of them until they've done some roof repairs."

"I'm so pleased that she's willing to let me have that room in her flat. Pimlico is such a convenient location. I thought I might have to go out to the wilds of somewhere like Wimbledon to find a place."

"I think her father had the flat as a kind of *pied-à-terre* before the War," said Ruth. "He was something in the City. But he was in the Territorials, like Daniel, though his was a very posh regiment, the Honourable Artillery Company. So he was called up in '39, and Dodie was able to move into the flat when the hostel was taken over for war work. I'm sure you'll like living there."

"I'm sure I shall but, of course, I don't know how long I'll be there. It will all depend on where my new job is based, if I can find one."

"That vacancy in the Home Office you heard about, for the unit dealing with emergency applications from displaced persons, sounded interesting."

"Yes, I would like to get that one, even though I know it won't be permanent. But it would give me time to look around for something more long-term. And how are your long-term plans going? Are the wedding arrangements all complete?"

Ruth laughed. "I suppose they're as complete as they ever can be. Penelope's still not certain if she's going to be able to get leave, and Daniel's parents and sister were having problems about booking a passage from Belfast, though I think that can probably be sorted out. And, of course, we're hoping that when we go to the altar on this day fortnight our best man will be a Member of Parliament."

"Oh, I'm certain Arthur is going to win the seat. You could see how much support he had when people packed all those meetings he had in the week before polling-day. But isn't it strange having to wait for such a long time before we hear the results? I know it's because the servicemen's votes have to get back from all over the world and be counted, but it's never happened in an election before, has it?"

"No, and I hope it'll never have to happen again," Ruth replied. "Daniel thinks it might sway the voting in favour of the Tories because of Churchill's popularity with the troops, even though that Gallup opinion poll showed the Labour Party ahead. But Arthur says that from what he saw among the troops in Germany before he came home their mood was very much that it was time for a change. Anyhow, the results will be announced two days before the wedding and I'm pretty sure our best man will be having a personal celebration, even if his party isn't forming the next government."

"And I'm sure he'll be pleased that you and I will be moving out of his flat and letting him have Margarita all to himself. Have you noticed how, even when we are around, he can hardly keep his hands off her?"

"Yes, they're like a pair of newly-weds," said Ruth, smiling at the recollection. Her smile faded as she remembered a question she had been meaning to put to Rebecca but had several times postponed the asking. At Sloane Square their compartment emptied and she decided to postpone it no longer.

"There's something I wanted to ask your opinion about," she said. "I wouldn't say this to anyone else, and I know you'll keep it to yourself."

She glanced sideways at her friend's face and Rebecca said, "Of course. If it's something private you know I would never talk about it."

"It's about Daniel and me," she sent on. "I was so pleased that he still wanted to marry me when he came back. Just before he went off to the War we made a kind of agreement that we weren't going to take anything for granted when it was all over, because so many things were bound to happen to both of us that might change us – even though we believed we would go on loving each other. And I think I said I didn't want thoughts about me to stop him from doing whatever he felt was best in some totally new situation. He agreed that if we both survived we'd be, in a way, different people, needing to make our decisions all over again. But we've gone on writing to each other all through the War, and even though there were limits on what we could say – with other people having to read the letters – I think we did stay close to each other. And we're both quite sure we want to get married."

"So what's the problem?" asked Rebecca.

"It's something that happened a couple of years ago. I think we both meant what we said about needing to be free to do what we felt was best in completely new situations and… well, I did. Daniel had an American cousin called Sherman who came on holiday over here in '38. He came on one of our rambles with the group from Hannah More House that I told you about – I remember he was very certain then that America would never get involved in a European war. Anyhow, about the end of '43 he came to Britain with the American Air Force. He was based near Attleborough, in Norfolk.

"Soon after he arrived Sher wrote to Daniel's sister, Sarah, because that was the only address he had, and he asked if Daniel was still in England. Sarah had been in touch with me because Daniel had once asked her to send me a photograph of him that I wanted to have. Anyhow, she put him in touch with me and I agreed to meet him one weekend when he had some leave.

"He was a really nice chap and we got on well together, and so I agreed to meet him again the next time he had leave at a weekend. It was about six weeks later. I remember he brought me a pair of nylon stockings. But I could see he had changed quite a lot in that short time. He looked a lot older. And he told me he'd been on several missions over Germany."

"Was he a bomber pilot?" Rebecca asked.

"He was in a bomber, a Liberator, but he wasn't the pilot. He was the nose gunner, in that glass turret sticking out of the front of the plane. Just before he met me he'd been involved in something they called 'Big Week'. The American Eighth Air Force, which Sher was in, and the RAF between them flew round the clock to bomb German aircraft factories. His plane was hit a few times but it got back safely, although some of the other planes in his Group didn't make it, and he'd lost a few of his friends."

"It must have been a nerve-shattering experience being shot at day after day and never being able to relax for a moment," said Rebecca.

"When he opened up and started talking about it I could see how it was affecting him," Ruth went on. "And then he told me he didn't believe he was going to survive. He actually started to cry, and I put my arms around him. We'd gone back to the flat and there was no one else at home. He stopped crying and then he told me that what upset him most was thinking that his life would never be lived completely, because he would never have sex with anyone before he died. He'd had a girlfriend back home but they'd never gone to bed because they'd both been brought up to believe that you mustn't have sex before you were married."

The train jolted to a halt at Earls Court station and an elderly woman entered the compartment. In a lower voice Rebecca said, "I think I know what happened. You went to bed with him?"

"I did. It seemed the right thing to do, because I liked him enough to be able to give him some real affection. I still think it was right, even though it was all a bit… a bit awkward, because we were both first-timers. And he was killed about three weeks later, in a raid on Friedrichschafen. I only found out he was missing about a fortnight later, and even then I couldn't get any details. But I remembered he'd told me that the film actor, James Stewart was something called 'operations officer' in his Group, and was a very approachable chap. So I wrote to Major Stewart and pretended I was Sher's girlfriend, and he wrote back a very sympathetic letter, telling me Sher's plane had been shot down after losing an engine, and they didn't think he could have survived the crash."

"You must have been very sad; but it was better to know what happened."

"In a strange way it meant that I was able to think of what happened between us as something complete in itself and somehow separate from the rest of my life. But now I have to decide whether or not to tell Daniel about what happened. It's not that I'm afraid he won't want to marry me if I tell him about it. I know him well enough to be sure he wouldn't react in that way. But I'm thinking he's bound to realize that something has happened when he finds out on our wedding night that I'm not a virgin."

"So you and he never… got together before he went off to the War?" said Rebecca, looking surprised.

"No. We were actually planning to but Daniel got called up so quickly that we never had the chance to go through with our plan. In fact, I think there's a hotel in Broadstairs to which we might owe some money for bookings at the weekend when war broke out. We were different people then."

Rebecca patted her arm and said, "There's no need to worry about what happens when you get into bed. You can tell Daniel – and you ought to do it well in advance – that your cosmopolitan friend Rebecca has given you some advice about how to avoid the messy, painful business of a first penetration. Just using your fingers a few times you can – though in reality now you don't need to – open the entrance enough to make it easy. You'll be surprised, perhaps, when I tell you it was my mother who showed me how to do it. She was truly Viennese and she'd mixed with a quite 'progressive' set before she met my father, whose background was a lot more conventional. He actually grew up in Prague. When I was about eighteen I fell madly in love with a handsome fellow-student called Otto, and it was then that she took me aside and gave me some very useful pieces of advice – especially about making sure I didn't get pregnant."

"What happened to Otto?" Ruth asked. "I mean were you still in touch with him after you came to England?"

Rebecca shook her head. "In a way he was part of the reason why I came here, and perhaps I should be grateful to him for that. He graduated about a year after we met, and he went into the Austrian civil service. That was about the time when Hitler was really putting pressure on the Austrian government and it looked as if the Nazis were going to win. And somebody pointed out to Otto that his career would not go very far if he were to get married to a Jew. So he dropped me.

"Up to that time I'd never thought very much about being Jewish. My family thought of themselves as 'assimilated' and Mama was actually a member of the *Freidenkerbund* – the Free-Thinkers Association – although Papa still kept in touch with his family in Prague who were fairly religious. Now we realized that as far as the Nazis were concerned there was no such thing as an assimilated Jew. So we began to think about leaving; and because of my experience with Otto I didn't hesitate when Papa told me he'd heard that his friend in London was ready to give me a job in his antiques business. That was two days before the Germans marched into Austria. Mama and Papa were hoping to leave soon afterwards with my younger sister, Deborah, but they left it too late."

Ruth put her hand on Rebecca's arm, saying, "Oh, my problems seem so trivial when I think about what you've been through."

"Problems just have to be dealt with as they come along, whether they're big or small," Rebecca replied. "Now you've got to decide what you're going to tell Daniel. Will it make you both happier if he knows what you've done, or will your marriage be better if you forget about the past?"

"I know people say it's important always to be honest and open with your partner," said Ruth, "but I don't think there's anything dishonest about not telling him something that he doesn't need to know.

It's not even as if I'd been in love with Sher. We were both quite clear about that. And now he's dead; so there's no possibility that he might reappear and complicate things."

The train stopped in West Brompton and a fresh-faced young man in sailor's uniform with a giggling dark-haired girl on his arm entered the compartment. They seemed totally absorbed in one another.

"I bet their complications are all still ahead of them," said Rebecca, smiling. "But I think you've answered your own question about what you ought to do. I can't believe your marriage will be better if you tell Daniel something he doesn't need to know. And you said you'd both agreed in advance that you should be free to do what you thought best in wartime situations. For all you know Daniel may have had his own moments of getting away from the horror he went through. And last year he must have met lots of lovely Italian girls. Would it trouble you if he had done something?"

"No, it wouldn't; and I never wanted to know about what relationships he had before we met. The time he's been away at the war is a bit like that time. And I don't believe that when people get married they should stop having individual lives; do you? I think that when you get married you're creating a second life for both of you: you each have your own life, which includes your past, and as well as that the life you live together. For example, there'll be some friends that you share with your husband but there'll be others that are just your friends or just his friends. Do you think I'm right?"

"I'm sure you are. If I should ever get married that's how I'd want it to be. Good luck with the honeymoon. By the way, where are you going?"

"We've found a small hotel in Brockenhurst that's still open. I think American officers on leave kept it in business. It'll be the first proper holiday that Daniel has had in six years, even though it will only be for a week. He wants to show me part of the New Forest that he discovered when he was in a Territorial Army training camp just before the War. I think he'll be more used to walking than I am now. I've not had much opportunity this year."

"You won't be walking all the time," said Rebecca with a knowing grin as the train drew into Putney Bridge station.

When they began walking across Putney Bridge Ruth caught sight of a figure in Army uniform standing on the pavement near the centre of the bridge, looking down over the parapet at the river. Glimpsing a staff officer's red tab on his collar she knew that it must be either Daniel or Arthur; and as she drew closer she could see that it was Arthur.

She said to Rebecca, "Arthur seems to have a thing about the Thames. He loves looking at it."

Possibly because he'd heard her voice Arthur looked round and saw them approaching. "Hello you two," he said, "Any luck with the place in Pimlico?"

"It's great," Rebecca replied. "You'll be rid of me next week. Dodie's happy for me to move in straight away."

"It's been wonderful for Margarita to have you both with her while I've been away. I hope you'll keep in touch. Old friends are the best friends. I was actually on my way back to the flat; so we can walk together."

He fell into step beside them and they walked together into Putney Bridge Road, talking about Dodie and other former residents of Hannah More House. As they turned the corner leading to home Arthur asked, "Is Daniel going to be with us this evening? I've hardly had a chance to talk to him properly since the Election began."

"Yes, he's coming to dinner," Ruth replied. "He's been visiting Mrs Compton, his old landlady, this afternoon. She lives very close to where he's been staying, at the Great Central Hotel. The government took it over to provide quarters for officers temporarily in London."

When they got to the flat they found that Daniel had already arrived and was helping Margarita lay the table for dinner. Arthur seemed to be comfortable again in his own home Ruth observed, as he offered them all a drink.

"Are you still on the wagon, Daniel?" he asked and added, when Daniel confirmed his abstemiousness, "You would have fitted in well on Monty's staff. As you probably know, he's strictly teetotal. I've only known him break it once. I wasn't actually present, because I'd had to go back to Antwerp to sort out a supply tangle, but I heard about it afterwards. On the night he took the German surrender he had a glass of champagne at dinner."

"The other Ulsterman, the one that I've been working for, isn't so puritanical," said Daniel, "but Alexander is an ideal boss – courteous and considerate. I didn't have a lot of direct contact with him, of course, but everyone spoke well of him. However, I don't suppose I'll be seeing him again." He turned towards Ruth and continued, "I had a letter this afternoon telling me to report to the War Office on 6th August for what is described as an 'interview'. I expect it will be about my next posting."

Ruth felt her mood of happy anticipation drain away into cold apprehension. "I hope they're not going to send you to the Far East," she said. "Haven't you done enough already?"

"I suppose some of the chaps out there might say they've been doing even more," he replied. "It must be no picnic fighting people who've been taught that suicide is better than surrender. I read last week that the Yanks suffered about sixty-six thousand casualties, with over fifteen thousand dead when they occupied Okinawa in June. What's it going to be like when we go into Japan itself?"

"I hope you won't be one of the guys that have to go there, Daniel," said Arthur. "I'm sure if they do decide to send you east they'll want to use your skills liaising with the Yanks."

"Your interview will be on the Monday after we get back from honeymoon," said Ruth.

"Well, between now and then there's no point in worrying about it," said Daniel. "And from then onward I'll be getting a marriage allowance; so I'll be charging them more for my valuable services. And you, Arthur, will be a Member of Parliament."

"Yes, with any luck," said Arthur. "I'm pretty optimistic about winning the seat; but I'm not so sure about the Party being in government. I was at Transport House today, trying to catch up on what Party policy is really all about, and the mood was very divided. Some people believe we're going to win with a working majority, but others are being more cautious. The *News of the World* has said Churchill's going to win and the *Financial Times* seems to be taking the same view; but one of the researchers told me the betting on the Stock Exchange is six to four on Labour."

"Whoever's in Downing Street, he's going to have a pretty full agenda," said Ruth. "I see that Mr Churchill will be taking Mr Attlee with him to meet Mr Truman and Marshal Stalin in Potsdam tomorrow; so there ought to be some continuity whoever wins the election."

"The strange thing is that nobody here seems to be interested in foreign policy any longer," Arthur observed. "I don't think I had a single question about it during the whole campaign. And certainly nobody was talking about it at Transport House. It's as if people are thinking, 'We've won the war and that's got the foreigners out of the way; so now we can concentrate on sorting things out at home.'"

"And they couldn't be more wrong," said Daniel. "If that's really what they're thinking then events could turn out to be frighteningly like what happened in the 'Twenties. A lot of wrong decisions were taken because not enough people cared about them, and that was what started us down the road to this bloody war that we're just finishing. If you get into the House, Arthur, I hope you'll remember your League of Nations Union days and help to get a debate going about how to do things better this time."

"I'd like to, but I'm not sure anyone's going to pay much attention to a new backbencher who doesn't even know his way to the gents'. I've heard that some people in Britain have already started a 'United Nations Association'. That might be a help," Arthur replied.

"I'm glad to hear it," said Daniel. "But Parliament has to give a lead if people are going to understand what the issues are – and how important they are. For example, what's going to happen to all the grand schemes for rebuilding Britain if the Americans stop lending us money? And, of course, the biggest question of all – how do we get both the Russians and the Americans to come in this time on a peace-keeping scheme that will really work? That's going to be a tough one to answer. Do you think Mr Attlee would be up to it if he got the job?"

"I really don't know," said Arthur, "but there certainly is a hell of a mess to be sorted out in Europe, quite apart from what may happen in Asia when we've finally beaten the Japs."

"They say the first proper assembly of the United Nations is going to meet here in London at the beginning of next year," said Margarita. "It will be interesting to see what's on the agenda. I hope they will have something to say about Spain."

"I should think a lot of work will have to be done between now and then if it's going to function properly. I wonder who will be working on the preparations," Rebecca added.

Daniel looked thoughtful. "It's an area I wouldn't mind working in," he said. "It's very easy to criticize the guys who have to make the decisions, but they must be very dependent on the blokes who do the research for them. However, if I'm going to be sent off to help with taking out the Japs it could be a long time before I have a chance to think about a new job."

"I should think it'll take at least a year to decide how the new organization's going to work – especially if the decisions are being taken by a committee," said Arthur. "With any luck the War will be over by then, and if it is the timing would be just right for you."

"Always an optimist, Arthur. I hope you're right – about the War being over," said Daniel. "But you must be tired of talking about politics all the time. I'm completely out of touch with what's been happening in the theatre. I suppose a lot of the theatres were bombed; but I looked at the advertisements in today's paper and there were still a few familiar names."

"Things got going quite well again after the Blitz," said Ruth. "Margarita and I saw a lot of good performances, though it's not been easy to get seats. There have been some brilliant films, too. Last year Laurence Olivier made a spectacular film of *Henry V* – very patriotic, of course."

"I saw on a poster at the station that *Arsenic and Old Lace* is showing at the local flea-pit this evening. Why don't we all go and see it after dinner?" Rebecca suggested.

"That sounds like a very good idea," said Ruth. "A bit of pure escapism is just what we need."

CHAPTER FIVE: 6th August, 1945 - RUTH

Ruth glanced up at the kitchen clock and remarked, "Daniel will probably know by now where they're going to send him." She was taking tea with Margarita, having been invited to stay at the flat in Putney with Daniel until he knew where and when the Army was going to post him.

"If the interview began at four o'clock I suppose he might," said Margarita. "If they do send him to the Far East at least he will have to have all the injections first, and get fitted out with his tropical kit. He won't be leaving straight away. You know you can stay here for as long as you want to. I was actually quite lonely some days last week, with both you and Rebecca gone, and Arthur working late at the House. By the way, I've asked Rebecca to come to dinner this evening."

"That's good. I'd like to know how she's settling into the flat with Dodie – and whether she's got that temporary job with the Home Office."

"Yes, she has. She'll be starting work there tomorrow. It seems that, unlike the War Office, the Home Office doesn't work on a Bank Holiday. This afternoon she's attending some kind of committee meeting at an organization she's volunteered to help in her spare time. It's called the Primrose Club. I think its aim is to help rehabilitate some boys who survived the Nazi death camps and have been brought over here to Britain."

"I find it hard even to imagine what kind of effect that experience must have had on someone's mind – quite apart from how it must have damaged their bodies," said Ruth.

"Arthur told me about what he saw at the Belsen camp," said Margarita. "He didn't really want to talk about it, but I asked him to tell me. When he got there, he said, it was several days after the camps - there was one for men and one for women – had been liberated and the worst of the horror had been cleared out of sight. He was helping to organize transport. But he still saw things he said he was trying to forget. He told me he couldn't believe that one group of human beings could treat another group in that way and not be sickened by what they were doing. I think I find it easier to believe because I saw for myself in Spain how fascism changes the way that people think about their neighbours, even when they're all of the same race."

"Rebecca was so lucky to escape," said Ruth. "She seems not to have any hope that other members of her family might have survived. Maybe it's her way of coping with her grief."

"We have to learn how to bear the unbearable," said Margarita, and for a moment her face was altered in a way that Ruth had never seen before. Then, with a little shake of her head, she continued, "But now we have a chance to start again. Arthur is very excited about being in Parliament with a Labour government. Of course he pretends not to be, but that's because he's English. You understand."

Ruth laughed. "Not only English but a Yorkshireman," she replied. "I hope he's enjoying his day at the Victory Test Match, but I'm afraid he won't have seen much play this afternoon. That thunderstorm at lunchtime must have put a damper on the proceedings. It's such a shame. Arthur must have been so looking forward to it, because he can't have seen much cricket in the past six years. You know, I went to a Test Match with him in 1938. It was just about a week before we first met you. I've always been keen on cricket. I hope I can get Daniel interested. He used to play rugby, but he says that in Ireland there was so much rain in the summertime that he never really got into cricket."

"I think maybe he is so serious-minded that he wouldn't want to spend a whole day watching a game," said Margarita. "You will have to persuade him that sometimes it is good to let your brain have a fiesta and stop thinking about how to solve the problems of the world. Then, when it starts to think again it will have lots of new ideas."

Ruth laughed. "I think you might be right. But when he's with me he does know how to enjoy himself. I don't have to persuade him." Delightful memories of the previous week flashed through her mind, and so strong were they that she gave an involuntary shudder, as though her body still retained an afterglow of the passion it had experienced.

"Are you feeling cold," Margarita asked solicitously. "The temperature has really dropped since that thunderstorm. I'll light the gas fire in the sitting-room if you like."

"No, no – thank you," said Ruth, embarrassed even though she thought Margarita couldn't possibly guess the reason for that sudden tremor. "I'm not really cold. Just adjusting to the sudden change in temperature, I expect." The doorbell ran and she exclaimed, "Surely that can't be Daniel back already. Even if he took a taxi he couldn't have got here in the time."

"I expect it will be Rebecca," said Ruth, standing up and moving to the door. "I told her to come straight here, whatever time her meeting finished."

The new arrival was Rebecca, looking a little damp because she'd earlier been caught in the tail-end of a shower. They all went into the sitting-room, where Margarita lit the gas fire to help her dry out.

Rebecca told them about the meeting she'd been to, and the discussion there had been about the best ways in which to help young concentration camp survivors get back to health and as normal a way of life as might be possible for them. Margarita recalled experiences she'd had helping Basque children who'd arrived in Britain in 1939. "But they were lucky," she said. "They escaped before they could be brutalized."

"Something I found very strange," said Rebecca, "was being with a group of Jewish people – people who were self-consciously Jewish, if you understand what I mean. As you know, my family were 'assimilated' – or we thought we were till Hitler appeared – but when I used to visit Papa's family in Prague I had some sense of being Jewish. They weren't orthodox but they used to keep the main festivals and go to the synagogue on special occasions. But I used to think of that as being their religion – 'superstition' my mother used to call it – and not as something that defined who they were. What connected me to them was family.

"Then this afternoon I had the feeling that if I didn't accept my Jewishness as the most important thing about me I was in some way being disloyal to the dead. They were killed because they were Jewish. All the same, I couldn't help feeling uncomfortable. It's as if we're going along with Hitler's sick idea that the world is made up of different races who have to be kept separate from each other. I believe I'm a member of the human race, and if I have a special loyalty it's first to my family and then to the community that I'm a part of, which happens to be Britain. But the dead were killed because they were perceived to be like me, and so I feel I have to be loyal to them, too. Does that make any kind of sense?"

"I think it makes a lot of sense," said Ruth. "We want to make the future free of the old prejudices, but we can't escape the fact that the past is part of us and it forces us to make compromises. If you try to be totally consistent you can end up hurting people you want to help. I suppose if we'd acted consistently in the War we wouldn't have made an alliance with Stalin, and that could have meant that Hitler would have been the winner. I think we just have to keep on deciding what's the best thing to do in each set of circumstances as it arises."

"Well, I'm going to help some of these lads from the camps to learn English, and I think that's the right thing for me to do," said Rebecca.

"Will you excuse me for a few minutes while I start cooking the dinner?" asked Margarita. "The butcher advised me that the piece of mutton he sold me would be best cooked slowly for a long time, which means, I expect, that it's old and tough. So I'm going to put the casserole on now, and maybe by the time Arthur comes home it will be edible. It was the only meat he had left, apart from some doubtful-looking sausages."

When she had left the room Rebecca asked, "How was the honeymoon? I don't want to pry, but did it all work out like you hoped?"

Smiling broadly, Ruth replied, "It did. Daniel asked no questions; but I think you were right when you suggested that he could... could have had some experience himself. We had a lot of fun, and we didn't do nearly as much walking as we had originally planned. Thank you again for helping me to think straight about what I ought to do. It was the right decision."

"I do hope they're not going to send him away from you again," said Rebecca.

The doorbell rang and Ruth said, "I think we might be going to find out." She felt her heartbeat quicken as they heard Margarita moving to open the front door. Time seemed to slow down while she waited for Daniel to enter the room.

When he finally appeared in the doorway he seemed to sense her anxiety, for he immediately said, "I'm not going to the East," and grinned broadly, like a schoolboy who had just won a prize.

Ruth ran to him and kissed him on both cheeks, knocking his officer's hat askew and making him look even more schoolboyish. "Are they going to let you come home?" she exclaimed.

"No, but its quite exciting, and a bit complicated. Sit down and I'll tell you about it. Sorry, Rebecca. I didn't mean to ignore you. Please stay. I think you'll be interested; and you, too, Margarita." He removed his hat and his raincoat and they all sat down.

"I've been given another liaison job," said Daniel, "but it's something entirely different. You could say it's actually about keeping the peace. I'm going to be attached to an Anglo-American consultative committee that will feed ideas to the official representatives at the United Nations who'll be drawing up plans on how to implement the parts of the UNO Charter that are concerned with preventing aggression in the future.

"Of course, I'm not going to be having any real input into the planning. I'll only be the messenger boy. But it's something I'd really like to be part of – a serious attempt to work out a way to prevent wars in the future. It's the ideal job and it's starting straight away."

Ruth saw the enthusiasm shining in his bright blue eyes and remembered how often, since the dark days of 1939, she had wondered whether she would ever see it again. "Where are you going to be based?" she asked.

"To begin with here in London," he replied. "It looks as if the Americans are going to host the permanent secretariat for the UNO, but the organization's first General Assembly is going to be held here, in November. And of course a lot of the American army's top brass are still in Europe. After that I'll go to America, and they said I'll probably be officially called an Assistant Military Attaché at the Washington embassy – and you'll be able to come with me. And while I'm still in London I'll receive a 'housing allowance' so that we'll be able to live 'at home' – wherever that may be. One other bit of good news: my brevet rank of major is going to be made permanent; so I'll have a rise in salary."

"Congratulations!" said Margarita. "I'm so pleased that things are working out for you. And it sounds like such an interesting job."

"If we go to America I hope you'll be able to give me some tips on how to manage there, Margarita," said Ruth.

"I'm sure a lot will have changed in the ten years since I was there," said Margarita. "And Washington will be different from Boston. But I'll try to think of things that could be useful to you – like words that have completely different meanings over there. Because I was a student working hard on learning about English Literature I didn't meet very many ordinary Americans, apart from students. I suppose a lot of things will have changed by now, just like they have over here."

"The Army must think very well of you, to pick you for that job," said Rebecca. "I'm sure a lot of other people would want to be given it."

"I may be wrong, but I would like to think Field Marshal Alexander put my name forward for it," said Daniel. "It's not that I ever had much direct contact with him, but just once he indicated that he was very pleased with a report that I'd made. It was at that time when we got bogged down at Anzio. When I visited the HQ of the American commander, General Lucas, at Nettuno, several American staff officers talked to me about how unhappy they were with his tactics. I reported back – that was part of my job. Needless to say, my report was only one small piece of the picture; but a few weeks later Lucas was replaced by General Truscott. Ironically, things had just begun to get better by then. Anyhow, a few months later when I was ordered back to the staff after the short time I spent in the front line, somebody told me Alexander had mentioned my report as the reason he wanted me back in liaison."

"But presumably he'd earlier decided to let you go when you volunteered for the front line?" Ruth asked.

"I doubt if he would have been consulted when that decision was made. I think he would have been much too busy trying to sort out the mess at Monte Cassino. I can hardly believe all that happened only last year."

"Maybe in your new job you'll meet some of the Americans you worked with in Italy," said Margarita.

"I'd be happy if I did. For the most part they were very decent chaps."

Ruth wondered if there had been any connection between the report that had helped to get General Lucas sacked and Daniel's decision to volunteer for front-line service. She remembered that he had some peculiar ideas about what was required of him by his 'honour'. But that was not an issue to be explored in the company of other people. Maybe one day she would discover the answer.

"I must get back to the kitchen," said Margarita. "If Arthur has been sitting on the grass at Lord's in this dreadful weather he's going to need something to warm him up just as soon as he gets home."

When she had left them Daniel told Ruth and Rebecca more about his interview at the War Office, and said, "This is probably the last time I'm going to be able to talk truthfully about the new job. I was told that when I report to the Intelligence Corps next week I'll be briefed on the official description of my job, but it won't be what I'll actually be doing. The advisory group I'll be working for won't officially exist. It will be feeding ideas to the ostensibly quite separate British and American representatives on a UNO committee."

"If you have to report to the Intelligence Corps does that mean you're going to be a kind of spy?" asked Rebecca.

"No, I don't think so. But liaison work is all about communication in two directions, and very often the messages you deliver aren't just what you've been told, but also what you've seen or overheard." He went on to tell them about a few of the more light-hearted moments in his 'errand boy' activities in North Africa and Italy until Ruth, glancing at the clock on the mantelpiece, said, "It's six o'clock. Shall we switch on the News?"

The Bakelite wireless on the sideboard took a few seconds to warm up and then the familiar voice of the BBC news-reader said:

President Truman has announced a tremendous achievement by Allied scientists. They have produced the atomic bomb. One has already been dropped on a Japanese army base. It alone contained as much explosive power as two thousand of our great ten-tonners. The President has also foreshadowed the enormous peace-time value of this harnessing of atomic energy.

The staccato formality of the announcement momentarily prevented Ruth from taking in its full significance and then, seeing the looks of astonishment on the faces of her two companions, she exclaimed, "An atomic bomb! They've actually made one!"

"And dropped it," said Rebecca.

"That sounded like a very carefully worded statement," said Daniel. "Never mind the 'enormous peace-time value' – this is the most important change in the making of war since the invention of gunpowder."

"Do you think it will make the Japs surrender? Does it mean the War will soon be over?" asked Rebecca.

"I don't think we can bet on that," said Daniel. "Since February the Yanks have virtually flattened a couple of dozen Japanese cities with incendiary bombs. Hundreds of thousands must have been killed, and yet they haven't shown any sign of surrendering. No doubt the men who are running the War have deep shelters to hide in; and they're the ones who will lose everything if they surrender. So why wouldn't they keep on with the War for as long as the poor sods they've brainwashed are still alive and willing to fight for them?"

"I hope you're wrong about that," said Ruth, "but you're right that the people getting killed now are not the ones who can do anything to stop it. It's a pity the bombs haven't hit Hirohito and Tojo."

"On the other hand, it might be better if Hirohito stays alive," said Daniel. "He's probably the only one who could surrender and make all the rest of them lay down their arms – since they apparently believe that he's a god. It could be a very messy business if some of the generals decided to go on fighting after an official surrender."

The news-reader had now returned to the 'Atomic Bomb' story and was saying that the name of the army base was Hiroshima. There was no information yet about the extent of the damage because a huge pall of dust and smoke was still hanging over the city.

"I must tell Margarita the news," said Rebecca, moving towards the door. "This is a day that's going to be written about in all the history books."

Ruth switched off the wireless and looked at Daniel. "It's going to add a whole new dimension to the job that I'll be doing," he said. "Do you think the horror of so much destruction might finally persuade people that war isn't any longer an option they ought to consider?"

"I don't think so," she replied. "I'm sure Hitler would have loved to have this bomb – and was probably trying to make it. And I'm sure Marshal Stalin will be telling his scientists right now that they'd better produce one for him if they want to stay out of Siberia. Do you remember how, when we were setting up the Fraternalist Party, we used to hope that all the terrible statistics about the effect of bombing on cities – I think Bertrand Russell predicted that London would suffer fifty thousand casualties on the first day of a war – would persuade people that they must never go to war? But what it actually did was to persuade them to spend more money on air raid shelters – luckily for London. I think the best thing that your United Nations committee could do might be to work out ways of preventing conflict situations getting out of hand and drawing in any countries that might by then have made the new bomb. Am I being cynical?"

"No. You're being realistic, as usual. But the new bomb might just give people a sense of urgency. I hope it will. Back in the 'Twenties everyone seemed to think there was plenty of time to play with ideas and argue about what was the best way forward in foreign policy, and then suddenly time had run out. I think this time we're only going to have a breathing space for as long as America remains the only country to have the new bomb. After that the chance to find a completely new way of doing things will have gone."

"I hope the people you're going to work for will take that view," said Ruth.

"Even if they do it will still be the politicians, not the soldiers, who decide what's going to be done," said Daniel. "The UNO committee will only be offering advice. I hope it gets started very soon and gives the politicians some firm proposals to get their teeth into."

"Talking of politicians," said Ruth, "I think I heard the front door opening. Arthur must have come back."

As they both stood up and moved towards the door she heard Margarita's voice exclaiming, "Arthur, the Americans have dropped an atomic bomb on Japan. It's just been on the news."

"An atomic bomb!" she heard Arthur reply. "So they've finally made one. Nothing's ever going to be the same again."

Ruth paused with her fingers on the handle of the door and looked at Daniel. "Some things aren't going to change," she said, and kissed him passionately on the lips.

CHAPTER SIX: 25th August, 1945 - ARTHUR

When Dodie Ferguson's invitation to a 'reunion party' had arrived Arthur's first inclination had been to decline it politely; but then he'd remembered a conversation he'd had on the previous day, following a meeting of Labour MPs at the House. Somewhat to his surprise the new Minister for National Insurance, Jim Griffiths, had stopped to talk to him, having discovered that Arthur's father had been a miner. His own roots, he had said, were deep in the mining communities of South Wales, and for a few minutes they had exchanged reminiscences. Arthur had felt uneasy about his own credentials, because he had left Barnsley as a toddler, following his father's mining accident; but he had warmed to the older man's evident concern that he should have a successful career in Parliament. And then Griffiths had said: 'This place can eat up all your time if you allow it to; but don't lose touch with people outside this hothouse. They have a completely different view of the world and it's important we understand how they see things.' - or words to that effect.

So Arthur had told Margarita he was going to be available after a morning visit to his constituency office and they had decided to accept the invitation. Now, as he looked around the dozen people assembled in the spacious living-room of Dodie's Pimlico flat, he reflected that it was also important for Margarita to have a wider circle of friends. With the huge programme of legislation that was being planned he was almost certainly going to have to spend a great deal of his time at the House over the next few months and he feared that she might be lonely – especially because Ruth and Daniel would probably be going to America.

Just then Daniel approached him, skirting a group of animatedly chattering young women with a glass of orange squash in his hand. "It must have been pretty exciting in the House on Monday," he said.

One of the young women, whose name Arthur thought was Alison, turned around and exclaimed, "Oh, that 'Red Flag' business! Did you join in the singing?"

Arthur laughed. "I didn't actually. I can never remember the words, after the first two lines. But I couldn't understand why some of the comrades were so annoyed when the Tories greeted Mr Churchill's arrival in the House by singing 'For he's a jolly good fellow'. It seemed a natural enough thing to do. Anyhow, the new Speaker was good-humoured in the way he handled the situation. He said afterwards, 'I wondered whether I was going to be Speaker or director of a musical show'."

"Speaking of musical shows, did you hear Roddy saying that he hopes he may get a part in Novello's *Perchance to Dream*? He's going for an audition on Monday," said Alison.

"Roddy? I haven't spoken to him yet," said Arthur. "Do you know, it's six years since I last saw him, and that must have been just after he'd heard about getting his first West End part. I think it was in *Pygmalion*. He came to the house-warming lunch that Nancy and Freddie gave when they moved into their flat in Finchley Road."

"I'm so glad that Nancy decided to come today," said Daniel. "It was good of Rebecca to volunteer to baby-sit for her. Ruth says she hardly ever gets out on her own these days; but it will be a bit easier when little Leo starts going to nursery school next week. I really must pay them a visit soon – I've never seen the little lad."

"Becoming Lady Newingham doesn't seem to have changed her at all, does it?" said Alison.

"I think she very strenuously doesn't want to be changed," said Daniel. "But having access to a good deal of money must be making it easier for her to cope with bringing up Leo on her own."

"What are you doing now, Alison?" asked Arthur. "Margarita said you've been in the ATS."

"Yes. I ended up in an Ack-Ack battery in Regent's Park. I was a loader. I was demobbed in June," she replied.

"And what are you going to do now?"

"I've been given my old job back. From next week I'll be teaching Latin to little girls. I expect it'll take a bit of getting used to."

"Who's the girl in WRAF uniform?" Arthur asked.

"That's Monica. Don't you remember her?" Alison replied. "I suppose she has changed quite a lot. She married a pilot a couple of years ago and he's in India now. So I should think she must be very pleased the War out there is over."

"Someone else who has good reason to be pleased is Polly. She was telling me her brother was taken prisoner in Singapore. He was in the Middlesex Regiment. They've just had confirmation that he's alive in Japan, and now that the Americans have landed there it shouldn't be very long before he's home," said Daniel.

"Didn't she work at Church House before the War?" asked Arthur, vaguely remembering that he had heard her express strong views on moral questions.

"Yes," Alison replied. "When she joined the ATS she was drafted into the Royal Army Chaplains' Department as a secretary; and now she's engaged to a chaplain. She was demobbed last week, but she won't have to worry about finding a job. They're planning to get married before Christmas and then, I suppose, she'll become a vicar's wife."

"Wasn't there one other girl in your little group at the hostel who isn't here today, a tallish fair-haired girl who was a science teacher?" Daniel asked. "I can't remember her name."

"That was Harriet Rice," said Alison. "We keep in touch; but she couldn't be here because she's still in France. She's a Wren – a wireless operator at a Navy shore base when I last heard from her. I think she's enjoyed it."

Arthur nodded his head. "That's one of the odd things about this War," he said. "There are quite a few people who've enjoyed their experiences, even though for others it's been pure hell."

"I suppose a lot depended on what job you had to do and where you were doing it," said Daniel. "Most of my time in Italy was pretty awful but there were a few intervals of huge enjoyment. I want to go back there, and take Ruth with me, as soon as they've got themselves straightened out. But I've no desire to see North Africa ever again."

"Nor have it," said Arthur. "I think I'd prefer a holiday in Iceland."

"I must ask Dodie what's happening at the National Gallery. I wonder if they can take visits from schools yet," said Alison, and moved away.

"I want to ask you more about what's been happening in Parliament, but first I really must have a word with Nancy," said Daniel; and he, too, moved away.

Arthur looked around the room at the several little groups engaged in lively conversation, and remembered the summer day when he had first met some of them, on a ramble in the Hertfordshire countryside. Margarita hadn't been there, of course, because she hadn't yet arrived in England. It must have been the summer of 1938. He'd snatched an opportunity to invite Ruth to go with him to an exhibition of Picasso's picture of Guernica that was coming to London.

Seeing Ruth put her hand on Daniel's shoulder when he joined her in conversation with Nancy, Arthur remembered how, on that outing, he had wondered whether she might be romantically interested in Daniel even though only a few weeks earlier it had been him she'd invited to fill a gap in her father's village cricket team. And then he'd become uncertain about his own feelings for her. There had been no doubt about the physical attraction, and she'd been a delightful companion on the several occasions they'd gone out together, including that incredible Test match when Hutton hit his record three hundred and sixty-four. But when he'd begun to think seriously about making a proposal the difference between their backgrounds had started to bother him. How would she feel when he took her to visit his Mam and Dad in their shabby flat about the tea-room in York?

And then there had been another outing of the group at the end of the summer and he'd met Margarita. He'd known nothing about her except that she was a refugee whose father had been killed by the fascists – and that she had the most beautiful body of any woman he'd ever seen. And he had instantly made an irrational decision that had turned out to be the wisest thing he had ever done.

"Am I interrupting your cogitation on some critical vote in the House next week?" asked Roddy, approaching in company with a striking blonde who was wearing a scarlet dress that saved even more material at hemline and neckline than might have been required by Utility regulations. "I think the last time you met Cecily she hadn't become my wife – and the War hadn't even begun."

"I remember it well. We were all hoping for the best and fearing the worst – and the worst happened," said Arthur. "You've been working together in ENSA, I hear."

"Yes, we've been doing our bit to keep up morale, though sometimes I've wondered if we might be having the opposite effect," Roddy replied. "For the last few months we were performing mainly at American bases. You could call it a kind of Lend-Lease in reverse."

"And now that you've stopped doing it the Americans have stopped doing Lend-Lease," said Arthur.

"Is that going to be as serious a problem for us as Mr Attlee seemed to be suggesting yesterday?" asked Ruth, who had joined their little group.

"Well, I was in the House when he made the announcement, and he did look seriously worried," said Arthur. "Nobody wants to be cutting imports when there are so many shortages already. And we've got to boost our exports to earn the money we need to get back to normal; so that's going to mean selling things abroad that we would rather be using at home. It's not going to be popular but I don't think there's any alternative. The Yanks have lent us a huge amount of money already. It's not too surprising they wanted to stop."

"Somebody said we're not going to be able to buy nylons. That would be absolutely awful," Cecily complained.

"Up till now you've never had to buy any," said Roddy. "There's always been some obliging GI only too anxious to give you a pair."

"I know; but they're all going home and we shan't see them any more," said Cecily. "We were with some of them on VJ Day and they were just so happy that they weren't going to be sent to the Far East."

"Dodie and I went down to Whitehall to listen to Mr Attlee and there seemed to be more American servicemen around than British civilians. Actually, we couldn't hear what Mr Attlee was saying because so many people were shouting 'We want Churchill'," said Alison. "It's a pity he hadn't invited Mr Churchill to be on the balcony along with him and Mr Bevin and Mr Morrison. People would have thought better of him if he'd done that."

"Have you listened to the new Light Programme on the wireless?" asked Cecily. "Roddy thinks it might provide some new opportunities for actors. I think we're going to need some, with all these chaps soon coming back from the forces. They're going to be given priority for any jobs that are going in the theatre. So I hope the BBC will be using a lot more actors."

"I'm going to put out some feelers in that direction," said Roddy. "But if I'm successful at the theatre audition on Monday it'll only be to help Cecily. Unfortunately the wireless people won't be interested in a beautiful face; so it will all be up to whether or not they like the sound of your voice."

"Where are you living now?" Arthur asked.

"Just after we were married – that was in February 1940 – we found a one-room flat in Chelsea and we've been able to keep it right through the War. Actually, we've been out of town for most of the time, but usually there's been some friend in the profession wanting to stay there while they've been working or visiting in London. So it hasn't been left empty for much of the time."

"And Hitler's bombs kept missing it," Cecily added. "A house just round the corner from it was completely demolished. I suppose we're lucky still to have it; but if we can both find work in London I hope we'll be able to move to somewhere bigger."

"Do you think it will be long before the Government gets started on a big housing programme, Arthur?" asked Ruth.

"I think it's going to be a priority," he replied. "There's quite an argument in the Party, however, about whether we ought to be going for smaller units that can be built quickly, like the prefabs, or concentrating on better quality and durability, to get right away from the old idea that if the working class can't afford anything better they ought to be content with slums."

"If it's not possible to do both – build quickly and have good quality – that must be a hard choice," said Ruth. "But with so many people not having proper homes now I don't think they're going to wait patiently for very long."

"I knew a girl in the Battery whose parents have a prefab and she said they think it's marvellous. They even have a little garden," said Alison.

"Oh, I wouldn't want to live in one of those. They look like oversized hen-houses," said Cecily. "But you're going to be moving to America, Ruth. Everything's so big and modern over there. Do you know yet where you'll be living?"

"Nothing is certain yet," Ruth replied. "Daniel's been told that he'll be formally attached to the embassy in Washington, but his work will be to do with the United Nations Organization and they think that's going to be located somewhere around New York. So I don't know where we're going to be living – even assuming that when the General Assembly meets here in January it agrees to have its offices in America. I think we'll still be in England until sometime next year.

"Daniel's starting on a short course at Camberley next week; so I'll probably go and stay with Mummy and Daddy during the Autumn, now that I'm jobless. It's a very strange feeling, not having to get up in the morning and go off to do something definite. I hope it won't last for long, but until Daniel knows exactly where he's going to be, and when, I can't start looking for a permanent job."

"You might be able to find translation work that you could do at home," said Arthur. "Margarita has been put in touch with a publisher who's probably going to give her some Spanish translation work."

"What a very good idea. I must start making some enquiries," said Ruth.

Remembering how Ruth had helped through her cousin at the Foreign Office to find a job for Margarita at the beginning of the War, Arthur felt pleased that he had, in his turn, been able to help her. "I hope you'll find something interesting," he said. "You might even think about writing something on your own account to help kids with learning German – if you can still remember your teaching days."

"That's an interesting proposal," said Daniel, joining the group with a glass of orange squash in his hand. "I seem to remember that you used to have some strong views on how German ought not to be taught."

"Yes, I did," said Ruth. "I must give some serious consideration to Arthur's suggestion. It would keep me out of mischief while you're off learning how to deal with the military top brass – if that's what they're going to teach you at Camberley."

"Roddy, you seem to have done a great job in helping Nancy to sort out the legal side of little Leo's inheritance. She sounds really happy about the arrangements," said Daniel.

"I didn't do all that much, really," Roddy replied. "I think I helped to point her in the right direction. An English chap who was at Trinity with me handled the business for her. His eyesight kept him out of the Army, and he seems to have got himself well established in a thriving practice. What really pleased me is the way she's been able to get into a good relationship with Freddie's mother. I remembered what my father used to say: 'If you can persuade the parties in a dispute to be reasonable with each other you may not make as much money out of the case but you'll have done a job you can be proud of.'"

"It's a pity more solicitors don't take that view," said Daniel. "Nancy tells me that the old lady is staying on in the big house and running the estate, while she and Leo go down to visit her once a month. And Leo's name has not been put down for Eton. She was talking about somewhere called Dartington Hall, but it sounds a bit peculiar to me. Seems to be based on the proposition that children should only be taught what they want to learn. However, it will be a few years yet before she has to make a final decision about that."

"I think there's going to be a big shake-up in education over the next few years," said Arthur. "I hope there'll be a lot more choices available by the time Leo's ready for secondary school. I've just been reading up about last year's Butler Act, and it ought to open doors that have been closed to the majority of kids until now. Of course, Nancy will have money to spend if she wants to, but if she prefers to be egalitarian there ought to be a well-funded grammar school with a decent curriculum that he can go to."

"I thought a lot of people in your party wanted to get rid of grammar schools and put all the kids into huge 'multilateral' schools where everybody would be given the same education, no matter how bright or how dim they might be," said Alison.

"There are quite a few who take that line," Arthur replied, "but Ellen Wilkinson, who's the Minister, seems to be a realist, and she must know it's going to be hard enough to find the money just to repair the existing schools and train enough teachers to make sure the Butler reforms are properly implemented. Starting all over again with a lot of big, new schools just wouldn't be possible."

"Well, if there is a new curriculum I hope it will produce a better result than the one that G M Trevelyan was so critical of – 'a population able to read but unable to distinguish what is worth reading,'" said Alison.

"Did he say that in his *History of England*? It's a shrewd observation but I don't remember it," said Daniel.

"No, it was something he said in a book he published a couple of years ago called *English Social History*. One advantage of my last posting was that it gave me a lot of time to read some of the latest books. Most of the time we were just sitting around waiting for something that wasn't going to happen. Even when the V2s were coming over there was nothing we could do about them," Alison replied.

"I'm going to have a lot of catching up to do with my reading," said Arthur. "Actually, I've decided to go to a weekend conference in Oxford in September that will probably give me some pointers to which people are having the most interesting ideas at the moment."

"Who's organizing the conference?" Ruth asked.

"The Fabian Society. I've had to take out membership in order to go, but I think it should be worthwhile. Some of the Party's best thinkers will be on the platform, like Michael Young, who wrote most of the manifesto, and G D H Cole; and there'll also be talks by people like John Bowlby, the psychiatrist. I expect he'll be taking a very different angle on politics. I'm quite looking forward to it."

"Sounds as if it should be very stimulating," said Daniel. "Will anybody be talking about international affairs?"

"I don't think so. The title of the conference is 'The psychological and sociological problems of modern socialism'."

"In my opinion one of the basic psychological problems is the difficulty that most people seem to have in recognizing the connection between their own aspirations for a better life here in Britain and events in the wider world that will make those aspirations either possible or impossible to achieve," said Daniel. "The things that are happening which will make us go on having to spend a lot of money on armaments are a good example. And is there going to be agreement on an open trading system that will keep the world away from the kind of protectionism that did so much damage in the '30s? I think those are problems that are psychological and sociological as well as economic and political."

"I'm sure you're right," Arthur agreed. "If I get an opportunity in the discussions I'll try to remind people about the international dimension."

"I saw something in the newspaper yesterday about a United Nations Association starting up here in London," said Ruth. "I presume it's going to be the same kind of organization as the old League of Nations Union. You were a member of that, weren't you Arthur?"

"Yes, I was. It was trying to do just what Daniel was talking about – getting people to understand that the really vital problems we have to solve are the international ones. I don't think it really succeeded, any more than the League itself did."

"Why do you think it failed?" asked Alison.

"Essentially because of the split between the idealists and the realists," Arthur replied. "The idealists believed that the League should stop aggressors using force to achieve their aims. But they also believed that the League should never use force itself – or rather that its members shouldn't, since it didn't have any force to use. And the realists, who could see that the League would never be effective if it wasn't able, ultimately, to deploy superior force against aggression, were too few to win political influence without the backing of the idealists. So the message kept getting fudged. The popular slogan was 'Peace and Justice', but the idealists refused to admit that you couldn't have both at the same time."

"I know that's right," said Daniel. "I was one of the idealists until it was too late. From my own experience I can recognize that human beings have a huge capacity for self-deception, even when facts to the contrary are staring them in the face. We've paid the price for that mistake and I hope we're not going to repeat it in the future. That's why I count myself lucky to have been given a job now that may make some tiny contribution to working out a better way of tackling the old problems than the League was able to devise."

"I'll be very interested to hear how you get on – if you're allowed to tell me," said Arthur.

Dodie approached their little group, saying, "I can see you're talking politics. This is supposed to be a celebration. The food's all ready now, over here. It's not very festive but it was the best we could do."

"So let us eat, drink and be merry," said Roddy.

And Ruth added, "For yesterday we might have died."

"Your substitute ending for that quotation is very apt," said Arthur, putting one arm around her shoulders and the other around Daniel's. "All the evils of human existence were let out of Pandora's Box and they've done their worst; but now we have Hope. We've got to hang on to her."

Together they walked across the room to the table where the spam sandwiches awaited them.

CHAPTER SEVEN: 26ᵗʰ November, 1945 - DANIEL

A gust of chill November wind ruffled the grey surface of the river as Daniel put an arm around Ruth's shoulders and hugged her to generate some mutual warmth. "I think we'd better turn back now. It's starting to get dark and I shouldn't be surprised if it starts to rain before very long," he said.

Ruth agreed with his suggestion and they turned around and headed back towards Putney Bridge with the wind now behind them. Because it was his first day back in London after the staff course at Camberly he had some free time, and they had taken the opportunity to walk along the Embankment.

"It's jolly nice of Margarita and Arthur to let us use my old room again," she said. "I would hate to have to be visiting you in a billet in some run-down ex-hotel for the next few weeks."

"I expect it will be the last time we lodge with them in Putney, now that Margarita is pregnant," said Daniel. "Before we come back to London again from the States, if that's where we go, they're going to be using the spare room for the baby – that's if they stay in the flat."

"I know that Margarita would love to move to a house with a garden, somewhere in the constituency, but of course at the moment there's absolutely nothing available," said Ruth.

"That should change if Arthur's colleagues are able to get on with their house-building programme," he commented. "But I'm not sure where the Government's going to find the money, especially after the cut they made in income tax last week. Maybe the new loan the Americans have agreed to give us will keep the wheels turning. I read in the paper that some of Arthur's colleagues on the Left were against the idea because they didn't want to be seen to be dependent on American capitalists, but I wonder where they thought they were going to find the money to pay for all the social welfare schemes they're planning. And the article also said that some American politicians had been opposed to giving us the loan because they didn't want to subsidize socialism."

"I saw somewhere that a group of Tory MPs are planning to oppose the loan when it's discussed in the House next month," said Ruth. "Apparently Lord Beaverbrook thinks we would be surrendering the independence of the Empire."

"He's going to have a few more bitter pills to swallow before very long," said Daniel. "We're in a new kind of world now, where countries are going to have to work together if they want to get back to some kind of prosperity. I think that's a very good thing. If we all become interdependent there'll be fewer temptations for countries to attack their neighbours."

"That could be very relevant to your job, couldn't it?" she said. "Do you have any clearer idea yet what this group you'll be working for are going to be proposing?"

"They haven't really started talking to each other yet – apart, I think, from agreeing who's going to be involved in the discussion. But it seems pretty clear to me what the focus of their discussion is going to be. As you know, the main job of the UNO is going to be 'maintaining peace and security', and the Security Council will be the body ultimately responsible for doing that."

"Who's going to be on the Security Council?" Ruth asked.

"There'll be representatives of five permanent member countries – Russia, China, the USA, France and Britain. And there'll also be ten non-permanent members elected every two years by the General Assembly, with quotas for different parts of the world, so that membership will really move around. But the permanent members will each have a veto, so that nothing important can be done without their agreement."

"Isn't that going to make it impossible to get anything done if one of them, or an ally of one of them breaks the rules?"

"Of course it is," he replied. "And I expect one of the main topics for discussion is going to be what procedures could be introduced that might help to get around that problem. The Covenant of the League of Nations actually contained what I think could have been the answer. Its Article Sixteen said that if a country committed an act of war against another country it would be deemed to be at war with all the other members of the League and they would have a responsibility to respond accordingly. Unfortunately the League never really implemented that Article and so it became an irrelevance. So my guess is that they'll be talking about ways to prevent the same thing happening in the UNO. But it's not going to be easy, and I suppose that's why they decided to have this informal Anglo-American consultation before the official five-power committee is set up to advise the Security Council. It's going to be called the Military Staff Committee.

"Incidentally, the group I'm working for doesn't exist officially; so from now on I have to be careful what I say about my job, even though I'm only the messenger boy. If anyone asks, I'm going to be just an assistant attaché at the Washington embassy, involved in the bureaucratic work of setting up the UNO."

"Apart from what's written in the Charter, has anyone publicly made any suggestions yet?" Ruth asked, leaning closer to him as a gust of wind from behind forced them into an involuntary quickening of their pace. He tightened his protective grasp on her shoulder and suddenly remembered the very first time his hands had encountered the softness of her body, as together they had pushed their way through the crowd in Downing Street listening to Mr Chamberlain on his return from Munich.

"I've been trying to find that out myself," he replied. "It's not been part of my briefing. But it looks as if the first positive proposals were made by Mr Cordell Hull at the end of 1943. He said that if it was confronted by some future aggression the UNO would need to have a permanent armed force of its own or else national governments would need to earmark in advance units of their own forces that would be available for it to use in an emergency. The third option was that the Security Council would have to call on national governments to provide forces after an emergency had happened. Personally, I think those are the three options they're going to have to choose between."

"It reminds me of those discussions we used to have in the old days at meetings of the League of Nations Union," said Ruth. "But by the time I joined I think a lot of people had begun to realize that none of the idealistic solutions was actually going to work. Do you think there's really going to be a second chance to set up an international system that will keep the peace?"

They had reached the Embankment's junction with Putney Bridge and Putney High Street and Daniel did not reply to her question until they had safely negotiated the streams of traffic flowing north and south across the river. Once they were across the street, in the lee of the church tower, he said, "You're right about idealistic solutions. There are still some of those around. I came across a book published last year, by an American chap called Ely Culbertson. He had a beautifully worked out scheme for a world police force, which would have a monopoly of all the powerful armaments, with nation states being limited to a kind of pre-1914 range of weaponry. It was all worked out in detail and perfectly logical. But can you see Marshal Stalin being willing even to discuss that kind of arrangement? They're going to have to do some hard talking to arrive at any kind of solution that might be workable."

"But it would be wonderful if they did," said Ruth.

"It would; and that's why I'm pleased to be involved in the process, even if I'm only a messenger boy. I suppose it's just possible the existence of the atom bomb may persuade Marshall Stalin that using force isn't likely to work so well for him in the future."

When they turned into Putney Bridge Road the wind seemed to lose some of its force and they slackened their pace. "I heard on the wireless on Saturday that the Mayor of Chicago has come over here with a proposal that the UNO headquarters should be built in his city," said Ruth. "I can't feel very enthusiastic about the idea of going to live in Chicago."

"All I know about Chicago is that it processes huge quantities of meat and used to have a nasty gangster problem – oh, and politics there are said to be very corrupt," Daniel replied. "I suppose like most generalizations that's very unfair. All the same, I would certainly share your lack of enthusiasm. In saw in the paper this morning that the UNO Preparatory Commission held its first meeting in Church House on Saturday. I expect it will be making a recommendation to the General Assembly in January. The word is that the location will certainly be America, because the Yanks are prepared to put up the money to pay for it, and also everyone is keen to make sure they don't duck out at the last minute like they did when the League was set up. But I should think it will be up to them to decide which city it goes to. Anyhow, the probability is that we'll be living in Washington, because that's where the military have their headquarters, and they're the people I'll be carrying messages to."

"I don't much care where it is so long as we can really be together," said Ruth, giving him an unexpected hug.

"When we get there I hope you're going to be able to find something satisfying to do," he said, returning the hug. "Unfortunately, I have no idea how long I'm going to be stationed there."

"I've found out a bit about this United Nations Association that's been set up to mobilize popular support for the UNO," said Ruth. "I went round last week to its offices in Maiden Lane. A very nice man called Judd, who's the head of it, told me that a branch has been set up already in the States and it has an office in Washington. I was thinking I might be able to get involved in some work for them. Mr Judd was very enthusiastic about the idea that I might also be able to do something to strengthen the link between the London and Washington branches."

"That sounds like a really good idea." Daniel experienced a sense of relief. Talking about their move to America had reawakened his anxiety about what was going to be the future for Ruth while he was engaged in a job that offered him the prospect of real satisfaction. She was going to need something that would be equally fulfilling. "As soon as we know when we're going to be moving you could get in touch with the Washington office and see what the prospects are. My guess is that

Americans – especially the kind who support the UNA – are likely to be very welcoming," he added.

"Look! There's Margarita and Arthur," Ruth exclaimed as they turned the corner into the street to which they were heading. "They must be coming back from their visit to the doctor. Arthur was going to take time off from the House to go with her. I bet the doctor was surprised to see him."

Their friends saw them approaching and waited on the doorstep. "How did it go?" asked Ruth as they went into the flat together.

"Doctor Arkwright was very reassuring. He told me all the things about eating and resting and exercise that I'd read in the book," Margarita replied.

"What is his prediction for the time of the happy event?" asked Daniel, pleased to see that her usually serious expression had been replaced by a look of carefree contentment.

"It should be in June," she replied.

"Not too long before the parliamentary recess; so for a few weeks I'll be able to spend most of my time with my family," Arthur added.

"Did the Whips' Office let you have the afternoon off today?" Daniel asked as they removed their coats and hats.

"At the moment they're pretty relaxed because of the size of our majority," Arthur replied. "And the main debate today is about the Housing Bill, which isn't a topic I'm particularly involved with."

"Has the argument between those who want to go for quality and those who are pressing for speed and quantity been resolved?" asked Ruth.

"I think there's been a compromise. Being in government is all about learning to compromise."

While Margarita went to boil the kettle Arthur turned on the gas fire and they sat down around it. Daniel noticed that Arthur, too, had a look of contentment.

"I expect Margarita has told you we're hoping to find a house in the constituency that we can move out to when the baby's born," said Arthur. "I'm just a bit concerned about taking a house there – assuming we can find one – while there's still such a shortage. But I would like us to have a house with a garden. I've never lived in a house with a garden."

"Won't the Government's new housing programme have started to produce results by the summer?" said Ruth. "And anyhow, remember you're not just an MP. You're an ex-serviceman, and they're supposed to have priority. I don't think many people will want to criticize you – especially if you get your photograph into the local papers holding the baby."

"I think I ought to hire you as my election agent," said Arthur.

"You would be doing yourself a favour," said Daniel. "Ruth was shaping up for a career in politics back in '38 – and in what's now your constituency. Remember our great crusade with the Fraternalist Party, which I think you were rightly sceptical about?"

"Yes, I remember. I'm sure that must have taught you a lot about grassroots politics that I still haven't had time to learn."

Margarita entered the room with a teapot and cups and saucers on a tray. "Your mother would be pleased to see how well I have learned what is the right thing to do when people come into your house on a cold day," she said to her husband.

"She would indeed. Mam thinks Margarita has more Yorkshire qualities than any of the southern English women she has met – not that she has actually met very many. I suppose you haven't had much opportunity to get to know *your* mother-in-law, Ruth," said Arthur.

"None at all," she replied. "We met for a short time when Daniel's parents and sister came over for the wedding, but then we were off on our honeymoon. My mother said she'd had a really nice conversation afterwards, answering a lot of questions about me – and asking a few about Daniel. But we're going over to Portadown at Christmas; so I'll be under scrutiny then from the whole of the Hardstaff family."

Daniel sensed a note of apprehension in her voice. "They'll probably end up knowing more about you than they do about me," he said. "It's been an unspoken rule in the family that we respect each other's privacy, and I've always been a fairly private person. But it's also a family tradition – I think it's really an Ulster tradition – that we welcome those who want to be welcomed. So you've nothing to worry about, apart from being given too much food to eat."

"Speaking of food," said Arthur, "after we've had dinner Margarita and I are going to grab this rare chance to go out somewhere together for the evening. We were thinking about that play by Walter Greenwood at the Westminster Theatre, *The Cure for Love*. Have you seen it, Ruth?"

"No, I haven't," she replied. "I remember before the War his book *Love on the Dole* was a huge success on the stage when he turned it into a play. There hadn't been many plays before that by working-class writers; but I don't know what he's been writing since then. Do you remember we'd thought about asking him to support the Fraternalist Party? I don't think anything ever came of that."

"I'm completely out of touch with what's been happening in the theatre," said Daniel, "though in your letters you used to tell me about plays you'd been to see. That was something the censors couldn't object to. Looking in the *News Chronicle* on the train this morning I saw that Laurence Olivier and Ralph Richardson are doing *Henry IV* at the New Theatre. That's something I'd like to see, to get me back into Shakespeare. It's a funny thing, but when we liberated Venice in May I was there for only a couple of days and everywhere I went I kept remembering lines from *The Merchant.*"

"*What's new on the Rialto?* would have been very appropriate, I should think," said Margarita. "And you might even have included *Othello* and remembered *I have done the state some service.* You were lucky to go there. I'd love to see Venice."

"So you're still a Shakespeare enthusiast," said Daniel. "I remember that gave Arthur his excuse for the first date he had with you, when he took you to see *Midsummer Night's Dream* in the park."

"I'll take you to Venice one day – when the baby's old enough to travel abroad," said Arthur; and he gently patted her stomach.

"Why don't we go to the cinema this evening?" said Ruth to Daniel. "There's a new film with James Mason and Margaret Lockwood at the Gaumont in the Haymarket. I think it's called *The Wicked Lady.*"

"Good idea," he replied. "We'll get seats in the back row and you can be my wicked lady."

CHAPTER EIGHT: 26th December, 1945 - RUTH

Daniel's detailed predictions of exactly how Christmas would be celebrated by his family were turning out to be amazingly accurate, Ruth reflected, as she sipped the cup of tea which, he had told her, would bring to an end the gargantuan Boxing Day lunch. The lunch (called 'dinner') was being held in the home of his elder brother, Mark and his wife, Maureen. This was a comparatively new venue, having been instituted only two years earlier, when his Uncle Henry (his mother's elder brother) and Aunty Letitia had moved to a town too far distant for the rest of the extended family to accept their traditional hospitality.

There were so many new names to be learned and new faces to be recognized, but Ruth felt that she was coping reasonably well. And there were some new faces that even Daniel hadn't seen before – Mark's second child, William, born in 1941, and his sister Mary's daughter, Ann, born in 1943. His unmarried younger sister, Sarah, now a Ward Sister at the Royal Victoria Hospital, was being very supportive to Ruth in an unobtrusive way, often anticipating the questions she wanted to ask.

Meeting the family en masse at their Christmas and Boxing Day celebrations had some advantages, she reflected. At least she had been spared a round of visits to individual homes, each one no doubt involving generous offerings of food and drink (non-alcoholic). And at the festive gatherings the various family members had plenty of questions to ask each other about topics of mutual interest, so that she was spared from being the sole object of scrutiny. There could be no doubt about the sincerity of their collective desire to make her feel welcome, even if at times it was a little overwhelming.

The rather severe-looking middle-aged woman whom she recognized as Aunty Hilda ('lost her fiancé on the Somme', Daniel had told her) now addressed her across the table. "I hear tell you might be going to America for a wee while," she said. "That should give you a chance to put a bit of flesh back on our Daniel. He's gone a bit skinny in the Army. I suppose it was the heat in those places they sent him to – and not getting regular meals, I shouldn't wonder. You'll need to build him up; and I hear they have no shortage of food over there."

"Do you know yet when you'll be going?" Daniel's father asked.

"I think it will be some time in January," said Daniel. "The War Office told me they'll let me know what's been decided by January 10th and we should be ready to move any time after that. We'll probably be going on the *Queen Mary*."

"What exactly are you going to be doing?" his brother Mark enquired.

"I'm going to be running messages for some of the top brass who'll be trying to get an agreement on how the UNO is actually going to do its job of keeping the peace. Everybody says that's what they want it to do, and there's to be a Military Staff Committee that will draw up plans on the best way to do it. Behind that committee, of course, there'll be people putting up ideas about what's desirable and what's possible, and I'll be working for some of them – helping to oil the wheels, you might say."

"That sounds like a very important job," said his mother.

"The committee's job is just about as important as anything that needs to be done right now," he replied, "but my contribution to it will be a very small one. All the same, I think it's a terrific privilege to be allowed to help the people working on this problem. If they can get it right Andrew and William's generation will never have to go through what we've just been through; and if they don't get it right what could happen is too dreadful to think about."

"It certainly is," said Sarah. "You've only got to look at the ruins still around in Belfast to see that – and those were only small air raids compared with what was happening at the end of the War."

"You were involved with taking care of the injured, weren't you?" asked Ruth.

"She certainly was," said her mother. "I don't know who we were more worried about at the time, Sarah or Daniel. But at least we knew where Sarah was."

"I was right glad to hear what that new American fella, Truman, had to say about it," said Aunty Hilda. "These days he's the boy that can really make things happen; and he was talking in his Christmas Message about listening to the Sermon on the Mount, and working for the time when they beat their swords into ploughshares and their spears into pruning hooks. It was a lot better than the oul' Pope's message. He sounded more like a politician, talking about 'banning arbitrary action'."

"The Christmas Message I liked the best was the King's one," said Daniel's mother. "Do you remember what he said about young people who'd grown up during the War? Didn't he tell them they shouldn't judge life by what they'd just come through but… something about life being a joyous adventure, and merriment was the birthright of the young? I wouldn't be surprised if it wasn't his two young daughters that gave him the idea for that. By the look of them they're growing up to be really nice young ladies."

"I hope the Army'll be paying you properly if you've got to live over there in the States," said Mark. "I hear tell those big cars and refrigerators and things that they all seem to need cost them a powerful lot of money."

"I hope we're not going to need a big car, but I would like to have a refrigerator. I've never had the chance to use one," said Ruth.

"We'll be well looked after. I'm very lucky to get such a cushy job," said Daniel.

"Did you see last week that the MPs at Stormont are in for a big rise?" Tom asked. "They're going to get three hundred quid a year for expenses and another two hundred for loss of earnings. All they've been getting up till now was a salary of about four quid a week. I think there'll be a wheen of fellas putting themselves up for a career in politics."

"A good friend of ours got into Westminster at the Election," said Daniel. "I don't know whether I told you about it in one of my letters, Sarah. There's been so much to write about this year. But he certainly seems to be earning every penny he's paid. Maybe the chaps at Stormont should have to work a bit harder if they're going to be paid more."

"Did you see that the Papish archbishop in London has been made a cardinal?" asked Aunty Hilda.

"I hear he was in the RAF in the Great War," said Tom, "so he's not likely to be of the Fenian persuasion. He might be able to have a good influence on some of those priests over here who keep stirring up trouble."

"Wasn't it dreadful that De Valera actually sent a message of sympathy from Ireland to the Germans when Hitler's death was announced?" asked his wife, Mary, who was sitting on Ruth's right.

"I hadn't heard about that," said Daniel. "I suppose it wasn't exactly the main news that day. I think I was actually in Caserta when the news about Hitler came through. That was where General Alexander had his headquarters. He'd just taken the surrender of the German troops in Italy. But it was pretty stupid of Dev to do a thing like that. I always thought he was a cunning blighter, but backing a loser when it's all over, wherever your sympathies might lie, doesn't sound to me like very clever diplomacy."

"He's not as clever as he thinks he is," said Aunty Hilda. "Daniel, whatever happened to that Dublin pal of yours that got himself wounded in Spain? Did he go back to Dublin during the War?"

"No. Roddy stayed in England and married an English girl, an actress. They've both been working with ENSA, entertaining the troops. Towards the end of the War I think they were mainly playing to audiences of Americans based in Britain. And now Roddy has got himself a small part in a play that's running in the West End."

"We've had a lot of Americans based over here, you know," said his mother. "I think they've all gone now, but they've left a few sore hearts behind them."

"Sore hearts – what do you mean?" asked Daniel.

"Among the girls, of course," said his father. "They were great talkers, some of them, and they had the nylons and the chewing-gum and the tinned peaches to make them more attractive. They turned a lot of heads."

"They did that for sure," said Aunty Hilda. "Do you mind young Sally Balcombe that sings in the choir at Thomas Street? You might have seen her at the service yesterday."

"Yes, I remember her," Daniel replied. "She was at Sunday School with me – a dark-haired girl, quite pretty. She went to work as a clerk in Spence Bryson's when she left school."

"She fell for one of the Yankees," Aunty Hilda went on. "Very lovey dovey they were, and she went around telling everybody that he'd asked her to marry him, and after the War they were going to live in a place called Atlanta, Georgia, in a big house with a veranda at the front. And then one night at the Saturday social they used to give in the Lecture Hall for the soldiers, to keep them out of the pubs, this fella sat Sally down on his knee and told everybody he was going to have to say goodbye because General Eisenhower had sent for him to go over to England. Did you ever hear the like of that? As if Eisenhower would send for a fella like him – he was only a sergeant."

"He might have been speaking figuratively," said Daniel. "The order for his unit to move could well have come from Eisenhower. I expect they were being moved up to take part in the invasion."

"That's as may be," said Aunty Hilda. "But she never saw hide nor hair of him again – not even a letter."

"I suppose it's possible he might have been killed," said Ruth. Her own experience with Sher made a sudden and unwelcome intrusion into her thoughts. "At least he didn't leave her with a baby, which unfortunately happened to quite a few girls."

Instantly she realized from the expression on several faces that her implicit reference to sexual activity had been a cause of embarrassment. Daniel had warned her, she remembered, that sex was a topic which was never spoken about.

Sarah immediately came to her rescue with a rapid change of subject. "You must have got to know quite a lot of Americans in the job you were doing, Daniel," she said.

"I did. Talking to Americans was the biggest part of my job for quite a lot of the time. I found them, like every other group of people, a mixture of good, bad and indifferent. But by and large I got on very well with them – and I suppose that's why I'm going to be doing the job I've got now."

"I'm sure you'll be well able to hold your own among them," said his father. "And if you get the chance, don't let them forget how much America owes to Ulster. There's been a lot of talk about all those Irish-Americans supporting the Free State because their ancestors went over from there after the Famine. You just tell them that a third of all their presidents had ancestors that came from Ulster, and even their great Declaration of Independence is in the handwriting of an Ulsterman."

"Who was that?" asked Daniel.

"A fellow called Charles Thompson that came from Maghera. There was a very good article about it just a couple of weeks ago – I think it was in the *Newsletter*. Anyhow, you put in a good word for Ulster if you get the chance."

"I'll certainly do that," said Daniel.

"When you're over there you might get the chance to visit your Aunty Sarah," said his father. "I think she was very cut up when young Sher was killed – as you'd expect her to be. We had a letter from her at Christmas and she was still saying how things would never be the same again, even though it must be more than two years now since he was lost. You both met him when he was over here before the War, didn't you?"

"We did," said Ruth. "And I met him again a few times when he came over in the Air Force and Sarah put him in touch with me. They were having a terrible time on those raids over Germany. I think he told me about three of his friends being killed, one after another. And then it was his turn." As she spoke she could feel tears pricking her eyes, and she struggled to control a tremor in her voice. A picture of Sher's face smiling up at her from the pillow flashed into her memory.

"You must have been the last person connected with the family to see him before he was killed," said her mother-in-law. "If you are able to

65

visit Aunty Sarah you might be able to say something that would give her a bit of comfort."

Telling her I was able to give him pleasure he would never otherwise have enjoyed in his short life would hardly be appropriate, Ruth thought. But she nodded her head and said, "I could certainly tell her that Sher was facing up bravely to what he had to do; but I doubt if there's any real comfort to be found for the loss of her son. The best we can hope for is that she'll be able to learn to live with it."

"I'm sure the Lord will be a very present help in her time of trouble," said Aunty Hilda.

"Well, if we're all done I'll get cleared away and you make yourselves comfortable in the front room," said Maureen, assuming her role as hostess. "Mary, will you keep an eye on the wee ones while I get the washing-up out of the way?"

"Can I give you a hand with the washing-up?" Ruth asked, hoping she might get to know her sister-in-law a little better over the kitchen sink.

"That's very nice of you, but we can't have you working on your holiday. That would never do," Maureen replied. "Why don't you and Daniel go for a wee walk? I'm sure you'd like to have a bit of time together on your own; and it'll give you an appetite for your tea. The rain seems to be over now."

"You might like to take Ruth to Brackagh Moss," Mark said to Daniel. "When we went there before Christmas there were a lot of swans swimming all over the place. It's les than half-an-hour from here, as I'm sure you remember."

"I remember it well," he replied. "We used to have family walks out there on Saturday afternoons, right back to the time when I was no bigger than William." He nodded towards his four-year-old nephew, who was climbing down from his seat at the children's side table. "Would you like to stretch your legs?" he asked Ruth.

"Sounds like a good idea," she replied. "I thought moss was something that grew on old stones, but it can also be a place – right?"

"Right. In these parts it's a synonym for 'bog'," said Daniel. "You'd better take an umbrella, in case the rain comes back."

"You can borrow mine," said Maureen.

"Don't go letting her catch cold, Daniel," said Aunty Hilda. "She wouldn't want to be having that when she was starting out across the sea to America."

66

"No, indeed," said Daniel. "And we're going to have to wait till we get there to buy you a new winter coat," he added, putting his hand on her shoulder. "You have no clothing coupons left after the wedding."

"You were so sensible getting married in your going-away suit instead of splashing out on a white dress that you'd never wear again," said Sarah (the only member of the family apart from Daniel's parents who had been at the wedding).

"I'm afraid some of the parishioners thought it was bordering on irreligious," said Ruth, smiling. "I suppose it's inevitable that after a time people begin to confuse long-established customs with religious requirements."

"It can't always have been easy for you, growing up as the rector's daughter. I suppose people would have been looking at you and expecting you to be perfect all the time," said Daniel's mother.

"There was a certain amount of that; and not being perfect, I just had to learn to put up with it," she replied.

"Susan tells me it's a bit like that for Winifred and Mary," said her mother-in-law. "She's my niece," she added by way of explanation, "and she married a Methodist minister. Her two girls would be about ten and twelve."

"I think it was worse when they were in that wee place in County Fermanagh. In a village you can't so much as sneeze without everybody thinking you've caught a cold. It's not so bad for them now that they've moved to a church in Belfast," said Aunty Hilda. "Us Methodists aren't like your lot, you know. We shift our ministers around every five years, or sometimes less."

"Yes, that's something I learnt from Daniel," said Ruth, smiling again. "Daddy's been in the same parish for twenty-five years, with two more parishes added on to it over the years, just to make sure that he's kept busy. I didn't mind too much that everybody had a close eye on me when I was a little girl. But I think I've sometimes not done things that I wanted to do because I've thought that the gossip might be hurtful to Daddy. So I suppose you could say I've pretended to be better than I really am."

Everyone laughed, except Aunty Hilda.

"Let's get our coats," said Daniel. "If we don't hurry the light will have faded by the time we get to Brackagh and we won't be able to see the swans – or we'll see them only as ghostly shapes in the gloaming."

"Don't go getting yourselves lost," said Mark. "It's been a right long while since you went for a walk in this neck of the woods."

"I nearly got lost once in the Western Desert," he replied, "but I think I should be able to find my way on the Annagh Road. If we're not back by six o'clock send out the Boy Scouts."

CHAPTER NINE: 22nd March, 1946 - ARTHUR

In the Central Lobby Arthur was accosted by a tall, balding Member for a Northern constituency, whose name he tried desperately to remember as he returned his cordial greeting. The man had spoken to him on a couple of previous occasions and seemed to take an avuncular interest in him when he learned that Arthur was a Yorkshireman in spite of having a Southern constituency.

"I thought Wells was right on the ball with what he had to say about technical education," said his new acquaintance. "Without a doubt it's been the Cinderella sector of education, and we're going to have to do something about it if this country is to be successful in the post-war world. Wouldn't you agree?"

"I certainly would," Arthur replied. "Before the War I was lucky enough to see a good model of how it can be done when I had a stint of lecturing at the Regent Street Polytechnic; but I think that was the exception that proves the rule. I was really pleased, though, to hear about the plans for more scholarships to universities. It was one of those that put my own feet on the ladder; but I'm sure it's equally important to do more for the kids who aren't academically inclined. They could be helped to find really worthwhile jobs if their skills were properly developed. When my Dad was growing up there was only one place for a young fellow to go, and that was down the pit."

"We're really starting to get things moving now, aren't we?" asked his acquaintance. "But I was a bit disappointed yesterday to see that the National Health scheme won't actually be in place till 1948. A lot of people could die for the want of proper care in the next two years."

"That's true," said Arthur, "but something as big as what we're planning is going to take a huge amount of organizing, when you think of the millions of people who are going to be involved. It reminds me a bit of the preparations for D-Day. I had a small part in those myself. They took over a year and we were all working flat out. I just hope the health scheme will be as successful; but Mr Bevan seems determined to get it right. It's so important. I can remember when I was about seven years old my mother sending me with a loaf and a hunk of cheese to one of our neighbours because she knew the woman had been going without food to pay the doctor's bill for attending her sick child."

"I could tell you quite a few stories like that," said his colleague. "Do you have time for a drink in the bar before you go home?"

"I'd like to, but I've promised my wife I'll be home early this evening. I'm taking her to the pictures. We're going to see that new film, *The Corn is Green.*"

"Isn't that the one about the woman teacher who sets up a school in a Welsh mining village and discovers a bright young lad who wins a scholarship to Oxford? Just what we were talking about a minute ago – youngsters being given the chance to make the best of their talents."

"Yes, that's the one. I think it's based very much on the author's own life. Emlyn Williams wrote it as the story for a play, just before the War. I'll be interested to see how Bette Davis makes out as a Welsh schoolteacher. She's my mother's favourite film actress."

"You must tell me what you thought of it when we have that drink in the bar," said his colleague, "but I mustn't delay you now or you'll be in trouble with your missus. That would never do."

Arthur bade him farewell and walked rapidly to the tiny office which he shared with a Member from Glasgow, who by now, he knew, would be on his way to Euston Station. As he strode down the corridor he reflected that it might have been better if the Luftwaffe, instead of wrecking just one chamber of Parliament, had destroyed the entire building. Then they could have started from scratch and build a new Parliament with proper facilities for all the people who worked in it.

It was less than ten minutes' walk from the Tube station to his new home and Arthur strode out briskly, observing with pleasure the yellow flashes of forsythia blossom and daffodils in neglected front gardens, still bereft of the railings they had sacrificed for the war effort. A few, he noticed, had converted their small patches of lawn into vegetable plots.

A bend in the road brought him within sight of his own house, into which Margarita and he had moved only a fortnight earlier. It stood solid and reassuring, his semi-detached little castle, with wide bay windows protruding on both floors and a warm red-brick alcove sheltering its front door. As he turned into the short path – devoid of its protecting gate, of course – bordering a small patch of grass with several unidentified shrubs, he reflected on how fortunate he had been to obtain it. The High Street with its shops was just at the end of the road, and there were two pleasant little parks within easy walking distance. When the baby arrived it was going to be an agreeable place for Margarita to spend time while she was on her own. He had his agent, Bill Coverdale, to thank for alerting him to the fact that the house was coming on the market; and he'd had no difficulty in persuading the Prudential that a Labour MP would be a reliable borrower. As the manager had said when he went to apply for the mortgage, "I should think you can be sure of your seat for at least two parliaments."

Margarita had seen him coming and was in the hall to greet him with the passionate kiss that never failed to remind him just how lucky he was that she had chosen Britain as her place of refuge. Gently he placed his hand on the bulge in her stomach and said, "I hope he's been behaving himself."

"She's been no trouble at all," Margarita replied with a mischievous smile. They had a long-running debate about whether the baby was going to be a boy or a girl – although they were both, he knew, equally happy to have either.

As they went into the kitchen she said, "I've had a long letter from Ruth. You must read it. They seem to be settling in all right in Washington. And she says it's wonderful having so many kinds of food to choose from. I'm afraid it's going to be spam fritters for us this evening. I hope you had something more substantial for lunch at the House."

"Since it's Friday they had fish on the menu and I had a pretty decent herring, but it's such a nuisance to eat because of all the little bones. Can I see the American letter? I've been wondering how they've been getting on over there since you had that first letter from Ruth."

"American letter – did you see in the *Radio Times* that there's going to be a programme with that name starting on Sunday. It's a talk by a journalist called Alistair Cooke. I think he's an American."

"No, he's actually an Englishman. He's a good journalist. I've read stuff by him in the *Manchester Guardian*. But what has Ruth got to say about life in the Land of the Free?"

"Actually, she says that it's not really very free," said Margarita, handing him the envelope that was lying on the kitchen table. "They're not very happy about the way that Negroes are treated; but otherwise they seem to be enjoying themselves and having lots of oranges and butter and bananas to eat. She does say, though, that they do have shortages, mainly because people have a tendency to panic when the newspapers say that something like white flour is going to be in short supply."

Arthur sat down at the table and opened the letter. Ruth began with the usual greetings and then a short account of how they were settling into the apartment that had been found for them. He turned over the page and continued to read:

I wonder if you have seen any reports on the speech that Mr Churchill made at the beginning of this month, when the President took him to a little college in his home state of Missouri. It has made a huge stir over here, and not just because of Churchill's usual wizardry with words – talking about an 'Iron Curtain' descending across Europe. A surprising number of people are very upset because they think he may have antagonized Stalin; and they really believe that Stalin has no hostile feelings against the West. President Truman has even had to send an invitation to Stalin to come and visit the USA, although I'm pretty sure he's confident that his invitation will be refused.

My new friends in the United Nations Association are upset with Mr Churchill for another reason as well. They say that his talk about the need for a special relationship between English-speaking peoples to protect the peace could undermine the United Nations Organization. Some UNA supporters even held a protest outside his hotel in New York. Apparently they chanted 'Winnie, Winnie, go away. UNO is here to stay.' I pointed out to my friends that in the conclusion of his speech, which wasn't so widely reported, Mr Churchill said that if Britain and America 'adhered faithfully to the Charter of the United Nations' and moved forward together, keeping up their strength, peace could be assured for a century to come. But I don't think they were convinced. I really like the Americans I've met in UNA, but their attractive optimism does tend to spill over into naïvety at times.

Arthur looked up from the letter and commented, "It's very interesting what Ruth has to say about reactions to Churchill's 'Iron Curtain' speech. I've heard a lot of similar comments from people in the House. It's not only Americans who can be naïve about the Soviets. I heard one of our own Members in the bar last week, a chap called Tom Driberg, saying it was time we realized we had more interests in common with the Soviets than with the Americans. And I noticed he was sipping a very expensive white wine. He's one of those public schoolboys who fancy themselves as the voice of the toiling masses."

"You'll find something about another ex-public schoolboy further on in Ruth's letter," said Margarita. "A man called Cyril Hamberly at the embassy, who's been very friendly, and helped them to move into their new apartment. He was at school with Freddie. I remember Freddie telling us about him once, because he was surprised that Hamberly had applied for a job in the Foreign Office. He'd always been a trouble–maker at school and had actually joined the Communist Party. But Freddie said his father was a lord and would probably be pleased his son wanted to settle down, and so he'd use his influence to get him the job."

"I think I remember that," said Arthur. "It must have been the evening when we had that dinner to celebrate me getting my doctorate. Poor old Freddie was always good company; and he had some amazing contacts because of his background. It sounds as if his old schoolmate was one of the type who abandon their commitment to the toiling masses as soon as they start to think about their careers."

He returned to Ruth's letter and read:

Daniel has been spending a lot of his time at a huge new US government building called the Pentagon. It's so big that he once got lost inside it. Interestingly, he says it's the only building in Virginia (it's across the river from here) where the lavatories aren't segregated with 'Whites only' signs. It seems that President Roosevelt gave an order that the signs should be removed. That's one of the few things we really don't like about America – the way that Negroes are treated. It sometimes makes me really angry. If they want to go on calling themselves 'the land of the free' they're really going to have to do something about it. Arthur could almost hear Ruth's voice saying the words with quiet passion.

The passage about meeting Cyril Hamberly came next it the letter. It concluded:

Daniel has actually been a little bit embarrassed, because Cyril keeps asking about his job and he really isn't allowed to talk about it, but he doesn't want to appear rude. I think Cyril ought to have taken the hint by now. He's a diplomat and he ought to understand about security rules. Although I'm very grateful for the help he gave us, there's something about him that I don't really like. For one thing, he drinks too much; and Daniel thinks he might be a queer. But I don't want to be judgemental, and he may just be one of those lonely people who are desperate to make friends.

"I've sometimes wondered if there might be more to Daniel's job than he's been telling us," Arthur commented. "That course he was on before Christmas was run by the Intelligence Corps. But I guess it's none of our business."

He resumed reading the letter:

Yesterday when Daniel was leaving the Pentagon he bumped into a young Englishwoman we'd met on the 'Queen Mary'. She was one of the group of GI brides who were coming over here, and her fiancé is a sergeant on duty at the Pentagon. She invited us to go to her wedding next month, and I think we might go because she won't have anyone else there from England.

"That was quite a coincidence – Daniel meeting up with the GI bride," said Arthur.

"It was; and that reminds me – I had a phonecall from Roddy this morning," said Margarita. "Cecily has gone off to America, not exactly as a GI bride, but he's convinced that she's going to end up as one. He was very depressed. It seems that a man who was the organizer of entertainments at an air base in Norfolk where she and Roddy used to perform has kept in touch with her. He's become a casting director in Hollywood – I think he worked there before the War – and he's offered her a part in a film. It's not a big part but they needed someone with an English accent. But Roddy says he'd suspected there was something going on between them last year, and indeed, they'd had a row about it. I got the impression from the way he talked about it that it wasn't the first time things like that had happened."

"Poor old Roddy. He doesn't seem to have much luck with women," said Arthur. "I remember Daniel telling me he'd confided that the real reason he went off to fight in Spain was because he'd been jilted by a girl. We ought to invite him for dinner. He's going to need cheering up."

"That's a good idea. I admire Roddy. Whatever it was that made him do it, he went to fight for my country and he was wounded, but he doesn't complain about it. And he's a good actor. Oh, and he said he's just got a job with the BBC to act in a series of plays on the wireless. That should help to cheer him up."

"Why don't we invite Rebecca the same evening?" said Arthur. "You haven't seen her since she came back from working in the refugee camp. It would look less as if we'd invited Roddy just because we were feeling sorry for him, and that might help him to relax when he comes."

"Oh, yes. I'd love to see Rebecca again. But I'm sure she has some grim stories to tell. You know, she still hasn't been able to find out what happened to her family. She heard that some of their neighbours in Vienna were sent to that terrible camp in Poland called Auschwitz. So that's probably where they ended up, too."

"Poor Rebecca," said Arthur. "It's difficult to imagine how someone must feel in her situation. I've never talked to her about what I saw at Belsen, and I don't think I ought to. Find out when she can come. We really must keep in touch with her. She was a good friend to you during the War."

"I must finish making dinner," said Margarita. "Otherwise we're going to be late for the cinema. I managed to get some bananas today; so you can have one for dessert."

"That will be a treat. I haven't seen a banana since I was in Africa. When I've finished reading Ruth's letter I'll lay the table."

Margarita kissed the top of his head as she passed behind his chair. He felt a surge of desire and reminded himself that he would have to go on being restrained for at least another five months. Reaching out behind him, he gently patted her bottom.

CHAPTER TEN: 22nd September, 1946 - RUTH

Ruth made a resolution that she would not in future postpone getting fully dressed until after Daniel had left for work. It could become all too easy, she decided, to dawdle over breakfast and allow domestic chores to expand and fill the time. Three days a week she worked for six hours as a volunteer at the headquarters of the United Nations Association, but beyond that she had no routine to channel her energy into useful activities. It wasn't much more than a year since she'd been exercising her linguistic skills at the Foreign Office but now her brain had no challenges to contend with, beyond finding another channel to listen to on the shiny new Bakelite wireless set.

She had also wanted to hear what had happened at Daniel's dinner last night with Cyril Hamberly and a journalist acquaintance. It had kept him out so late that she was asleep when he returned; but he'd been in such a hurry to get off to a breakfast meeting at the Pentagon that he'd been able only to say "Tell you all about it when I get back this afternoon." Doing business over breakfast was an American custom that she suspected had more to do with creating an appearance of hard work and efficiency than the reality of being effective. Based on her own experience, she couldn't believe that people's brains would be working in top gear if they'd had to leave home at the crack of dawn with empty stomachs.

Nonetheless, she was resolved not to allow herself to cultivate the bad habit of sleeping late and lingering over a solitary breakfast. And she needed to find another challenge to occupy her when she wasn't involved with helping the UNA. Imbued with her new resolution to be a more efficient manager of her own time, she put aside the unopened letter from Margarita until she had finished washing up and tidying the kitchen. Then, with an easier conscience and a feeling of pleasant anticipation, she sat down at the kitchen table and slit open the envelope.

Dear Ruth, she read, *I am sorry to have taken so long to reply to your last, lovely letter, but getting used to looking after Vera was very exhausting to begin with. However, we are now back at home and I have worked out a good routine for each day. And Vera has also started sleeping at the times when she's supposed to sleep, which has made life much easier for me – and for Arthur, because he has been very good at getting up during the night. In the past week that has never been necessary.*

I am really glad that we went to stay with Arthur's parents the week after Vera was born. It was a little bit cramped, but Mrs Leyland (I think of her now as 'Mam') was so much help to me, without being interfering, that I don't know what I would have done without her support. I also had some good talks with Mr Leyland.

He is very friendly, and he had some enthralling stories – like one about what happened in the General Strike, in 1926. In the later months, when the miners were striking on their own, he and some friends used to go out at night and steal vegetables from farmers' fields to help feed their families. Even though he has been out of mining for a long time because of his injury, he is very happy that the coal mines are going to be nationalised. The Act had just been passed by Parliament when we went up to York. Of course he is very proud that Arthur is an MP.

Now we are back in London and I feel quite confident about looking after Vera on my own. However, when we had Rebecca and Roddy to dinner last week I found that I had nothing to talk about but the baby and queuing at the shops, and I realized that I need to rediscover other interests, especially when Arthur has to be at the House for so much of the time. I think I will accept an offer I've had from a publisher – Juanita, who used to work with me at the BBC put me in touch with him – to translate a Mexican novel into English. I just hope I can do it quickly enough to meet his requirements. It will probably be best to get on with it while Vera is still at the stage where she sleeps a lot of the time.

Rebecca has found a new job that she is really excited about. One of the friends she made at the BBC asked her to do a short talk on the voluntary work she has been doing, teaching young refugees to speak English; and they liked it so much that she has been given a permanent post with the BBC Overseas Service. She's actually working in the department that is called the German Service. Rebecca says she believes it is so important that people in Germany should be able to start hearing what's really happening in the world around them, after so many years of living behind a wall of lies. And in spite of what they did to her family she is pleased to think she will be helping them to make a new beginning. I admire the way she refuses to be bitter about the past. She still has not had any definite information about her family.

Someone else who is suffering from not having had any news is Roddy. Since Cecily went to Hollywood he has had only one letter from her. She said she was loving it there, and she had already finished acting her part in the film, but her 'friend' has already found her another part, although in order to play it she is having to learn to talk like an American from the Deep South. Roddy showed me her letter, and she doesn't seem to be very good at writing. He has had two more small parts in BBC radio plays, and he thinks he might even get a longer term contract with them. I hope he does, because he is very pessimistic about what is going to happen with Cecily. I feel so sorry for him, especially when I think about what he did in Spain. And still the UNO has not done anything about Franco, except make disapproving noises.

Arthur, who sends his love to you both, has been busy in the constituency while Parliament has been in recess. However, he is concerned that a lot of his efforts may be a waste of time, because it looks as if the constituency may be one that the new Boundary Commissioners will decide to split up at the next General Election. He is being very philosophical about it, and says he just wants to do the best job he can in this parliament. Something he has been pushing hard for with colleagues behind the scenes is actually going to happen, and it has just been announced that local authorities are going to be allowed to use military camps to house homeless families who are waiting for new houses to be built. He is very pleased about that.

Now that I am at home for most of the day I have been listening to the wireless a lot more in the mornings and afternoons. Did you know that the BBC is going to have three programmes? Very imaginatively, they have called the new one 'the Third Programme'. Arthur is enthusiastic about it because, as you probably remember, classical music is one of his passions and that's what the new programme will mainly be providing. I listen to a lot of book-readings and plays on both the Home Service and the Light Programme. At the moment I'm enjoying two different stories, 'Goodbye Mr Chips' and 'King Solomon's Mines'. They are both teaching me a lot about British culture as it was fifty years ago.

Listening to the wireless has been easier than reading while I've been getting used to looking after Vera, but I really do want to get back to reading books in English. Arthur has given me George Orwell's new book, 'Animal Farm' and says he thinks I will find it interesting. He thinks it is the best explanation ever written of the way in which the Communists used the Russian revolution to impose their dictatorship on the country. He read me one quotation that I thought was brilliant: 'All animals are equal, but some animals are more equal than others.' It could be the slogan for what is going on in so many places today. I saw the same kind of hypocrisy in Spain when I was growing up. Everyone who was greedy for power proclaimed very loudly that what they wanted to do was to set the people free — free from capitalism, free from communism; free from government, free from anarchy; free from priests, free from the atheists; and, of course, free from poverty. What they nearly all had in common (there were a few who were honest) was a strong desire to dominate everybody else. Unfortunately people believed them.

I mustn't bore you by ranting on about Spain, but I feel very angry when I read in the papers that, even though more than a hundred MPs signed a statement back in July urging that the UNO should take action to help the Spanish people regain their freedom, nothing seems to have been done about it. Arthur says he doesn't think any more action will be taken, apart from passing resolutions. He thinks that because getting rid of General Franco could involve going to war nobody wants even to suggest that. And Franco knows that he is safe from attack; so he will ignore anything else that the UNO tries to do. I think I might never see Spain again.

You might have read that since the end of July bread has been rationed here. It doesn't worry me because Vera isn't old enough yet to be eating it, and Arthur will be having a lot of his meals at the House. He is cross because the Opposition blamed the Government even though it was the world shortage of wheat that made the rationing necessary; but the Tories take every opportunity to make it look as if the Government is incompetent.

I saw that the UNO Security Council had been meeting in New York. Does that mean that Daniel's committee has been meeting there, too? I wondered if you might have a chance to visit the city with him. From what we see in Hollywood films it looks like an exciting place. You will be pleased to know that the United Nations Association over here seems to be making good progress. At the end of this month there is going to be a 'United Nations Week', and in October the King and Queen are going to attend a special service in St Paul's Cathedral. I hope your voluntary work at the UNA has become more interesting than it was at the beginning.

I must end this rambling letter now because it will soon be time for Vera to have a feed, and I can see that she's starting to wake up. I hope you will be able to write soon and tell me all your news.

Very best wishes from Arthur and from me, Margarita.

Thoughtfully Ruth folded up the letter and laid it on the table. So Margarita was going to translate a book, and that was something she could do while being at home with her baby. Something like that might suit her, too, she reflected, because she would be able to take her work with her if Daniel was suddenly moved to another place – as he thought he might be. But she wasn't attracted by the idea of translating someone else's thoughts. Writing a book of her own would be a tremendous challenge. Her wartime experiences weren't likely to provide the subject matter because the only bits that weren't boring were covered by the Official Secrets Act. And everybody knew for themselves what it was like to go through the Blitz – well, maybe not people who lived in the countryside, but they'd all heard about it ad nauseam.

She wanted to write a book that would do something useful for its readers, even if it was fiction. Maybe that was because she was conditioned to think like a teacher, she reflected, as she moved to the window and looked out at the quiet, sunlit street. Something that might be a valuable asset was her ability to read German. There was going to be a need for people to start thinking positively again about the Germans once the Nuremberg trials were over. If the Germans were ever going to become partners in a peaceful Europe the Nazi years would have to be put into perspective as a horrible aberration. Maybe she could write an historical novel about German characters who had done things that had been beneficial to everybody else in the world. Musicians would be too obvious a topic and there were already plenty of good biographies of people like Bach and Beethoven; but maybe the von Humboldt brothers could provide the background for an exciting story. They'd been the 'fathers' of modern education and modern geography as well as being much involved in the politics of the early Nineteenth Century. She decided to have a look at what was available about them in the library – if she could get permission to become a user.

"I've decided I'm going to try to write a novel," Ruth announced when Daniel had taken off his raincoat and was exchanging his shoes for slippers. "I think it was hearing from Margarita – her letter's on the table – that she's going to translate one from Spanish – that gave me the idea."

He looked up, surprised, and asked, "Do you have an idea for a plot?"

"Not yet," she replied. "I want to tell a story that shows Germans in a positive light, to help people stop thinking about them as enemies. I thought maybe something that had the Humboldt brothers in the background would provide the chance to bring in exciting discoveries and new ideas."

"I know that Alexander Humboldt was the Humboldt Current man and did a lot of exploring, but I can't remember anything about his brother. What did he do?" asked Daniel.

"Wilhelm was a diplomat and a philosopher who influenced John Stuart Mill; and he devised a state education system that included free elementary schools and grammar schools and technical colleges, and a university that was financially independent of state and church. His ideas were copied in countries all round the world."

Daniel looked thoughtful and nodded his head. "But you're planning to write a novel – not a biography?"

"That's right. My main characters would be fictional. They might be people who worked for one of the brothers, or maybe who disagreed with them. But they'd have to have their own adventures and their own love affairs, to keep the readers interested. The setting would be in the Goethe period, and I studied quite a lot about that for my degree – though nothing about scientific activities, unfortunately."

"I think it's a brilliant idea," said Daniel. "Your writing style should be just right for telling a story. All those letters you sent me during the War were like a conversation that kept being interrupted. It was as if I'd only gone away for a couple of days. I wish I'd been able to keep more of them. I lost the first lot when I was taken to hospital; and then I lost some more when I went back to the battalion in Italy. But I do still have quite a lot of them."

"I still have all of yours," said Ruth. "For safety I've left them in a shoebox – actually two shoeboxes – at the Rectory. I always felt frustrated because there was so little you were allowed to tell me about what you were really doing."

Into her memory came unbidden the recollection of writing to Daniel just after she'd heard about the death of Sher. She had been unable to tell him about it and instead had covered a whole page with news about changes in the new rationing period – a cut in the cheese ration was one of them. And she'd also rambled on about advice from the Ministry of Food that the nutritional value of potatoes could be increased if they were boiled in their jackets. She'd remembered Daniel had once told her that was the way in which potatoes were always cooked in his home, and that the side plates were known as 'skin plates' because it was on them that each diner placed the peeled potato jackets during the meal. She hadn't felt able to mention hearing about Sher's death until two months later, just before D-Day.

"Did Margarita have any exciting news in her letter?" he asked.

"Not really, but you can read it for yourself later. First of all, tell me what happened to keep you out so late last night. It's the first time I've ever fallen asleep before you got back. Did Cyril Hamberly get so drunk that you had to help him to get home?"

"I did actually help him to find a taxi, and he was pretty drunk; but that wasn't the reason I stayed out so late. It's something I'm seriously bothered about, and I want to know what you think. Let's go and sit down while I tell you about it."

"Before we do that take off your tunic. You must be very hot," she said, unfastening the buckle of his Sam Browne belt. When she had hung his tunic in the wardrobe – reminding him once again how difficult it was to iron out creases – they went through to the living room. From the refrigerator, which was still a source of special delight, she brought two glasses of Coca Cola (a drink to which Daniel had been introduced in Italy, but which Ruth had discovered only when she arrived in America).

They sat down in facing armchairs and sipped the cooling liquid. "As you know," said Daniel, "Cyril wanted to introduce me to this *New York Times* journalist, a young fellow called Reuben Sternberg, and we started off having dinner together. That went OK, though I still can't get used to the outsize helpings these Yanks indulge in. Maybe my stomach shrank during the War and it hasn't expanded again. Anyhow, the conversation was pretty wide-ranging. Sternberg has heard that New York is going to offer the UNO a site for its headquarters at a place called Flushing Meadow. But he was mainly interested in what's going to happen in the mid-term Congressional elections at the beginning of November. He thinks that the Republicans are going to do well, and that's going to make life difficult for Truman and, in particular, for his more generous international policies. I got the impression that he wasn't very enthusiastic about Truman but liked the alternatives even less. Meanwhile Cyril had another go at trying to get me to talk about my job – without success."

"It must be very frustrating for him," said Ruth, "but you'd think as a professional diplomat he'd be familiar with the idea that some people aren't allowed to talk about their work, especially if the person they're talking to has a tendency to get drunk and let his tongue run away with him."

"That's exactly the point," said Daniel. "Last night he excelled himself. After the meal we moved to the bar and Cyril started on his favourite tipple, Jack Daniels whiskey. Sternberg became morose and began talking about that rally we read about, in Madison Square Gardens, when thousands of Communist Party members protested about the American government's hostility to the Soviet Union. He seemed to be in sympathy with the protest but thought it wouldn't achieve anything. Cyril agreed with him, and said something I didn't quite understand, about 'the comrades in Hollywood' having a better chance of getting through to the workers, even if they had to wrap up the message in tinsel and lead them down a yellow brick road."

"Yellow brick road" said Ruth. "That's a song in a film called *The Wizard of Oz.*"

"Never heard of it," said Daniel. "But then I didn't see very many films during the War. Anyhow, it seemed that Sternberg and Cyril knew each other quite well. But soon after that Sternberg had to leave us because he was going to attend another of those business breakfast meetings this morning. At that point I was going to leave, too, but Cyril made a remark that worried me and I decided to stay on a bit longer. He said – in that confidential way that drunks sometimes address you when they're about to get maudlin – 'You know, old chap, these Americans can be frightfully naïve sometimes, even progressive-minded chaps like Reuben. They think that if they just keep pegging away at exposing the contradictions of capitalism, when the next big slump comes along the toiling masses will rise up in anger and then the bourgeoisie will be swept aside by their fury. We know that's not the way things really happen. Reminds me of a song we used to sing when I was a student: *We'll blow the bloody bourgeoisie to bloody Kingdom Come/When the red revolution comes.*' Those mightn't have been Cyril's exact words, but I think I've got the gist of what he said."

"You certainly got his accent," said Ruth, laughing. "It's very similar to the way that dear old Freddie used to talk. But do you think he was really being serious?"

"He went on to lecture me about the impotence of 'armchair progressives', and how they were unwilling to accept the fact that omelettes could not be made without breaking eggs. 'Like the eggs that are being smashed by the Red Army in Eastern Europe at this very moment' was the phrase that I think he used. Then he seemed to recollect where he was, and he asked me what had happened to Reuben. I reminded him that Sternberg had gone home, and at that point he decided it was time for him to go, too. He had to be helped into the taxi by me and one of the doormen."

"I hope he got home all right," said Ruth.

"Yes, he did. I know because I had a call from him this afternoon. He apologized for getting sloshed, and said he couldn't remember what we'd been talking about, but if he'd 'gone into a rant' he hoped I hadn't taken him seriously. He said he knew he sometimes had a habit of sentimentalizing about his student days, when he was an anti-establishment rebel. But that was all before he'd learned how to live in the real world. I said he'd only been making a few colourful generalizations about aspects of society that I wasn't too happy about myself; and I pretended I was more concerned about whether he'd got home safely. But actually I wasn't.

"Maybe I'm seeing trouble where there isn't any, but something about his behaviour bothered me. I may have been unduly influenced by some news I heard last week – it was from one of our security chaps at the Embassy. He said they've been told that the Soviet official who defected in Canada last year, Gouzenko – you remember, it was in all the papers a few months ago – brought with him information about a whole network of spies, in Britain and America as well as in Canada. They're still working on his information and they think the network might be even wider than they first thought.

"When Cyril started spouting his revolutionary rhetoric I couldn't help wondering why he'd had such a sudden change of heart before the War, abandoning Communism to join the Diplomatic Corps. Do you remember how Freddie said he'd been so surprised when Cyril told him he'd changed his mind about the best way to work for political change?"

"Yes, I do vaguely remember that," she replied. "Freddie told me I should warn my cousin Giles in the Foreign Office to steer clear of him because he had a habit at Eton of getting other people into trouble."

"That's my worry," said Daniel. "If he should have secretly kept his links with the Communists he could get a lot of people into a lot of trouble just by passing on information. I can understand why ten years ago people like us got involved with the CP, when nobody else seemed willing to take on the fascists; but to go on supporting the Soviets after all we've learnt about them and their methods must require a huge amount of intellectual dishonesty."

"I suppose some people might genuinely believe that Stalin is capable of changing for the better," said Ruth. "Those statements that he made on Tuesday, about there not having to be a conflict with the West must have been designed to give that impression."

"But can any intelligent person seriously think that a man who has murdered scores of his own closest colleagues, not to mention countless thousands of other people whose opinions he didn't like, could be trusted to keep his word?" Daniel asked. "And it's not just about one man. A system that can only stay in control by locking up hundreds of thousands in so-called 'labour camps' and by killing who knows how many more is hardly the model to choose for replacing our own way of doing things, however imperfect that may be."

"All the same," said Ruth, "otherwise intelligent people seem to be capable of making that kind of judgement. In days gone by the horrors of the Holy Inquisition were common knowledge and yet plenty of clever and compassionate people were still devoted to the Roman Catholic Church. And it took quite a long time for you and me to see that our well-intentioned activities were probably, in a small way, helping Hitler to achieve his aims."

"That's very true," said Daniel, loosening his tie. "The problem remains: what am I going to do about Cyril? I hate the idea of bringing suspicion on him if he's just expressing his silly opinions; but I also have a duty not to let other people be exposed to the risk of very real danger."

"Could you maybe have a discreet word with the security man at the Embassy who spoke to you last week?"

"That's a possibility, but unfortunately I didn't form a very favourable opinion of him. I might be wrong, but I got the impression he was in the job because he had good connections, and he might well assume that the Honourable Cyril, late of Eton and Oxford, couldn't possibly be capable of passing on our secrets to a bunch of Commies. I think I'll wait until my next visit to London – that's the first of two bits of good news I'll tell you about in a minute – and talk to a chap called Ted Frobisher. I got to know him in the last few months of the war in Italy. I think I mentioned in a letter that I went with him in Venice to look at some wonderful paintings by Carpaccio. He'd been liaising with the partisans and knew an Italian guy who got the Scuola di San Giorgio opened up for us."

"I remember that letter," said Ruth. "I remember wishing I could have been there with you to look at that picture of the monks running away from Saint Jerome's friendly lion."

"I'm going to take you there one day, when Italy gets back to normal – if it ever does," said Daniel. "But I must tell you about the trip to London. There is beginning to be talk about having a new UNO commission to look at the prospects for disarmament in conventional weapons, leaving the atomic bomb issue to be dealt with separately. At the moment it's just talk in the corridors of power, but that's exactly where the people I work for operate. So I have to go to London for a briefing session in October; and I've been told I can take you with me, making it look like a spot of leave."

"That's brilliant. How long will we have there?"

"Less than a week, I'm afraid. But we'll have five lazy days together each way on the *Queen Mary*. What I was going to say is that I should be able to talk to Ted Frobisher while I'm there. He's working now for the Secret Intelligence Service and he's based in London."

"You said you had two bits of good news. What's the other one?"

"We've been invited to Ottawa at the beginning of November. My former boss of all bosses, Field Marshal Alexander, is giving a reunion dinner at the Governor-General's residence for officers of the Canadian 1st Infantry and 5th Armoured Divisions who served with him in Italy. I've had an invitation, and you're included."

"But how on earth did he know that you were here?" Ruth asked; and when Daniel laid one finger along the side of his nose and winked she said, "Does that mean he's one of the group that you're working for?"

He grinned and replied, "You know that I can't answer that question, but there's nothing to prevent you from speculating, provided you don't share your speculations with anyone else."

"I haven't got anything posh to wear at a do like that," she said. "It's all right for you – you'll be wearing uniform. Oh, I know. I still have the dress I wore at the May Ball in Oxford – the only one that I ever attended. It's hanging in the wardrobe in my old room in the Rectory – just above the box that contains all your letters to me. If we're going to be in England I can bring it back. I just hope it will still fit me."

"Of course it will. You may have lost a pound or two during the War, but that's only made you more perfect than you already were," he said, standing up. "I'm going to take off this tie and hang it in the wardrobe, like you've taught me. If you come to the bedroom with me I might take off something more."

Experiencing a tingle of anticipation, Ruth stood up and moved towards the door. Daniel followed her and she felt his hand on her bottom. "Sometimes when I used to lie awake under the stars in Italy I would try to remember every detail of this beautiful bottom," he said, patting it gently.

"Flattery will get you anywhere you want to go," she replied, opening the door and quickening her pace towards the bedroom.

CHAPTER ELEVEN: 12ᵗʰ July, 1947 - DANIEL

As Margarita took Ruth's hat she remarked, "It was raining when you came to see us in October. You've been luckier with the weather this time; and according to the forecast the sunshine is going to continue for at least another day."

"We've been enjoying it," Ruth replied. "I love your long swishy skirt. Is that what they're calling the New Look? There was a woman on the ship who had one a bit like that, but not with such beautiful colours."

"I decided to treat myself after a year of being virtually out of circulation because of having to get used to looking after Vera," said Margarita. "By the way, thank you for her birthday card. You must have posted it the minute you landed. It arrived right on time, on Thursday morning."

Daniel noted that her figure was as eye-catching as it had been before her pregnancy, and remarked, "That's a beautiful skirt. I think I'm in favour of this new fashion. I expect they'll have it in all the New York shops when we get back."

"Unfortunately, a tight waist isn't going to suit me for very much longer," said Margarita, smiling a little shyly.

"You mean you're…?" Ruth asked, and Margarita nodded her head.

"We decided it would be better to have two close together so that we could get all the time-consuming stages of bringing up babies over in a few years; and then maybe I'll be able to get back to doing things again that use my brain," she said. "And, anyhow, we want Vera to be close to a brother or sister when she's growing up."

"That sounds like a very sensible plan," said Ruth. "Have you any preference for a boy or a girl?"

"We'd like a boy now, of course, but I think Vera might prefer to have a sister when she's bit older. So we don't really mind."

"Well, enjoy wearing your wonderful skirt while you can," said Daniel. "It may have gone out of fashion by the time you're ready to wear it again."

"Have you found New York very different from Washington?" Margarita asked, as they went through to the sitting-room.

"There's a lot more variety," said Ruth, "but I haven't really been able to make any new contacts yet, and we're not sure how long we're going to be staying there."

"The Commission for Conventional Armaments that I'm working to was supposed to issue its first report in June but I doubt if it will be able to reach agreement on anything until at least next year," said Daniel. "Whether the Security Council will agree to keep it in existence is anybody's guess. But at least I'm working on a job now that I'm able to tell people about – or parts of it, anyhow."

"Arthur was very pleased when he heard you'd been appointed to work with our man on the Commission," said Margarita. "He should be back quite soon. I made him promise not to linger at Lord's however exciting the game might be. He hasn't had the chance to watch very much cricket this year."

"I can't see him getting very excited about the Eton and Harrow match," said Daniel.

Margarita laughed. "Actually he went today only because a colleague at the House invited him. The man is a Labour MP but he actually went to Harrow."

"Like Mr Attlee," Ruth observed. "So Arthur will have to cheer for Harrow. Which reminds me – or rather, Eton does – have you seen Nancy recently?"

"She came for tea last week, and brought little Leo with her. He's growing up fast, and seems to be doing well at his kindergarten school. I think he's going to be good-looking, like his father.

"Nancy has become active again in the Peace Pledge Union. She's convinced that the atomic bomb will make everybody realize there can't be another war without destroying civilization, and so everyone will soon be in favour of disarmament and total pacifism. She sells *Peace News* in Trafalgar Square – I think it's on Wednesday mornings after Leo has gone to school."

"I wish it was as simple as that," said Daniel. "This Commission that I'm working for, indirectly, seems to be influenced more by the possibility that there could be a separate agreement to take atomic bombs out of the equation. Then, it is assumed, everything else will continue as before – only we should try to get everyone to scale back on their arms expenditure. From what I've heard about the discussions so far I don't think that's going to happen. For one thing, Stalin is already using a huge amount of conventional armaments just to make sure the East Europeans, from Estonia to Roumania, do what he tells them. And for another, he's working flat out to get himself some atomic bombs. I'm sure our Commission will come up with some good ideas, but it won't be the people of Russia who'll be deciding whether or not to accept them."

"But might your Commission come up with ideas about how to limit the arms trade, so that lots of smaller countries don't spend money on buying weapons, and then start using them against each other?" asked Margarita.

"I think it will try to, but even there it is bound to come up against the same problem. Uncle Joe won't agree to stop sending weapons to the people he supports – like Mao Tse-tung's rebel army in China; and when that happens Uncle Sam will go on sending guns to whoever opposes them. I'm sure you remember all too well how the League of Nations put a ban on supplying weapons to either of the combatants in Spain, and Hitler and Mussolini ignored it while Britain and France obeyed it – with the inevitable result. International law often works in favour of the criminals, because there is no policeman to enforce it. In that respect it seems to me the situation hasn't improved since the Thirties."

"Isn't that because we've had to back up one criminal in order to defeat another?" asked Margarita.

"Exactly so," Daniel replied. "But the situation is complicated by the fact that a lot of people don't want to admit that Stalin's regime is essentially criminal. Some of them are swayed in that direction simply because they admire the bravery of the Red Army soldiers and sympathize with the terrible sufferings of the Russian people. But that's irrelevant to what you think about their government. You can sympathize with the German people's suffering during the War without holding any brief for Hitler's regime.

"There are other people who say that, whatever we may think about Stalin, his government isn't going to change and we've got to work with it as best we can, just as we did during the War. So we ought to treat him as a friend and hope he will reciprocate, even though we have to remain wary of him. And, of course, that's what we're trying to do in the UNO. But he's already made it quite clear that he's an implacable enemy whose ultimate aim is to destroy us; and whatever 'rules' we may agree on with the Russians he will not hesitate to break them if he thinks it will be to his advantage.

"And, of course, there are the ones who believe, either openly or secretly, that Stalin's on their side. His methods may be a bit rough but he's the only effective champion of the downtrodden and oppressed, and he holds the key that will one day open the gate to the workers' paradise. I've met a surprising number who think like that in the face of all the evidence to the contrary."

Smiling broadly, Margarita stood up and said, "Oh, this reminds me so much of the days before the War, when we all got together and talked for hours about how to sort out the problems of the world. I hope you'll tell us more about what's happening in the UNO, Daniel, when Rebecca arrives. Like you, Ruth, she's very active in UNA. I think I told you we've invited her and Roddy to dinner. And Arthur's going to be interested, too. He's always saying that the House doesn't spend enough time on foreign affairs.

"But I've got to get some things started for dinner; and I think I hear Vera waking up." (Daniel had not detected the sound that had alerted Margarita's maternal ear.) "I'll bring her down to meet you, and maybe you can keep an eye on her while I'm starting dinner."

When she had gone to fetch the baby Ruth said, "You haven't told me yet what happened when you met Ted Frobisher at lunchtime. Has he made any progress on the check-up he was going to run on Cyril Hamberly? Do they think he's somebody who's in your third category of Soviet sympathizers?"

"Ted was very cautious, as chaps like him always have to be, but he indicated that they were still keeping an eye on Cyril. He told me he'd found out that two years ago, soon after the end of the War, our consul in Istanbul had contact with a Soviet agent who wanted to defect to the West. Actually, the Russian never made it, presumably because somebody on our side tipped off his bosses. But this agent had said he was going to bring with him information about people in our SIS, and in the Foreign Office, who are working for Moscow. So Ted has been very careful about who he shared my information with, about Cyril. It's not easy to check on him because he's in Washington, but Ted knows somebody in the FBI that he trusts and they've started to keep an eye on him. I hope it turns out to be a false alarm; but Ted agreed with me that there's so much happening just now we can't afford to take risks."

Margarita reappeared, holding a pink-faced, dark-haired infant in her arms, and Daniel made appropriate noises even though he could never understand the attraction that babies seemed to exert on adults – other than their parents and grandparents. He knew that Ruth, fortunately, shared his reservations, and smiled knowingly at her as she went through the 'Coochie-coochie-coo' routine.

"I hope Arthur will get back from Lord's before Rebecca and Roddy arrive," said Margarita. "I don't want to be inhospitable but I'm going to have to spend some time in the kitchen. And now I have to feed Vera."

"Don't worry," said Ruth. "We'll have plenty to talk about. It'll be like the old days – except, of course, Rebecca wasn't around then."

Rebecca was the first to arrive, and Daniel was pleased to have the opportunity to catch up on her news with undivided attention. There had still been no information about the fate of her parents and she seemed resigned to the possibility that she might never find out how they had died. In her spare time she was still helping survivors of the concentration camps to learn English; and she was enthusiastic about her job at the BBC Overseas Service, where she was discovering interesting differences of opinion among her colleagues.

"There are one or two who think we ought to concentrate on making our German audience understand the awful extent of their guilt," she said, "and of course we've been giving full coverage to the Nuremburg Trials. But I think we must also help them to start thinking of themselves as part of Europe again. Hitler tried to cut them off from the mainstream of European culture and we've got to give them opportunities to get back into it. I hope this new 'Marshall Offer' from America that's being discussed in Paris today is going to include Germany."

"I think it will," said Daniel. "Truman knows that it's absolutely vital to get the German economy moving again – not just for them but for the rest of Europe as well. But it's very sad that Stalin seems to have leant on the Czechs and the Poles to make them refuse to join in the scheme. They need all the help they can get, and he's not going to give them very much himself."

The doorbell rang and they were shortly joined by Roddy. Daniel was surprised by the way in which Rebecca's eyes lit up when he entered the room. The last time he'd seen them together they had scarcely known each other.

When the preliminary enquiries about each other's health and well-being were over Roddy said, "I'm sure you'll want to know what's been happening about Cecily. I heard from her last week that she wants a divorce. I don't know exactly how I'm going to arrange it, but I've seen it coming for a long time. Thank goodness we didn't get married in Ireland."

"Why not in Ireland?" asked Rebecca.

"Because divorce is impossible over there. It was made illegal in the 1937 Constitution. God knows, it's difficult enough over here. We could do it under the 'three years desertion clause', but that would mean waiting until the end of next year, and Cecily is dead keen to get married to this American guy."

"The Americans seem to think that changing your partner is fine so long as you get married every time it happens," said Ruth. "Why don't you let Cecily wait till the time limit has expired? Otherwise you're only going to have to tell lies, or else produce proof of her adultery, which you can't easily do without her collusion, and that could get the case thrown out. It's a law that seems to have been designed to promote the telling of lies."

"Or to maximise profits for lawyers," said Roddy. "I think you're right. She'll just have to wait. I'm sure it won't prevent her from having fun. I should have seen this coming, but I'm not sure if there was anything I could have done to prevent it."

"You shouldn't be blaming yourself, Roddy," said Ruth. "It's time for you to start thinking about the future now. Cecily has shown very clearly that she can look after herself."

Daniel heard the front door opening and guessed that their host had returned. "Sounds as if Arthur is back from his posh cricket match," he said, hoping to give Roddy the opportunity to end the public discussion of his divorce proceedings, if he so desired.

"Has he been at the Eton and Harrow match, then?" Roddy asked.

As he confirmed that information Daniel heard Arthur being greeted enthusiastically by Vera, and mentally approved of his friend's priorities. When Arthur entered the room he looked sunburnt and relaxed.

"Were the happy couple at the match again today?" Ruth asked him when the initial greetings had been exchanged.

"The Princess and her Greek chap? No, I didn't see them there," he replied.

"There is a lovely picture of them at the match in today's *Times*," said Margarita, who had accompanied him into the room, carrying Vera in her arms.

"I thought the King looked rather drawn in that photograph," said Rebecca. "I wonder if he has recovered yet from all that he went through during the War."

"There's still a lot of recovering to be done all round," said Arthur. "I hope these talks about the 'Marshall Offer' will go well in Paris today. We desperately need to get some more money back into the European economies if we're not going to be living in a state of perpetual crisis."

"I'll leave you to talk about politics while I finish preparing the dinner," said Margarita.

"Shall I come and look after Vera while you're doing that?" Rebecca asked, and her offer was accepted.

When they had sat down again Daniel asked Arthur, "Do you think Mr Bevin is serious when he says there's going to be no appeasement of Stalin's aggressive tactics?"

"I'm sure he is. I was very doubtful about how he would perform at the Foreign Office when Attlee first appointed him, but now I'm full of admiration. It looks as if being a trade union leader is good practice for diplomacy. Of course, not all my colleagues would agree. His namesake with an 'a' and others on that wing of the Party are saying that we ought to be aligning ourselves with Stalin and not with the Americans. Strange that having fought a war to get rid of one murderous dictator they think we should now cosy up to another one. Luckily Mr Attlee has no time for that kind of thinking. Do you see any prospect of your Commission getting some kind of agreement on disarmament?"

"Can't say I'm optimistic," Daniel replied. "If there's one thing that murderous dictators like to have a lot of, it's armaments. But the Commissioners keep on talking; and there's just a faint hope that the rising cost of weaponry might influence Stalin to strike a deal. I expect you know better than I do how much more armaments are costing now than they did back in 1939. I'd guess that the price of a single Meteor Mark III would have paid for quite a few Hurricanes. And who knows how much is being spent on developing atomic bombs? Marshal Stalin might just decide that the Russian people would like to have a bit more butter than guns for a change."

"Let's hope that's how he sees it," said Arthur. "I won't be holding my breath. Roddy, are you working on anything interesting at the moment?"

"I've had parts in a couple of radio plays; and I've done some reading for the BBC as well – extracts from books and things like that. But the most interesting development is something that came out of one of the plays. I had to act the part of an announcer on the wireless, and afterwards the producer asked me if I'd ever considered the idea of becoming an announcer. He said I had the ideal voice for the job."

"I'm not surprised," said Daniel. "I've often heard it said that the Anglo-Irish upper classes – to which you have to admit belonging, Roddy – have the most perfect spoken English. I suppose it's down to the schools you attended. Anyhow, your producer was right. You'd make an ideal BBC announcer or news reader. But you'd have to give up acting, I suppose."

"Yes, but I could probably revert to doing amateur theatricals in my spare time. I think this is the moment when I'm ready to make a real change in the way I'm living my life. And it would be nice to have a steady income, which is something that acting hasn't provided for me."

"Good luck," said Ruth. "I'll look forward to hearing your dulcet tones when I switch on the wireless. You must let me know which programmes you'll be working on. I suppose you might sometimes bump into Rebecca when you're going to work at the BBC."

"That's not very likely to happen. Since '41 the Overseas Service has been down in the Aldwych, at a place called Bush House. But I must have a talk with Rebecca some time. Her experience might well provide me with some useful tips, especially if I get to work on news and current affairs programmes."

"How long are you two going to be in London this time?" Arthur asked.

"For once they've given me a decent spell of leave," Daniel replied. "We'll be over here till the end of August. On Monday we're off to Hampshire, to stay with Ruth's parents for a week."

"I had only twenty-four hours with them on our last trip," said Ruth. "Penelope's going to be there, too, and so it'll be a proper family reunion."

"And then we're going to have a few days in Portadown. I have nephews and nieces I'm probably not going to recognize," Daniel added. And he was hoping there would be no awkward questions to Ruth about when she was going to add to the score. He was reasonably confident that his family would maintain their customary respect for each other's privacy… but Aunty Hilda might possibly find it difficult to contain her curiosity. Whatever happened, Ruth would be quite capable of coping without giving offence.

"Aren't you going to have any proper holiday time to yourselves?" asked Roddy. "When you're in Portadown you could always pop over the Border to the Free State. I was back in Dublin in May and I noticed that rationing's not nearly so bad there. You can get some quite decent food in the better restaurants. There's a nice little hotel in Bray that I know of, if you fancy a trip to the seaside."

Daniel looked at Ruth and she nodded her head enthusiastically. "That sounds like a good idea," she said. "And there are things I'd love to see in Dublin, like the Book of Kells – and that building in Trinity where you used to live, called 'Botany Bay'. It could be fun."

"When I was there I had an ice-cream called a 'Knickerbocker Glory'" said Roddy. "You should try one. It made me feel that at last the War was really over."

CHAPTER TWELVE: 25th May, 1948 - RUTH

As the chairlift soared into the open air Ruth squeezed Daniel's hand and said, "I can't believe there's a panoramic view anywhere in the world that's better than this one. To see a whole range of the Alps from the Breithorn to the Hasliberg – it's incredible. It reminds me of that verse in the hymn: *Where every prospect pleases....*"

"*And only man is vile,*" Daniel completed the quotation. "But the good thing about this place is that the people are very far from being vile. I've never met a friendlier lot; and they're also incredibly efficient. Sing me again that little verse you composed when we were coming up."

Ruth laughed. On the way up, to control her nervousness at suddenly finding herself gliding some twenty feet above the ground in a kind of double garden-seat with a foot-rest and a canvas canopy overhead, she had sung a little doggerel chant, based on the names of the intermediate stations on the chairlift to First:

The kindly men of Oberhaus,
The merry men of Egg,
And Berghaus Bort, Berghaus Bort,
Doing what he berghaus ort.

She sang it again as they glided slowly down towards Egg and Daniel joined in, dropping his voice half an octave on the final line. And then he called out, "Look over there, on the edge of the trees. It's a deer. Must be a young one. It doesn't have any antlers – or maybe it's a doe."

"Probably a young one if it's foolish enough to come out of the woods in the afternoon," said Ruth. "Weren't we lucky this morning to see all those chamois against the skyline – and that golden eagle hovering above them. I hope it didn't manage to grab one of the young ones when they went down the other side of the ridge."

"I suppose it was looking for lunch for its own young ones," Daniel replied. "I should think the young marmots were more at risk from it – though their sentries did seem to be very alert. You don't expect little furry animals to have such a piercing whistle."

They clanged and clattered at ground level through the little wooden station called Egg and then soared up again into the sunshine. "It was clever of the local people to build this chairlift so quickly after the War," Daniel remarked. "It's one more attraction that should help them to get back the tourists again."

"Actually I think that just now they don't need to have any more attractions than the scenery and the peace and quiet – and the food. Wasn't that rösti we had at the little restaurant up there delicious?"

"I'm glad a morning walking had given me the appetite for it. Oh, I meant to ask you – didn't we see the lady who was in charge at the restaurant in our hotel last night?"

"Yes, we did," Ruth replied. "I remember my friend, Liselotte, telling me about her when we stayed there on that weekend in 1938. She and her husband own the hotel, and Liselotte said it had been in the family for about forty years."

"What time did you arrange for us to go to Liselotte's this evening?" he asked.

"At seven o'clock. I think the Swiss like to eat fairly early in the evening. She lives on one of the roads that lead down to Grund; so it won't take us long to walk there. It's the same house where her aunt lived and where I stayed with her a couple of times when we were students together in Bern. Her aunt died in '44 and left her the house, and she was able to move in there when she got married at the end of the War. Her husband works in Interlaken; so it's very convenient."

"I can see Bort now," said Daniel. "Isn't that stretch of alp incredible? From this distance it looks completely yellow. It must be covered in dandelions."

"Maybe buttercups as well," said Ruth, "and I'll bet if you get close up you could see lots of forget-me-nots. This must be the best time of year for flowers, when you think of the acres of crocuses and soldanella we were walking through higher up."

When they had rattled through the larger station at Bort and crossed over a tiny lake formed by a dam across a swiftly flowing stream they heard the clanging of bells.

"We're getting to the level where the cows have been brought up," said Ruth. "Once they move higher there won't be much left of the dandelions."

"It's amazing how far the sound of bells seems to carry. I suppose it depends on which way the wind is blowing," said Daniel.

Soon they were floating over a herd of brown-and-white cows, each with a bell fastened to her neck on a broad leather collar. The cows munched away contentedly, oblivious to the people passing above their heads.

When the chairlift had taken them through the little station at Oberhaus, with its benignly smiling attendants, Ruth said, "I wish this journey was twice as long. I think it's suddenly become my favourite form of transport."

"We could come up again tomorrow and walk across to Bussalp, perhaps," said Daniel. "If we go through the forest we might see the woodpeckers or the goldcrests you said you saw when you were on holiday here."

"I'd love to see those again – and the crossbill. It's a strange-looking bird, and the males and females are completely different in colour," said Ruth. "With those strong binoculars of yours we could get a really good look at them."

"I'm not sure I should still have these Service binoculars. It's three years since I last used them 'officially', but nobody has ever asked me to hand them in."

"I'm sure Liselotte's husband, Ulrich, must have army binoculars that he keeps at home, along with his gun," said Ruth, "and he was demobilized three years ago."

"But in theory he's liable to be mobilized again at a moment's notice, and then he might need them," said Daniel, "whereas I'm still in the Army but I'm unlikely ever to use mine again."

"I certainly hope you won't have to. I don't want even to think about the possibility," said Ruth. "Oh, look at that gorgeous Oberlander dog on the path down there. He looks so dignified and yet so cuddly."

It was fortunate they had spent so much time walking in the open air, Ruth reflected, as Liselotte went to the kitchen to make the coffee. Otherwise they would never have been able to do credit to the sumptuous meal that she had prepared for them. "Can I give you a hand with the dishes?" she asked.

"Certainly not," her friend replied. "You are on holiday, and just for a little time you must enjoy having no responsibilities."

"Have you been back to Europe since the end of the War?" asked Ulrich.

"No, not since I left Italy in June '45," said Daniel. "As you probably know, we've spent most of our time in America because of my job."

"Now that the UNO has opened an office in Geneva perhaps you will be sent over here," said Ulrich.

"I'd like to think that would be possible but I doubt it," Daniel replied. "The people I'm working with report to the Security Council, and that's based in New York. But just how long their work is going to continue I don't know."

"Liselotte told me it was all about disarmament," said Ulrich. "Do you think there is any chance that the big countries will agree to some kind of disarmament?"

"I'm afraid it's beginning to look unlikely," said Daniel. "The way the Russians are behaving in Berlin just now is one more indication that Stalin is still thinking about pushing out the boundaries of his empire."

"Even here in Switzerland that is how we see it," said Ulrich, nodding his head. "We have begun to modernize some of the Army's equipment."

"Are you really worried about the Russians?" Ruth asked, surprised by this turn in the conversation.

"Of course we are. If we had not worried about the Germans a long time ago we would not have been able to stay free until 1945. And we haven't forgotten that Suvarov's army fought its way through the Saint Gotthard Pass a hundred and fifty years ago — even though it was the French they were fighting. In October I must attend a lecture with other officers to learn about the Russian army."

"How near do you think the Germans came to attacking Switzerland during the War?" asked Daniel.

"We think there were three times when they were getting ready to attack us, but each time Hitler changed his mind. In 1940 I was stationed in Basel. I was not happy because the plan was to retreat after the first battle. I did not like the idea of retreating."

"Sometimes retreat is the best strategy," said Daniel. "Kutuzov destroyed Napoleon's Grand Army by knowing when to retreat. I think the best decision I ever made during the War — luckily I didn't have to make very many decisions in action — was a decision to retreat."

"When did that happen?" asked Ulrich. "Was it at Monte Cassino? Liselotte told me you were there."

"Yes, it was. My company had been sent to attack an enemy position that was supposed to have been destroyed by a preliminary bombardment, but of course it hadn't been. The Germans were firmly dug in on a slope up above us and I lost one man dead and four wounded before we took cover and got our heads down. Luckily my walkie-talkie was still working and I was able to tell the battalion commander that if we attacked again we would certainly lose a lot more men and probably still not be able to capture the position. So he authorized a retreat, and we pulled back without any more losses."

"I remember reading about that siege, but I can't remember how it was that the Allies eventually broke through," said Ulrich.

"It was a classic example of attempting the impossible when everything else has failed – and succeeding," said Daniel. "The Free French had a division of North African troops called Goumiers who'd been trained in the Atlas Mountains. They crossed the Aurunci Mountains, which everyone thought were impassable, taking their supplies on mules, and attacked the Germans from the rear. At the same time the Polish Corps stormed up Monte Cassino itself and pressed on yard by yard for five days until one morning they discovered that the last of the German survivors had gone. But it was a costly business. The French later had to send the Goumiers back to Africa because their favourite relaxation was raping and pillaging the Italian population. In a war you can find yourself with some very strange allies."

"One of my regrets is that I've never experienced any real action," said Ulrich.

Daniel shook his head. "Don't ever regret that. As the Duke of Wellington said after Waterloo, 'Nothing except a battle lost can be half so melancholy as a battle won.' Whenever I think about the War – which I try not to do – the one memory that gives me a feeling of satisfaction is that decision to retreat. There are men alive now who would be dead if I hadn't made it – and that probably includes myself."

Ruth felt herself shudder involuntarily, and decided to change the subject. "We thought we might go down to Interlaken one day and sail across the lake to Brienz. Are the boats running at this time of the year?"

"Yes. They will take you all the way to Brienz and back. If you go to Brienz be sure to look at the small streets away from the lake. There are some beautiful old houses; and the church, too, is very interesting – up on the hill."

Returning with coffee, Liselotte asked, "Will you be in London for the Olympic Games?"

"Not unless my boss decides he needs me to be there for a high-level consultation," Daniel replied.

"A friend of ours, Arthur – I think I've told you about him – is on a committee advising about transport problems created by the Games," said Ruth.

"Arthur – isn't he the Member of Parliament? Are you going to need new laws to keep the buses running?" Liselotte asked, proffering a plate of little round biscuits that were called 'St Martin's Ringli', Ruth remembered.

"Arthur was one of the guys who kept 21st Army Group fully supplied all the way across Europe after D-Day. I think he might have a useful way of looking at the problems," said Daniel. "I just hope our own contestants in the Games are being given some extra rations in the run-up period. All that exertion is bound to need more than a shilling's worth of meat and one and a half ounces of cheese a week to keep it going."

"Are you really still so strictly rationed in England?" Liselotte asked.

"We haven't seen much of it because we've not been there for long; but my mother tells me all about her difficulties," Ruth replied. "Because she's constantly having visitors at the Rectory she hates not to be hospitable, but there's not much she can do about it – although I think local farm produce helps a good deal."

"I suppose I was being naïve when I thought that after the War we would start hearing more good news than bad," said Liselotte. "It doesn't seem to have worked out like that. Everywhere you look there still seems to be fighting. The Arabs say they're going to wipe out the Jews in Palestine, now that you British have left it. Hundreds of thousands of people were killed when you left India last year. The Communists have killed Jan Masaryk in Czechoslovakia, though they're pretending they didn't. And all the millions of refugees still don't have proper homes to live in. We have a little group here that raises money to help them."

"But not everything is bad," said Ruth. "General Marshall's new plan is getting started, and that's going to bring a lot of American money into Europe to help things get back to normal. I suppose we just have to accept that the War hasn't got rid of the old problems that were there before it started. It's just meant that we are the ones with the responsibility for doing something about them – which is a lot better than being at the mercy of the people who wanted to be in control."

"I suppose that's true," said Liselotte, "but I can't help wishing the UNO had been given more power to sort things out."

"Isn't that exactly what you've been working on, Daniel?" Ulrich asked.

"Yes, I suppose it is. Unfortunately, it's a bit like living in a town where the bench of magistrates includes the local Al Capone, whose only interest is to use the law to further his own interests and protect his criminal associates. But everybody has to pretend that he's a law-abiding citizen who means what he says. I think the difficulty springs from the fact that the United Nations began as a military alliance with the single aim of defeating Germany and Japan. It's key rules seem to be aimed at preventing those two countries from ever giving trouble again – but I don't think they're ever likely to, if they become genuine democracies. What we have now is the kind of situation we might have had if Germany and Italy and Japan had stayed inside the League of Nations.

"But I'm sorry, I mustn't start banging on about politics when there are so many more cheerful things to talk about. Is your tourist industry here beginning to pick up again?"

"It certainly is," said Ulrich. "Of course, a lot of old friends still cannot afford to come here, but we are getting some new visitors. American servicemen in Germany, for example, are finding out that Switzerland is a good place to have a holiday. And we've been investing in new attractions so that we will be able to compete when better times return to other parts of Europe – like the First chairlift you enjoyed today."

"That was an incredible experience," said Daniel. "I wish we could stay here longer; but you can be sure that we'll be back." He smiled at Ruth and she nodded her head vigorously.

"I expect little Bettli will have started skiing next time we come," she said. "I remember you said you put on skis soon after you learnt to walk."

"If you come in the next winter sports season she might have a brother, or a sister," Liselotte replied, blushing.

"Everyone we know seems to be adding to their families," said Ruth, as they walked up the steep slope leading back to their hotel. "Liselotte looks as if she's more than content to settle for the rôle of housewife and mother. She was quite different when we were at university. We used to spend endless hours talking about what we could do to make the world a safer place. Now she says she's even lost interest in the women's suffrage movement."

"It's incredible that Swiss women still don't have the right to vote," said Daniel.

"Liselotte said – only half joking – that she wasn't too bothered because she was sure that Ulrich would vote the way she told him to. All she seems interested in now is books about education and how to bring up children."

"I expect that's what is going to give her the greatest satisfaction," said Daniel. "I suppose it's just as well that there are a lot of women with strong maternal instincts, so that the race can go on renewing itself while those of us who aren't turned on by the patter of tiny feet can use our talents in different ways."

"Luckily I think Liselotte understands that," Ruth replied. "She's not one of the smug brigade who think that every other woman must secretly be longing to produce an infant, and those who haven't succeeded are only engaged in other activities to suppress their disappointment. Their implicit assumption that we somehow don't have a choice in the matter is mind-boggling in the middle of the twentieth century."

"Unfortunately I think an awful lot of people are still not able to exercise that choice," said Daniel, putting his arm around her waist as the slope became even steeper. "Aren't we lucky, being able to stay in control of our bodies without being compelled to cut back on opportunities for having fun?" His fingers tightened on her waist as he continued, "Do you think the walls in our bedroom are sound proof?"

Without slackening her stride she turned her head and kissed his cheek. "I don't care whether they are or not," she replied.

CHAPTER THIRTEEN: 3rd October, 1948 - ARTHUR

When Roddy put down his knife and fork and proclaimed, "That was about the best Yorkshire pudding I've ever tasted," Arthur glanced at Margarita and savoured the happiness that lit up her face.

"Arthur's Mam taught me how to do that," she said, "and his Dad told me it was the one sure way to keep a Yorkshireman happy. But I wish the beef could have been better. The ration book would only stretch to a fairly small joint and she told me a bigger one always cooks better. I've never actually seen a big one."

"Well, at least Bramley apples aren't rationed, and I know that's what you have coming next for us," said Arthur, as he stood up and helped her to clear away the plates.

When everyone had received their apple pie and custard Rebecca asked Nancy how her son, Leo, was getting on at school.

"He's really enjoying it," Nancy replied. "I'm sure the Montessori method is the best way of getting children to develop their full potential. It ought to be compulsory in all the primary schools."

"That would need a lot of retraining for teachers," said Arthur, amused to see that Nancy had found yet another cause for which to campaign.

"If you stopped spending money on making atom bombs and spent it on education instead they could all be retrained in a year," Nancy retorted.

"I seem to remember hearing a similar argument when Mr Chamberlain announced that he'd ordered a thousand Spitfires," said Arthur. "But I'm glad to know you're still engaged in the debate. There aren't any easy answers to the uncertainties we're having to face up to nowadays. I don't think I'd want to have Mr Attlee's job. And I wish the people Daniel's been working with at Lake Success had had more success with their efforts. In his last letter he sounded pretty despondent about the prospects for any kind of agreement on limiting armaments."

"Did he say how Ruth is getting on with the novel she's writing?" asked Roddy.

"Yes, he said she was hoping to finish it at Christmas. Then she'll have to begin the whole business of trying to find a publisher."

"I wonder if the publisher I translated that Mexican novel for last year might be interested," said Margarita. "When I write to Ruth I'll ask her if she'd like me to speak to Juanita about it. She's still working for him. The one I translated was a historical novel, and that's what Ruth is writing; and she told me part of it is set in South America. So he might well be interested."

"Did you go to any of the Olympic Games? Weren't you on a committee that was doing some of the planning for them?" Rebecca asked Arthur.

"It was only connected indirectly with the Games," Arthur replied. "We were trying to make sure that the transport system would be able to handle all the visitors – and I think we succeeded. But it didn't get me any free tickets. However, we did manage to have a day at Wembley. We actually saw Fanny Blankers-Koen winning the 80 metres hurdles. She's an incredible woman – thirty years old, with kids at home to look after, and she won four gold medals."

"Rebecca and I were there on the day that Zatopek won the 10,000 metres. It was good to see the Czechs winning some golds, after all that they've been through," said Roddy.

Arthur exchanged a quick, covert glance with Margarita. So Rebecca and Roddy were going out together. Would anything come of it, he wondered. Roddy's divorce wasn't through yet, but it was under way. And Rebecca had never before mentioned male friends – only colleagues. When they'd gone he would find out what Margarita thought about their prospects.

"Did you go to more than one day at the Olympics?" he asked.

"No, there wasn't another day when we both had time off," said Rebecca. "I'd have loved to see Fanny Blankers-Koen in action."

"What did you think about those Jewish terrorists killing Count Bernadotte?" asked Nancy, who was clearly not interested in sport and wanted to steer the conversation back to politics.

"I surprised myself by feeling deeply ashamed when I heard about it," Rebecca replied. "I've never identified with Zionism in any way, though I've had sympathy with those refugees who were just looking for a place where they could live in safety. But for Jewish people, after all they've suffered at the hands of nationalists over the centuries, to murder the representative of the one international organization that is trying to find a way of solving their problems, a man who had actually saved hundreds of Jews from the Nazis during the War, is beyond my comprehension. And killing somebody because he doesn't agree with your arguments – that's pure fascism. It's doubly depressing that Jewish people should be guilty of a crime like that."

"It's a sad fact of history that persecuted people often become like their persecutors when they get the opportunity," Arthur observed.

"I think that's why I've never been happy with the idea of Zionism," said Rebecca. "I couldn't see how a Jewish state could be set up in part of Palestine without it getting involved in violence against the people who were already living there. And then we saw how it was working out. They were even killing the British soldiers who were protecting them, because the soldiers had to protect the Arabs as well.

"I've argued about this with Jewish people who don't actually want to live in Palestine themselves, but who say it's good that the refugees from Europe can find a place where they feel safe. I'm a refugee and I feel safe in Britain, but I wouldn't feel safe in this new state of Israel. It's surrounded by countries that want to destroy it, and even if they don't succeed it will have to keep itself in a constant state of siege for as long as anybody can foresee.

"I admire the courage of people who've gone there, but I think it's crazy they should say this bit of land belongs to them because some imaginary god that half of them don't even believe in is supposed to have 'given' it to their ancestors five thousand years ago."

"And if their ancestors' records are to be believed," said Roddy, "this god told them that in the cities they occupied they should 'leave nothing alive that breatheth' – but be careful not to cut down the fruit trees. It doesn't sound to me like a very good basis for claiming ownership."

"Where does that quotation come from?" asked Margarita.

"The Book of Deuteronomy," he replied. "Some well-meaning soul gave me an English bible when I was in hospital in Barcelona, and with nothing else to read at the time I read bits of it that I'd never looked into before. Bombs were being dropped outside every day by airmen urged on by priests and bishops who thought they were defending religion, and I started wondering just how much of the violence in the world had its roots in religious ideas that were deep-seated, maybe sub-conscious. Do people find it easier to kill when they think some god has given them permission to do it?"

"But most of the people I know in the Peace movement are there precisely because they believe God doesn't give anybody permission to kill," Nancy objected.

"And they all use the same collection of writings to justify what they believe," said Roddy. "One writer says that their god told the Israelites when they captured certain cities they should kill all the inhabitants, together with their animals; but another writer says that the same god's son told them they had to love their enemies. It occurred to me that they couldn't both be right – and more likely both of them were wrong. It's beyond belief that intelligent people in the twentieth century should be basing their politics on the myths of their ancestors – and even of other people's ancestors."

"Unfortunately that's exactly what they're doing," said Rebecca, "and I don't want any part in it. On the other hand, it would have been a catastrophe if the Arab states had succeeded in their attacks; and the UNO had no forces there that could have prevented them. It's lucky that the Israelis were able to hold them off. I just hope that Count Bernadotte's successor will be able to persuade the two sides not to start fighting again and accept the borders they were given by the UNO."

"Are you still doing voluntary work with that refugee aid organization?" Margarita asked Rebecca.

"Yes, I feel more comfortable with it because it's not just Jewish refugees that they're helping. There are millions of people still in those camps in Europe, waiting to be resettled. But I'm only doing translation work for them at the London office. I don't have a lot of spare time these days."

"The BBC is quite a demanding employer, whichever bit of it you're in," said Roddy. "I'm finding that the shift system can make life quite awkward at times – but I'm enjoying it. I meet more interesting people than I used to in the theatre."

"Do you ever go to the theatre these days?" Arthur asked him.

"Occasionally. Rebecca and I saw that wonderful American musical that's running at Drury Lane."

"*Oklahoma?* I've heard that it's very good," said Margarita. "I'd love to see it, but I don't want to leave Danny with a baby-sitter just yet. Vera's all right now – she goes to bed and usually sleeps right through till next morning. But Danny still needs a lot of attention."

"Why don't you think about a matinée?" Nancy asked. "I'd be happy to come over one Saturday afternoon if I can bring Leo with me. It would be no trouble."

"That's a very kind offer," said Arthur, remembering how restless Margarita had been in recent months because of being housebound for so much of the time. "Can I telephone you when I've found out whether I can get the tickets?"

106

"You must go," said Rebecca. "There's a wonderful song near the beginning of the show – *Oh what a beautiful morning*. It made me wish I could wake up one morning and feel like that – feel that everything was going to be new and fresh and going my way."

"Maybe one morning you will," said Roddy; and then, looking slightly embarrassed, he went on hastily to add, "But the play is quite realistic, too. There's a bad guy who messes things up for everyone else, just like in real life. In an odd way it reminded me of *All's Well that Ends Well*."

Through the open dining-room door they heard the sound of an infant wailing. "That will be Danny," said Margarita, rising to her feet. "I'll go and see what's the matter."

"Better now than in the middle of the night," said Arthur.

"It'll probably be both," she rejoined, over her shoulder, as she left the room. "I hope he doesn't wake Vera."

"I see that there's going to be a State Opening of Parliament at the end of the month, for the first time since before the War," said Roddy.

"Yes. I hope they'll remember how it ought to be done. A lot of the old stagers in the House have either died or retired by now. Even the King himself has only done it twice," said Arthur.

"I think they ought to get rid of all that dressing up and strutting around," said Nancy. "Parliament in a democracy should be just about the MPs and the people they represent."

"I don't agree," said Roddy. "Pageantry is like theatre; it entertains people and helps them to feel happier. But it also encourages them to think about their traditions, and I believe that's important, especially when so many things are changing."

"I think it's very important," said Rebecca. "You are so lucky in Britain where being loyal to your country doesn't mean you have to belong to one particular party. I remember when I was growing up in Austria people used to say 'We've got rid of all the out-of-date traditions and from now on everything will be controlled by the ordinary people.' But we all know that's not what actually happened. When nobody respects the rules it's the thugs who take over in the end."

"But I don't see how dressing up in fancy robes and making the King pretend that he's in charge when he reads a speech that was written for him by the Government contributes to that," Nancy objected.

"I think it's a reminder of how we got to where we are today," said Arthur. "We're a country where the Government is nominally responsible to the King, and the King is symbolically the representative of the whole population, not just one part of it. And we call the MPs on the other side of the House 'His Majesty's Opposition' because that symbolizes their willingness to abide by the rules. When I was a student my sympathies were republican, but eventually I realized that what we actually have in this country is a republic that, for reasons of practical convenience and continuity, pretends to be a monarchy. In contrast, the Americans have a monarchy – with an elected king – that pretends to be a republic."

Roddy laughed. "I think I see what you're driving at. Incidentally, I was reading De Valera's new constitution for the republic that Ireland is going to become next year, and it looks to me more like the constitution for a theocracy. I remember before I went to Spain the biggest pro-Franco organization in the country was the Irish Christian Front. I happened to be in Cork, visiting my Aunt Beryl, when they had a huge rally there, and I went along to hear what they had to say. There were tens of thousands of people at it, and some Monsignor – I think he was the Dean of Cork – told them that the Civil War was all the fault of 'a gang of murderous Jews in Moscow.' And up on the platform beside him was Douglas Hyde, the man who's now the President of Ireland."

"I'm afraid there must still be a lot of anti-Semitism over there," said Rebecca. "I know that the year before last the Minister of Justice in Dublin refused a request to let in a hundred Jewish orphans from the Bergen-Belsen camp."

"People make a joke of it now, but De Valera's message of sympathy to the German embassy when Hitler's death was announced may not have been just a diplomatic formality," said Roddy.

"I can understand why you've chosen to live over here," said Arthur. "I wish people who try to excuse their own ambivalent attitudes to the Nazis in past times could have been with me when I arrived at Belsen – and that was a day or two after the first horrors had been cleared away. I remember talking to a major who'd had the job of creating a burial ground for the thousands of corpses that the Germans had dumped into pits. He said he'd not been able to prevent his men from whacking the camp guards with their rifle butts when they made them carry the corpses to the graves. All of us were familiar with the shocking sights you come across on battlefields, but to see the evidence of cold-blooded cruelty on a mass scale – it was beyond comprehension. The only people who can feel comfortable about what they were doing before the War started are people like you, Roddy, who actually did something to try to stop the spread of fascism."

Roddy smiled and shook his head. "As you know, I only did it by accident – but I'm glad now that I did."

Margarita came into the room with a smile on her face. "He's gone back to sleep," she said. "I think it's the start of teething. Vera started at just about seven months, too."

"Everywhere you look nowadays there seem to be teething troubles," said Arthur. "The governments in India and Pakistan, our government's Parliament Bill and the plans for nationalization and, from what Daniel says in his letters, the proposals his disarmament commission has sent to the UNO – they're all having teething troubles."

"In Israel it's more like birth pains," said Rebecca.

"When everything is changing that's the way it has to be, I suppose," said Margarita, resuming her seat at the table. "We think we've solved a problem and then we discover that we've created two new problems."

Roddy chuckled. "That's exactly what you and Arthur have done. Your new problems are sleeping upstairs; but I'm sure you're enjoying them."

Arthur looked into Margarita's smiling eyes and replied, "Yes. Some problems can provide a lot of pleasure while you're searching for solutions."

CHAPTER FOURTEEN: 3rd November, 1948 - DANIEL

As he entered the kitchen Daniel pressed a tiny scrap of toilet paper to the cut on his chin, where the razor had nicked it. Ruth was sitting at the table with a half-finished bowl of cornflakes and several unopened letters in front of her.

"Anything in the post that looks interesting?" he asked.

"There's a letter from Margarita, and one from Mummy, and something from Trinity College, Dublin for you."

"They're probably trying to raise money to stop the place from falling down," he said, drawing up a chair and reaching for the cornflakes packet.

"Would you like your egg sunny side up today?" she enquired as she finished eating her cornflakes.

"Yes, please. I'll make the toast in a minute."

When they had eaten their eggs and bacon Ruth opened the air letter from Margarita and Daniel slit the envelope with the Dublin postmark. It was, as he suspected, an appeal for donations.

"Anything exciting been happening to Margarita and Arthur?" he asked.

"Well, Arthur has been to the first State Opening of Parliament since before the War, and apparently it was all very splendid. And baby Daniel is teething and keeping her awake at night. Takes after his namesake. Oh, and she thinks there might be something going on between Rebecca and Roddy, although his divorce hasn't gone through yet. That's as far as I've got."

"Has the paper come yet?" he asked. "Oh, yes. I see it on the dresser." He stood up and brought the copy of the *New York Times* to the table.

"I just glanced at the headlines," said Ruth. "They seem to think Governor Dewey's victory might be a lot narrower than they were predicting yesterday. It looks as if these 'opinion polls' that they had aren't as reliable as everybody seems to think. Is it going to make a lot of difference to the UNO if Truman isn't in charge any more? Some people at my UNA group last Friday were very worried about it."

"I'm afraid it might," said Daniel. "The Republicans have a strong isolationist streak in them; and nobody knows if Dewey will really back the plans they started making last July for a permanent alliance between

America and the West European countries. If that falls through it will be a great encouragement to Marshal Stalin to push ahead with his expansionist policies – like he's doing now over Berlin." A strong sense of foreboding took hold of him as he turned the pages of the newspaper.

"I saw somewhere that Shostakovich and Prokoviev are the latest victims of his displeasure," said Ruth. "Their new compositions aren't in line with Party ideology." She resumed reading the letter. "Oh, Margarita says that she's spoken to the publisher she did the translation for, and he says he would be interested to look at my manuscript."

"That's great news. Even if he doesn't take it, getting a publisher's reaction could be very helpful for you. Come to think of it, there might be a chance for you to talk to him face to face sometime early next year. There's going to be a meeting in Washington about the North Atlantic treaty idea early in December, provided Governor Dewey doesn't upset the apple-cart. If those talks go well I think my boss will be heading back to London for consultations, and with any luck he'll take me with him. You could come too."

"I'd really like that. Can I tell Mummy it's a possibility when I reply to her letter?"

"Maybe not. There are still a lot of uncertainties – not least about who's going to be the President. I wouldn't want to disappoint her."

"OK. I won't mention it until you're sure it's going to happen; but it's very exciting. This treaty idea – is that the reason why the chap from London you're going to see today is coming over here?"

"I don't think so; but like all these secret service types Frobisher doesn't give anything away, even if it's totally unimportant. He says he'll be on his way to Washington for a 'briefing', which is why we're meeting at Penn Station, under the clock."

"I expect he's going to bring you up to date on what's been happening about Cyril Hamberly. I wonder if they've found any evidence he's been spying."

"I'd like to think that maybe he's been frightened away from his Soviet contacts by realizing that someone's keeping a watch on him, but I suppose that's being too optimistic," said Daniel. "But tell me, what are you going to be doing this morning?"

"I'm going to Central Park with my UNA friend, Julia. She's a member of the National Audubon Society, and several of them go the Park regularly to watch the migrant birds that pass through at this time of year. Apparently you can see as many as two hundred different species in the autumn, although most of them will have gone through by now."

"Sounds interesting. You used to go bird-watching when you were in your teens, didn't you?"

"Yes. Where I grew up was quite a good place for it; but unfortunately my binoculars must still be somewhere in the attic – if Mummy hasn't given them away. Over here they call it 'birding'. But I'll be back home before you get in from work. I want to know what Frobisher has to tell you about Cyril Hamberly. I hope you won't be barred by the Official Secrets Act from telling me."

"Well, since you also signed up to the Act in days gone by I think I could treat you as an insider," he said. "I wonder if FBI agents pretend to be 'birders' with binoculars if they're watching out for illicit contacts being made in Central Park."

Ruth laughed. "It's more likely that people making illicit contacts would do it under the clock at Penn Station."

The hands on the great clock were showing ten minutes past twelve, Eastern Standard Time, when Daniel caught sight of Ted Frobisher approaching in the never-ending stream of passengers. Waving to attract his attention, he stepped forward to meet him.

"Have you seen the newspaper placards? Dewey has conceded defeat. So Truman's going to be carrying on after all," were Frobisher's first words to him.

"The new editions must just have come out," he replied. "Well, that's going to make life a lot more predictable for all of us. Did you have a good voyage?"

"Weather was a bit rough on Sunday and Monday, but the old *Queen* stays steady whatever it's like. Disembarking is always a bit of a pain – so much hanging around."

"Will you have time for a spot of lunch before you catch your train? I know a pleasant little Italian place a couple of hundred yards from here, if that would suit you."

"Good idea. It'll be a reminder of old times in '45, though I expect the menu will have a few more items on it. Things are beginning to look up a bit now in Italy. I think the Marshall Plan is going to give them a real boost. You haven't been back there, I suppose."

112

"No, but I'd like to go one day and show Ruth some of the things we only managed to catch a glimpse of. I take it you've been back recently."

"Yes; at the moment it's my principal place of work, but I think that's going to change fairly soon, now that the Christian Democrats seem to be firmly in the saddle. As you probably know, Italy's going to be joining the new North Atlantic treaty, and everyone seems to think we can depend on De Gasperi to keep the country stable."

As they pushed their way through the incoming throng Frobisher commented, "This really is an incredible building. It's like a cross between a Greek temple and the Crystal Palace, and inside here it reminds me of those gigantic ruins in Rome, the Baths of Caracalla. Did you ever see them?"

"Yes, I did; and it's interesting you should say that. I remember reading in the guide to New York we bought when we moved here that the architect actually had the Baths of Caracalla in mind when he designed the main waiting room – all that imitation travertine on the lower walls. When I first saw the station from the outside I thought of it as a kind of Neo-Classical response to the Gothic of Saint Pancras. I expect a student of architecture would have something profound to say about that. But it's certainly one of the most impressive buildings in New York."

"Do you remember the ceilings in that villa we used as HQ in Rome?" Frobisher asked.

"I do indeed. They were the last word in Neo-Classical grandeur. And then there was that cupola with semi-naked girls dancing around among the roses. No wonder Mussolini got grandiose ideas when he was living there."

When they had given their order to the waiter at a corner table in 'Fratelli Bonici', shady but somewhat removed from other diners, Frobisher's face became serious and he began to talk in a quiet voice. "I wanted to bring you up to date on the Cyril Hamberly situation, since it was you that tipped me off about him. There have recently been some developments. As you probably know, the Yanks set up this new Central Intelligence Agency and, in fact, I'm on my way to visit it."

"There was quite a lot of publicity about it last year," said Daniel. "Unlike your outfit it actually exists officially."

"I think that's one of its problems," said Frobisher. "It has to justify its existence to the great American public. Anyhow, it has taken over the Hamberly case from the FBI and it wants to pull him in. I think it may have been influenced by the recent disclosures about Alger Hiss.

He's going to be coming up before a grand jury in about a month's time, and the FBI are handling that one. My contact in the FBI says he thinks the CIA want to interrogate Hamberly themselves because they believe he had American contacts as well as his Soviet embassy controller. But if they have him arrested he can claim diplomatic immunity, and that's something the Foreign Office would probably be very reluctant to waive. On the other hand, if they let the FO recall him to London to be pulled in by us or by MI5 they'll lose the chance to give him the third degree. I suspect that's what they want to talk to me about today. Up till now I'm the only person on the UK side – apart from yourself – who knows that Hamberly's under suspicion, and even that is unofficial because I simply gave a personal tip-off to Palmer, my FBI acquaintance. Now the CIA want to make it official, although my bosses think I've only been invited here for a briefing on the new set up and, in particular, how it will work in Italy."

"That puts you in a tricky position," said Daniel. "I guess you can only advise them on what you think will be the most effective way of achieving a result."

"My main worry is how to pull in Hamberly without frightening him off before it happens," said Frobisher. "You remember all the fuss a couple of years ago, when that Soviet clerk, Gouzenko, defected in Canada? The information he gave broke up the Canadian spy ring, but he also gave them leads on Soviet agents in the US and Britain and I don't think those have been completely followed through. There was talk that he knew about agents inside the FO and the Service, but I don't believe that's ever been thoroughly investigated – which is suspicious in itself. What I'm concerned about now is that, when I take their message back to HQ, it may be told to somebody who's actually an accomplice of Hamberley's and who'll give him a tip-off before there's time to go through all the formalities, whatever they may be."

"I see your problem," said Daniel. "There's no easy way round it. Maybe you should share it with whoever briefs you at the new Agency. If they were able to keep things unofficial for a while longer might you be able to talk to someone higher up in your own outfit that you know you can trust?"

"That's a good thought," Frobisher responded. "Now that I come to think of it, there's one chap who ought to be OK. He was head of our counter-intelligence section at the end of the War but he's based in Turkey now. His wife has had a health problem recently, and I heard that he's going to be in London next week. I've never actually met him but the reason I'm inclined to trust him is that he was known to be rather pro-fascist when he was in Spain as *Times* correspondent in '37; and that was when he was recruited by the Service. I don't think the Reds would have seen him as a likely contact. His name is Philby. I might be able to have a quiet word with him next week if I can persuade the Yanks to hold their fire in the meantime."

"Sounds like a good contact to advise you if he's worked in counter-intelligence," said Daniel. "It must be tricky when you don't know whether you can trust your own colleagues."

A waiter approached with Daniel's gnocchi verdi and Frobisher's cannelloni, and they began to eat.

"This place reminds me a little of that restaurant in Rome where we went on the day we heard that Monty had crossed the Rhine," said Daniel. "It was that partisan liaison officer, the Englishman with the Italian name, who took us there."

"I remember. Actually I saw quite a lot of Isolani last year, because he's in the Service now, though technically he's a diplomat, at the Embassy in Rome. They gave him an MBE for his work with the Resistance. We had lunch together a couple of times at Mario's. It hasn't changed much, except that they've been able to redecorate. It was starting to look tired when we were there in '45."

"I really must get back to Italy soon. There's so much that I want to see there," said Daniel. "I've been reading a book about art that Ruth gave me for my birthday. It's passed the time on railway journeys on the days when I've had to go to Lake Success. In fact, one day I nearly forgot to get off the train at the station the regulars call 'Great Bottle Neck'. Anyhow, a great many of the really important pictures I've been reading about seem to be in Florence. I'm sorry I never got there, but I suppose at that time most of the pictures would have been hidden away somewhere in caves to keep them safe from bombing. I expect by now they'll be back on display."

"Just a few weeks ago I managed to spend the best part of a day in the Vatican Museum," said Frobisher. "There's a heck of a lot to see there, if you've got the stamina to traipse around all the corridors and stairways. I wonder if the Pope ever takes the time to look at it."

"I should think he's busy these days worrying about what's happening to his flock in Poland and Czechoslovakia. Do you have people keeping an eye on what's happening there?"

"It's hardly been necessary. Everybody who can is getting out and bringing the latest news for whoever wants to listen to them. But it's not a part of the world I know anything about. My job's been helping to make sure that Italy doesn't go the same way." He broke off a piece of bread and began to mop up the sauce on his plate.

"I still find it hard to understand why a chap like Hamberly persists in helping the people who are spreading this plague of repression – unless, of course, he's so deep in the mire that he can't extricate himself," said Daniel, refilling his glass with *aqua minerale*.

CHAPTER FIFTEEN: 26th March, 1949 - RUTH

As Rebecca paid the bill for their lunch she remarked, "I'm so glad Guiseppe was able to re-open this place after the War. Being interned as an enemy alien can't have been much fun. My old boss, who took me in when I came to Britain, didn't enjoy the two years he spent in the Isle of Man."

"Locking up a Jewish man because he happened to have come from Germany was a daft bit of bureaucracy," said Ruth. "But of course Guiseppe could have been a supporter of Mussolini – though I know he wasn't. Actually, the first time I came here was with Arthur, back in 1937. He was lecturing at the Regent Street Poly then, before he got his PhD."

"Were you and Arthur going out together?" Rebecca asked, as they stepped into the sunlit street. "I thought you told me that you and Daniel were virtually engaged to each other when the War started."

Ruth laughed. "We were, but that was nearly two years later. For a while I used to see both of them in turn – and sometimes together, when we were in our little group of friends. With Arthur I used to go to concerts and cricket, but with Daniel it was usually political activities – we were working together to save the peace, or so we thought."

"But did you also have a… a romantic thing about both of them?"

"I did, actually; and I was very undecided about which of them I wanted to get serious with, if you understand what I mean. In those days courtship was a much more cautious business, and they were both very polite young men. They never tried to 'take advantage', as Mummy would have put it. But I was getting to the point where I thought I was going to have to make a choice between them when Margarita solved the problem for me."

Rebecca's eyes widened. "You mean she snatched Arthur away from you?"

Ruth laughed again. "Not exactly. It was more the other way round: Arthur snatched her up the moment she appeared. I'm only guessing, but I think he was totally bowled over by her gorgeous figure."

"That's ridiculous," said Rebecca. "You have a lovely figure, too; and it's better now than Margarita's, since she's had two babies."

"Nice of you to say so. But she was spectacular when she first arrived. Her waist was tiny, and her other attributes were… well, in the proportions men seem to find irresistible. I'm only half-serious; but I actually feel quite grateful to Margarita for settling the question. I like Arthur very much, but I think his aim would have been to have the kind of family that now he has with Margarita and that wouldn't have been the direction I wanted to take; and so I doubt if it would have been a 'happily ever after' situation."

"I hope you don't mind me asking, but I wondered whether you've stayed with the decision we talked about – not to tell Daniel what happened with the American airman," said Rebecca.

"Of course I don't mind. You gave me good advice and I took it, and I'm sure it was the right thing to do. And if Daniel had any wartime secret I hoped he'd have done the same. Actually, I have a feeling that he may have had. When we first... got together it was quite different from the first time with poor Sher. Then we were both admitting we were virgins, of course, and it was all a bit clumsy, even though it was passionate. With Daniel we were sort of pretending to be virgins, though nothing was actually said, but I was a bit surprised about how confident he seemed to be." She felt herself blushing and laughed to counteract the serious tone that had crept into her voice. "Anyhow, I thought afterwards if he *had* been with someone before she'd done a good job with him and I ought to be grateful to her."

"Roddy and I didn't have that problem," said Rebecca. "His marital status was out in the open; and I had already told him about my experience with Otto."

"Do you have... any plans?" Ruth asked.

"Do you mean are we going to get married?" Rebecca answered, smiling broadly. "Yes, we are; but not until the whole divorce think has been completely wrapped up, of course. In the meantime I've moved in with him, but not officially, so please don't mention it to anyone. The BBC can be a bit stuffy about 'irregular arrangements', even though we work in completely different parts of it; and Roddy doesn't want to shock his parents when it isn't going to be too long before we can make it official. I've kept on my place in the flat, but I'm letting a friend at the refugee agency use it temporarily."

"Actually, Daniel and I had been thinking about having the same kind of arrangement before the War," said Ruth, suddenly remembering an emotion-charged conversation in Daniel's bed-sitter in Dorset Square. "It was even trickier in those days, because if we'd got married I'd have had to give up my job, and that was something I didn't want to do immediately. But if we'd lived together openly everybody and his dog would have been shocked to bits. I think we'd even have been shocked ourselves."

Rebecca laughed. "Things haven't changed all that much, have they? But Roddy and I have both known what it's like to think with good reason that there might not be a tomorrow, and we don't want to waste precious time now because of other people's prejudices."

"I'm sure you're right," said Ruth. "Oh, look at that placard." On the front of a newspaper vendor's stand she read the announcement, '*Cam beats Ox by whisker*'.

"Are you disappointed?" asked Rebecca. "You were at Oxford, weren't you?"

"I was, but I never had the least interest in the exploits of sweaty youths spending half their time at university rowing up and down the river. If the two universities want to compete for public attention it should be about something more important than which of them has the fastest boat."

"I take it you won't be putting any money on the Grand National this afternoon?"

"Never been interested in horses, though my sister, Penelope, was mad about them when she was young. Fortunately my father couldn't afford a pony, or she'd probably have ended up with a cracked skull or a broken collar-bone. I stuck with cricket, and that has given me a lot of pleasure. I've missed it while we've been in the States."

"Have your parents been listening to the Dorothy L Sayers play on the wireless on Sunday evenings? It's been causing a lot of controversy among church people," Rebecca asked.

"They haven't mentioned it. What's it called?"

"*The Man Born to be King*. It's a dramatization of the life of Jesus. I understand that some of the pious are saying that nobody ought to mess about with the Biblical text."

"I suppose that's just because it's on the wireless and you can listen to it in your own home," said Ruth. "There have been Passion plays and Nativity plays since medieval times; but even in those days I expect there were holier-than-thou types who voiced their disapproval. They ought to be pleased that the BBC is willing to give them free propaganda."

They had reached the junction of Great Portland Street and were waiting on the pavement to cross over to the Tube station. "Are you going back to your hotel now?" Rebecca asked.

"Yes. Daniel's going to meet me there. He's having an early lunch with an old comrade from Italian days and then going on to report at the War Office. He thinks they may be going to change his job now. It's becoming clear, he says, that the Commission he's been working for isn't going to get anywhere. The Russians are happy to go on talking about disarmament but they're never actually going to do anything about it."

They crossed the street, and Rebecca said, "But I thought last year the General Assembly had asked the Commission to go on working on proposals. Margarita said you'd told her in a letter that Daniel was pleased because they'd had approval for their work."

"That's right: I did," said Ruth, as they walked down the steps to the station. "But it's become pretty clear to everyone that the Russians are only concerned about the propaganda value of the negotiations, and in the end they're not actually going to agree to anything workable. You can see from what's been happening in Berlin that they only stop pushing when they meet firm resistance. That's why Daniel's beginning to think he could be more usefully employed if he was involved in something that would persuade Stalin he has no chance of making any more gains and might as well accept the status quo."

As they reached the ticket barrier Rebecca said, "Well, I hope when you see him he'll have some good news for you."

When Daniel tapped on the bedroom door (they had only one room key) Ruth jumped up and ran to open it. Smiling broadly, he removed his hat and kissed her even before the door was closed behind them.

"We're going to Paris," he announced.

"To Paris?"

"Yes, that's where the new alliance might be going to have its headquarters, and I'll be attached to the staff that will be setting it up. First of all I have to do a three-month course at Camberly on strategic planning. So as soon as we've tidied up in New York we'll be back in England for the summer. And one other bit of good news – they're making me up to lieutenant-colonel. I think it's so that I won't be outranked by the guys I'll be working alongside."

"Paris will be great – but are you happy about the new job?"

"I am. Disarmament was a great idea but it's not going to happen; and it's not what's going to keep the world safe from another war, at least while Stalin is alive. But a North Atlantic alliance might just help to do that. If the Russians know they can't hope for easy victories they may stop taking us all to the brink, like they did over Berlin. That's why I think I'll be doing something useful in the new job, and not just wasting my time. And Paris should be a nice change after New York."

"Will you get any leave before we go to Paris?"

"I think I'll have a fortnight; so we can make a quick visit to Portadown and then have a bit of relaxation. And maybe you can stay with your parents while I'm at Camberly. With any luck I might be able to spend some of the weekends with you."

"Mummy would love that – and Daddy, too, I'm sure. They might even be starting to plan Penelope's wedding by that time. She seems to be thinking about a date in June."

"Will she want you to be matron-of-honour?"

"I shouldn't think so. We've never been particularly close; and she's bound to have ex-FANY friends she'd want to have as bridesmaids. But tell me, what about your lunch with Frobisher? Did he have any news?"

"He certainly did. But let me take off this Sam Browne." He removed his belt and unbuttoned his tunic, and then sat on the edge of the bed while Ruth settled in one of the two wicker armchairs.

"Frobisher was hopping mad," he continued. "Hamberly has done a runner – down Mexico way when last sighted, but no doubt he's in Moscow by now. Apparently the Central Intelligence Agency had come to an agreement with the FO about waiving diplomatic immunity. They reminded the FO that the Americans had waived immunity for a cypher clerk in London back in 1940, when he was just about to send Lord Haw Haw some stuff on Roosevelt's correspondence with Churchill. So the Yanks were just about to pull in Hamberly when he disappeared. Somebody must have tipped him off. The Americans say it must have been someone at our end. Frobisher thinks it had to be from inside the FO because the only person in the Service who knew about it was this chap Philby that he consulted. Anyhow, they all want to keep it quiet, so please don't mention it to anyone else."

"I think my cousin Giles is the only person who knew that we'd had contact with Hamberly in Washington," said Ruth. "He's bound to hear eventually that Hamberly has disappeared, though I suppose the FO will cook up some story – maybe a mysterious accident while on holiday in Mexico, and probably under the influence of drink."

"You ought to be a scriptwriter for them," said Daniel.

"I used to be," Ruth reminded him, "though then I only translated the words that other people had written."

"Talking about writing, how did you get on this morning with the publisher?"

"It was great. He seems to be really pleased with the concept of the book. Of course, he's still got to read through the whole manuscript; but he even raised the possibility of doing a translation in German. He said he thought the Germans also need to be reminded of the good things in their own past. And he has some contacts with a new publisher who has opened up recently in Munich."

"Mention of Munich always reminds me of the night when Mr Chamberlain came back with his piece of paper," said Daniel. "It's a night that will always be vivid in my memory – making our way into Downing Street behind the rump of that policeman's horse..."

"... and having our very first kiss in the lamplight beside the Guards' Memorial," she continued, rising out of her chair and moving towards him. He held out his arms to embrace her.

Snuggling against him, she murmured, "The one thing I would never have dreamt of that night would have been that one day I'd be hugging you in the uniform of an army officer."

"But we're both still trying to keep the peace," he said, and kissed her firmly and hungrily on her parted lips.

CHAPTER SIXTEEN: 28th November & 1st December, 1949 - DANIEL

As he walked in the cool, late November sunshine across the bridge that spanned the dry moat Daniel tried to remember what he had read about the Château de Vincennes. The tall gateway in the tower ahead of him had a Gothic archway, but the massive walls stretching into the distance on either side were pierced by three parallel rows of tall windows. He wondered whether it might have been in this stretch of the moat that the Duc d'Enghien was shot on the orders of Napoleon; and he presumed that when Henry V of England died of dysentery it must have happened in the ancient donjon which, although reputed to be the tallest in Europe, wasn't even visible from this position.

The sentry positioned at the side of the open gateway was wearing a gleaming white kepi, green epaulettes with scarlet fringes, and a wide, dark blue sash under his white, pistol-bearing belt. Daniel recognized the uniform of a Foreign Legionary and was puzzled, because he'd heard that the Legion was not allowed to be deployed in metropolitan France. The problem was solved when, having shown his pass, he walked through the shadowy tunnel of the gateway and into wide, sunlit space ahead. Glancing to his left he saw a short flight of steps leading up to a doorway, over which hung a red and green signboard emblazoned with the name *Légion Etrangère*. It was, he presumed, the Legion's central recruiting depot.

His first concern, however, was to find the department of the Defence ministry to which he had been summoned. To his right he saw a free-standing, weatherbeaten signboard with an arrow pointing to *Ministère de la Guerre*. Presumably they hadn't bothered to update the nomenclature when the *Ministère de la Défense* was created last year. He followed the sign and had just arrived at a massive wooden door leading into what looked like an eighteenth century building when he heard footsteps overtaking him. It was his Dutch colleague, and together they went into the building.

"I hope Commandant Poivre will agree to conducting the business in English," said the Dutchman. "It takes up a lot less time."

"He probably will," Daniel replied. "In spite of his name he's really quite a mild chap. He spent part of the War in London and enjoyed it. Some of his colleagues aren't so accommodating. They seem to think that national honour requires them to speak only in French. With us British it's just a question of being not much good at other languages."

Inside the building they were met by an orderly, who escorted them up a flight of stairs and through a huge, high-ceilinged room in which about a dozen male clerks were busy on typewriters. At the far end of it a door led into a smaller room in which a long table had been laid out for their committee meeting. Eight colleagues were already present and soon they were joined by two more.

Commandant Poivre conducted the business of the meeting in English. Their task was to complete the practical arrangements for a meeting of the NATO Defence Committee in three days' time. "I suppose if tomorrow's meeting of the Military Committee doesn't reach a conclusion we might have to make some changes to the timetable," Daniel remarked.

"Don't you worry, it'll reach a conclusion all right," his American colleague replied. "General Bradley's in the chair. Nobody'll be going home till they've come up with the right answers."

When the formal business had been completed Commandant Poivre produced a pile of envelopes and distributed one to each of them. "It is an invitation to a reception at the Elysée Palace on Thursday evening," he said. "Wives are included – for those of you who have been staying in Paris."

"Unfortunately Mr Johnson is going to have to leave for Washington right after the Defence Committee meeting," said the American officer, "but I guess all you guys' ministers will be staying on for the reception. I reckon General Bradley ought to be able to stick around as well. He's an interesting guy to talk to, if you get the chance."

Commandant Poivre escorted them out through the large office, where now half-a-dozen men, mostly young and shabbily dressed (though Daniel noticed that one was wearing a smart suit) were shuffling between the desks with dusters under their feet, polishing the floor. "Do you use convicts to do the cleaning?" Daniel enquired.

Poivre laughed. "No; those are Foreign Legion recruits waiting to be taken south. I think the theory is that they've got to be kept occupied all the time or they might start to brood and regret their decision to join."

Outside in the Château's open space – too huge and rambling to be thought of as a 'courtyard' – Daniel regretted that he had no time to explore some of its buildings. The church, he'd read somewhere, was an outstanding example of medieval architecture, built to house an alleged thorn from Christ's crucifixion crown. One day he would come back and have a look – with Ruth.

"All these overpowering red and gold walls and glittering chandeliers make me think of decadent goings-on in the Belle Époque," said Ruth, when Daniel's Danish colleague and his wife had moved on and left them momentarily to themselves in the midst of the chattering throng.

"I hate these formal receptions," said Daniel. "A complete waste of time and money. But it is interesting to see inside the Elysée Palace. Trouble is, there are too many people cluttering up the space to get a proper look at it."

"Well, I'm going exploring to find the loo," she said. "Stay at this end of the room, so I can find you when I come back."

Left on his own, Daniel began to study the décor. It was very classical, and must date from long before the Belle Époque, he decided. But he recalled reading that Napoleon III had had it renovated and used it as a place to meet his mistresses – so no shortage of decadence.

He noticed that the group nearest to him included Mr Alexander, the British Defence Minister, a man he had never met but greatly admired. Alexander's father had been a blacksmith, and he had entered politics through the Co-operative Party, becoming First Lord of the Admiralty in Ramsay Macdonald's second government, and again in Churchill's coalition government. Daniel remembered Arthur telling him how he had listened to Alexander talking informally at a Labour Party conference, and recounting his decision to leave school at thirteen because he thought the increased charge of sixpence a week was going to be too great a burden on his widowed mother. Daniel decided to move closer to the little group, even though it included a French admiral and a Belgian general, in the hope of being able to join in the conversation.

"Why, hello there, Danny Boy!" said a soft voice directly behind him.

He spun around and looked into the laughing blue eyes of Charlotte, the nurse in whose arms he had spent many happy hours in the late autumn of 1942. His first reaction was momentarily one of panic, but then he steadied himself and responded, smiling, "Charlotte, what brings you to this auspicious event?"

"The arm of my husband," she replied. "He's over there, talking to the Norwegian ambassador." She nodded her head in the direction of a tall, good-looking young man in evening dress (but no medals), wearing thick horn-rimmed spectacles. "He's a Third Secretary at our embassy here – name of Sawyer."

The tremor of her honey-blonde curls as she moved her head aroused a vivid memory, together with a startling desire to kiss her, but he suppressed it. "I had some difficulty in recalling your Christian name, Nurse Brightling. Matron was very strict about no familiarity," he said, with a conspiratorial grin.

"Yes, indeed, Lieutenant Hardstaff. And I see you're now a lieutenant-colonel," she continued, glancing at his shoulder. "That's not bad going in seven years. Are you attached to this new Treaty Organization?"

"I've been working for the planning group that's been setting it up. I'd been hoping they were going to establish the headquarters here, because I'd quite fancied living in Paris; but for the time being it's going to be in London. The permanent HQ won't be decided on until a supreme commander has been appointed, and that might take months."

"Are you married? I thought I saw an attractive lady by your side a few minutes ago."

"Yes, that was Ruth. We got married soon after the War."

"I remember the name. And that means we do both have good reason to be a little vague about recalling each other's names – right?" She smiled knowingly, and he remembered the way in which she used to tease him about being a virgin.

"Right," he replied. "The past is nobody else's business."

"I'm glad you agree; and that being the case I'll introduce you to my husband when he's stopped doing his boring diplomatic duty."

"When did you get married?"

"Not long after I was demobbed. As you very well know, I wasn't a real nurse – just in for the duration, and only because the brass in Cairo were too bloody prejudiced to let me be a driver. Stuck out there, I had to do something while Daddy was using his archaeological skills to interpret aerial photographs for the Army. But I told you all that a long time ago; didn't I? Anyhow, I stayed in Egypt for a few months after demob because Daddy wanted to get back to his digging. And then Bertie was posted to the embassy and I met him at a party. He speaks good French and there was a lot of liaison with the French just then about what was happening in Syria and the Lebanon. We got on well but" – she lowered her voice – "Bertie's a bit old-fashioned. His father's an archdeacon. He wanted everything to be proper and above-board, and so we got married out there, and the family celebration had to wait until we came back to London in '47."

"Are you enjoying Paris?"

"Oh, yes. I don't think I'd want to be living in England just now. It's a pity you're not going to be staying here... or maybe it isn't?" She gave him a quizzical smile, and unaccountably he found himself remembering the first time he touched her breast, through her silk blouse, and discovered to his delight that she wasn't wearing a bra. And then he saw Ruth coming through the door, and he beckoned to her.

"Ruth, this is Mrs Sawyer, who was one of the nurses who looked after me in Cairo," he said when she had joined them. "Her husband is a diplomat at the Embassy here."

"I'm so pleased to meet you, and to have the chance to say thank you for sending him back to me in one piece," said Ruth, extending her hand.

"He was a good patient. He never complained about all the tedious things we had to do to him," Charlotte replied. "Did the wounds give you any more trouble after you left us, Colonel Hardstaff?"

"There was just one blip while I was in Haifa. A tiny fragment of poor old John George had been overlooked and it worked its way to the surface when I started exercising my arms again. But they were able to extract it without too much trouble. Though I have to say, the nurses lacked the delicate touch that you... and your colleagues in Ward Four had."

"You never told me you had another operation when you were in Haifa," said Ruth.

"It was just a minor blip – no point in bothering you with it. And I bet you didn't tell me about all the bombs that were falling around you every night."

"I would guess that my grandmother, who was the main person I wrote to back in England during the War, thought I was having a great time in Cairo," said Charlotte. "It was partly because we didn't want to depress ourselves, I think, that we didn't want to write about the bad things."

Her husband approached them and Charlotte introduced "Colonel and Mrs Hardstaff."

"It's the first time I've met one of Charlotte's ex-patients," said Bertie. "By the time I arrived in Cairo she was trying to forget about her nursing career. I hope she was actually a better nurse than she pretended to me that she had been."

Daniel smiled. "She was a very good nurse, from the patients' point of view; but I think Matron didn't always approve of her disregard for petty regulations. Calling patients by their Christian names, for example – I wonder if you can even remember mine?"

Charlotte wrinkled her brow and then replied, "It's Daniel, isn't it? I remember because you didn't like being called Danny."

"Right first time. What job do you do at the embassy here, Mr Sawyer?" he asked.

"Call me Bertie, please. At the moment I'm helping the Cultural Attaché, but I'll shortly be moving to Commercial."

"The Frogs aren't interested in other people's cultures," said Charlotte, with a mischievous grin that prompted instant memories for Daniel. "They think their own culture is the only one worth knowing about."

"Not entirely accurate, my dear," said Bertie, "but they certainly do have a number of... prejudices. Are you on permanent attachment to NATO?"

"I am, which means that we'll shortly be heading back to London after an all too short stay in this stimulating city. But it's good to feel that the first stage of the job has been completed."

"You must have been finding it a lot more expensive here since the pound was devalued in September," Charlotte remarked.

"We have indeed," said Ruth. "When we first arrived in August everything seemed to be incredibly cheap."

"It's a pity the alliance wasn't in place last year, before the Russians made the mistake of thinking they could get their own way over Berlin," said Bertie. "Stalin might not have pushed his luck so hard and caused us all so much trouble and expense."

"You're absolutely right," Daniel replied. "I hope NATO's main job will be to ensure that nobody in the future miscalculates our determination not to allow any more serious erosions of freedom. That seems to be even more important now that the Russians have tested their first atomic bomb."

"That bomb test makes it look as if their Germans are as clever as our Germans," said Charlotte. "It's all a bit scary. Where were you based before they sent you to NATO?"

"I was working at the United Nations Organization, with the Disarmament Commission."

"Did you have much contact with the Washington Embassy?" asked Bertie. "Earlier this year I heard a sad report from there about a young chap who disappeared on holiday in Mexico and hasn't been heard of since. Can't recall his name, but I think he was very well connected. Must have been dreadful for his people."

"As it happened we met him a few times," said Daniel. "His name was Cyril Hamberly. It was a sad business indeed."

"The rumour was that he had a drink problem and that could have led to getting involved in a fatal accident. Do you think that's likely?" Charlotte asked.

"It's possible," Daniel replied. "Once or twice I saw him drinking more than was good for him. He seemed to have a weakness for vodka."

Daniel observed that, just for a second Charotte's eyes widened and then she gave an imperceptible nod. And into his memory flashed pleasurable moments when they had enjoyed the thrill of exchanging secret messages under the nose of Matron as they conversed on matters of medical routine.

"I've seen one or two good chaps in danger of going the same way," said Bertie, nodding his head sagely. "Some of the day-to-day work can be a bit boring, and over here there's the added temptation of some excellent wines on offer when we have meetings with contacts who want us to do them favours. It's always been a rule of mine never to let my guard down when dealing with Johnny Foreigner, however amiable he may appear to be."

"I suppose everyone has some weakness," said Charlotte. "I remember my father once telling me, 'If you're going to have a weakness choose one that you can keep out of sight when you're with people who would disapprove of it'."

Her husband looked surprised. "That sounds very cynical," he said.

"Daddy isn't cynical: he's a realist," she retorted.

"How is your father?" Daniel enquired. "I remember meeting him once when he came to visit you... at the hospital."

"He's in fine fettle, but he's spending more time in London these days, because he's been given a post at the British Museum. He's doing some exciting research on discoveries that were made just before the War and haven't been properly examined. So that's keeping him happy. But he thinks Egypt's heading for big trouble. He says that King Farouk ought to stop posturing on the international stage and put his own house in order. I remember during the War people used to say Farouk was really pro-Nazi. And there was also a story going around about how he used to eat six hundred oysters every week."

"He had certainly put on weight when I last saw him" said Bertie. "That would have been at a reception a bit like this one, except that I recall there was a lot more food on offer."

"I remember there was no shortage of colourful stories about him," said Daniel.

"I once met his mistress, a girl called Irene Guinle," said Charlotte. "She said he was very playful, like a naughty schoolboy, but he didn't have much… staying power."

Bertie cleared his throat nervously and said, "Actually that kind of personal tittle-tattle doesn't add much to our understanding of Farouk. His army's failure in Palestine hasn't done his reputation any good. I'm told that the French are concerned, as we are, that he might try on something like nationalizing the Canal to win back popularity."

"He might well make noises about it, but I suspect he has enough self-knowledge to realize that he lacks the determination and energy he would need to cope with the consequences," said Daniel.

"Are you suggesting that lazy, self-indulgent autocrats cause less trouble than energetic, ambitious ones?" asked Ruth.

"I suppose I am," he replied. "But of course the lazy ones may just be storing up trouble that others will have to deal with in the long run."

"And nobody knows how long the long run is going to be," Charlotte added.

"That reminds me of something my supervisor at LSE said to me when he was reading a chapter of my dissertation," said Daniel. "He quoted the words of John Maynard Keynes: 'In the long run we are all dead'. If you don't get it right you'll not be there in the long run."

"Do you think NATO is going to have a long run – if I may continue to use that expression?" Bertie asked.

"My guess is that it will have a very long run," Daniel replied. "If it doesn't then none of us will."

Arthur had reached his peroration. "This General Election is your opportunity, as voters, to decide whether you want to go on being governed by the party that puts equal opportunities for everyone before protection of privileges for the few; the party that has put an end to the scandals of a poor mother not being able to afford to take her coughing child to see the doctor, or an ageing man no longer capable of reading the newspaper because he can't afford an eye test; the party that has avoided the mass unemployment that blighted the lives of so many ex-servicemen after the last war; the party which has played a leading rôle in creating the United Nations Organization to guard against the outbreak of any more wars in the future. The past five years have not been easy for any of us, but the burdens have been shared as equally as they could be, and the foundations have been firmly laid for the building of a new, a fairer and a more prosperous Britain. This is not the time to change direction. I hope you will keep this country on the course it has chosen by voting Labour, and by helping us over the next four weeks to persuade other people in this new constituency to do the same. Thank you."

He sat down to a rattle of applause that echoed round the half-empty church hall. The small group of personal friends he had persuaded to occupy seats in the front row were the last to rest their hands. He was glad they had agreed to come to this first public meeting of the campaign. His fear that public interest in the Election would be not nearly as great as it had been in 1945 seemed to have been justified by the sparse attendance. Maybe interest would increase when the newspapers began to pay more attention to the issues. He was pleased to see a young reporter from the local *Chronicle and Advertiser* in the second row. The lad would still have been at school in 1945 and was unlikely to make clever comparisons with the overweening optimism of that campaign.

"The candidate will be happy to take questions from the floor; so now's your chance to let him know what you want the next Labour Government to be doing for you," said the chairman, Bill Christopher, who was a local official of the National Society of Operative Printers and Assistants.

The first to raise a hand was an elderly man wearing a threadbare imitation Crombie overcoat and a misshapen grey trilby. "When are they going to do something about the bomb-sites?" he asked. "At the far end of Pertwee Street there's one where a V2 took out four houses, and all they've done is tidy up the rubble and cart away the big stuff. It's not good enough after six years. And they've not got round to building enough houses. My son and his wife still can't even get a prefab; and they don't want to start having a family till they've got somewhere of their own to live. It's not good enough."

Arthur was glad that he knew the location of the bomb-site referred to by the questioner. "Those are two very important questions that you've raised," he replied. "The Pertwee Street bomb-site is not in a part of the constituency that I previously represented at Westminster, and so I wasn't aware of it. As you know, we've had a boundary change. But if I... when I get back in the House I will certainly raise the issue with the proper authority. And as you rightly point out, there's a space in that street that ought to have new houses on it. The problem with the housing shortage is that there have been so many jobs needing to be done after the War and they can't all be done at the same time."

"And your Government's been doing them in the wrong order," interrupted a loud-voiced young man sitting in a group of four in the third row. A quick glance at the cut of their coats made Arthur suspect that they had come from the local Conservative Association with the purpose of heckling. "Nationalizing businesses comes before building houses for your lot. And you're leaving the bomb-sites so that people will forget there isn't still a war on, and put up with being rationed at a time when even the Germans are getting rid of rationing."

One of his companions, a fair-haired young man who was wearing what looked like a college tie, joined in. "The Minister says we can have an extra ounce of bacon and half an ounce of sweets a week from next month," he said. "Would that by any chance be because we're also going to have an election – or has he suddenly discovered some more pigs?"

"I think most people prefer a system in which the scarce food that is available is shared out equally, rather than allowing people with a lot of money to buy up as much as they want and leave those who aren't so lucky to go without," Arthur replied. "What this country is still short of is spending power overseas. But our exports are increasing at a very encouraging rate; and if the American government can be persuaded to continue with Marshall Aid after July the situation will be a lot easier. One of the reasons they're likely to do that is because they can see we're acting responsibly, and not trying to live beyond our means. I know it's annoying if Saturday comes round and there's no bacon left to go with your egg, but we all have to look at the broader picture. We emptied the country's coffers in order to fight the War and defend our freedom, and now we're slowly but surely earning the money we need to be prosperous again. This isn't the time to go on a spending spree."

There were several 'hear, hears' from the audience, and the chairman pointed to another questioner.

A middle-aged woman in a close-fitting red felt hat stood up and asked, "Are you aware that the Ministry of Education is cutting back on the funds available to help youth clubs? We're getting to a situation where the staff of charities and churches that run the clubs are having to spend half their time on activities to raise money, and there's a real risk that young people are going to be left spending their leisure time on the streets. What that's going to do to the juvenile crime rate is anybody's guess."

It was a subject in which Arthur was interested and he was pleased to be able to make a well-informed reply. "The lady is referring, I think, to Circulars 209 and 210 from the Ministry of Education to local education authorities. It is the local authorities that have responsibility for expenditure in this area of work, but the Ministry has been making small grants for the renovation of buildings. In Circular 209 it has indicated that it can't make grants at the present time for any new building projects – only for maintenance. And in 210 the Ministry has said that spending in the current year has reached the limit of what is available and so local authorities will need to cut out projects or activities that they think are least essential.

"Once again, this is a question of priorities at a time when money is in short supply. The government is putting a limit on how much support it can give to local authorities at the present time, and they have to judge, taking into account local circumstances, where their priorities should be." He knew, however, that his answer wasn't going to satisfy anyone who believed that their own activity must inevitably take priority.

A bald-headed man in a duffle coat stood up and asked, "If money is short why are we going to be spending so much on this exhibition jamboree next year?"

"I take it you are referring to the Festival of Britain," said Arthur. "There are two very good reasons why the money spent on it is going to be money very well spent. The first reason is that it's going to provide a shop window to the world for all the exciting new developments in British industry. For three or four years after the War we had no problem selling our goods overseas because everything was in such short supply. But now other countries are getting their industries back into production – even the West Germans have been quicker than anyone would have expected – and we're moving into a competitive situation. The exhibition on the South Bank is going to demonstrate that Britain can match the best of them. It's going to show that the skill and inventiveness the Victorians displayed a hundred years ago, in 1851, is still very much a part of our tradition.

"And the second reason why the Festival is a good idea is that, all over the country, people are beginning to plan for a big celebration of the fact that we're moving into a new era. It's been tough going since the end of the War, just trying to get things back to normal, but now we can start looking forward to the better times that we've worked hard for, and that we all deserve. It's time to give ourselves a party. I've been on a committee looking at what might be the transport problems next year, and it seems very likely that huge numbers of people are going to be coming to London to see the exhibition, as well as organizing events of their own, all the way from Land's End to John o'Groats. This is going to be money well spent."

His riposte was greeted with vigorous applause, and Arthur suddenly felt an enthusiasm for the Festival of Britain that had hitherto eluded him. There were a few more questions about rationing and the housing shortage, but Arthur could see that the meeting was not going to produce any fireworks, and it limped listlessly along to the concluding attempt by his agent, Bill Coverdale, to rekindle the revolutionary fire of 1945 in a speech that was too long for the mood of the audience.

As people began to move from the chilly church hall to the wintry street outside there were a lot of hands to be shaken. Arthur knew he could count on their votes – apart from the Conservative claque – but wondered about the attitudes of those who weren't bothering to attend meetings. Would they listen to the Election broadcasts on the wireless, and if they did would they find the Radio Doctor, Charles Hill, who was talking for the Tories, more persuasive than the bluff Yorkshire commonsense of J B Priestley, who was still arguing for Labour?

"You handled that well, Arthur," said Daniel, looking unfamiliar in a civvy suit, as he and the small group of friends prepared to be the last to leave. "I understand we've all been invited back to have dinner with you and Margarita. Ruth and I are really looking forward to seeing her again. Let me help you on with your coat." Together they walked to the exit.

The conversation over dinner avoided politics. Roddy was sad about the early death of George Orwell, his fellow-combatant in the Spanish Civil War, and wondered to what extent the wounds he received there might have contributed to it. "I thought the obituary that said 'he lived his convictions' really summed him up," said Ruth.

"I think that's right," Arthur agreed, "but his state of mind seemed to be altering. I felt that *Nineteen Eighty Four* had been written by someone suffering from depression, unlike *Animal Farm*, in spite of its pessimistic ending. I'm sure there'll still be a lot wrong with the world in 1984, but I don't think it will be nearly such a hopeless picture as the one he painted."

"There's an interesting exhibition of Yugoslav folk art at the Academy in Oxford Street," said Nancy. "They seem to have been able to wriggle out from under the Iron Curtain."

"We're just beginning to catch up with the cultural scene in London," said Ruth. "We went this week to see a play at the Haymarket called *The Heiress*. Wendy Hiller gives a brilliant performance. We actually saw her in the play when it was in New York, but I think this production is even better. And next week we're hoping to see the new Anouilh, *Ring Round the Moon*."

"I want to see that one," said Roddy. "I've heard that the young director, a chap called Peter Brook, is an up-and-coming talent in the business. I'd be interested to hear what you think of it."

"You're about to make your own contribution to the cultural scene, Ruth," said Rebecca. "Do you have a date yet for the book launch?"

"It's going to be at the beginning of April. The publisher is looking for a day when it won't clash with any other literary event – not that it's likely to be an 'event'."

"Have you decided on a title yet?" Nancy asked.

"They've finally persuaded me to go for 'Loving by letter from the last frontier'. I'm still a bit doubtful about having a long title, but I suppose it draws attention by being different."

"Is the story made up of letters?" asked Rebecca.

"No, it isn't; but I have used them for quite a large part of the narrative. I didn't want to tell it all in the first person, because I didn't think I could sustain the 'voice' of an eighteenth century German man the whole way through. But I did want to have first person accounts of some events and I also wanted a long distance love interest in the story."

"Is the letter-writer the central character, then?" asked Roddy.

"Yes, Heinrich is a fictional character, but he accompanies Alexander von Humboldt on his journeys in South America while trying to sustain his love affair with the beautiful Caroline, back in Berlin. Humboldt himself wasn't going to provide me with a love interest. Very little is known about his private life, and what little information there is suggests that I wouldn't have got it past the censors."

"I must confess I'd never heard of Humboldt. I'd heard about the Humboldt Current – I think in a geography lesson. It must have been interesting doing the research on him," said Nancy.

"It certainly was. I really enjoyed my trips to the library on 42nd Street. And I came across all kinds of unexpected snippets. There was a piece in an Augsburg newspaper pointing out that two of the three translations of his great book *Kosmos* into English were by a woman. That was in 1849. And the article went on to say that 'in Germany most men do not understand it'. I also found an interesting quote that said 'He was to science what Shakespeare was to drama'. But I did agree with my editor that not many people would be interested in a story that was just about a German scientist and explorer, and so I played up the love interest."

"Well, I hope your publisher can attract the attention of some of the reviewers," said Rebecca. "I think I can make sure we get some coverage of it on the German Service. I might even be able to persuade them to do an interview with you."

"That would be terrific. I hope you can," said Ruth.

"Talking of colleagues at the BBC reminds me of something I meant to ask you, Daniel," said Roddy. "There's a chap in my department who came originally from Portadown, and he went up to Trinity just after we came down. His name is Waldo Maguire. Did you happen to know him when you were at school? He said he remembers your name."

"I remember his, too, mainly because his academic success was much talked about at home. I must have been aware of him at the College, but I can't honestly say I remember his face. There's always a great gap between seniors and juniors. By all accounts he was an incredibly bright lad. So he's ended up in the BBC."

"He's a very pleasant guy, though I haven't actually had a lot of contact with him. I know that during the War he was doing something very hush-hush that even now he's not allowed to talk about. It seems he met his wife while he was doing that job. I've heard that she's incredibly good at crossword puzzles; so it makes you wonder what the work might have been."

"I think I could guess," said Rebecca. "For a couple of months before D-Day I was switched temporarily to doing a different kind of translation work, and I know that some incredibly clever people were involved in producing the material. But I'm also not allowed to talk about it. I think maybe one day the historians might have an interesting tale to tell."

"Why should there be all this secrecy now that the War is over?" asked Nancy. "It only makes people suspect that things were being done that shouldn't have been done, like maybe torturing prisoners."

"Some people will always want to believe the worst, and there's not much you can do to convince them otherwise," said Daniel. "But I know – and I think Rebecca knows – that there are clever ways of obtaining information that's more reliable than anything you're likely to get by torturing random prisoners. Unfortunately we live in a world where there are still people who want to do us harm, and the less they know about the ways we're able to find out what they're up to the better it is for everyone. I think that's a good reason for keeping the Official Secrets Act in force. Those amusing posters we had during the War summed it up very seriously when they said 'Careless Talk Costs Lives'."

"Have you ever been involved in that kind of work?" asked Nancy.

"No, but I've known a few people who have been, and I admire them," Daniel replied.

"Are your NATO offices going to be permanently in London now?" asked Roddy. "I remember you saying last year that you might be moving to France."

"The set-up in Belgrave Square is temporary, until it's been agreed who is going to be the Supreme Commander. It'll be an American, of course. I think the probability is that HQ will be located in France; but I think by that time I might have finished my job."

Taken by surprise, Arthur asked, "Are you getting a transfer, then?"

"No. I'm hoping to move on from the Army. My CO is agreeable, and with any luck I should be able to hang up my hat before the winter, about the time when they'll move to the new HQ. I think I've done my bit for peace-keeping, though I'd still like when I'm back on civvy street to do something that'll contribute to the climate of opinion we need to sustain it – maybe from an academic base. And it would also be nice to have a permanent home of our own at last, and be able to see more of our friends."

Arthur observed an exchange of glances between Daniel and Ruth, who then said, "I'm looking forward to having some furniture that we've chosen ourselves. Ever since we got married we've been living in furnished accommodation of one kind or another. I've already started looking at catalogues. There's a firm called Ercol whose stuff I really like the look of."

"We got our kitchen furniture from Remploy," said Margarita. "It's a government-owned company that gives employment to people who are disabled. Their furniture is good quality and it's not expensive."

"I confess I hadn't heard about it," said Daniel.

"It was set up by the wartime government, but it's only become well known in the past couple of years," said Arthur. "Have a look at our stuff before you go. It's interesting you should be thinking about finding a new job, because I've also had to give some thought to that possibility. I was wondering what it might be like to go back to academia."

"You!" Nancy exclaimed. "Aren't you confident you're going to hold on to your seat in the election?"

"Well, as you know, the boundaries have been changed, and that means nothing is certain. The national opinion polls are giving Labour a reasonably good lead, but the odds are that we'll not have such a huge majority again. Some seats are bound to be lost. Bill Coverdale, my Agent, knows more about these things than I do and he seems pretty confident we'll scrape home. But there's still four weeks to go and all kinds of things might happen that could change the public mood. So I'm not taking anything for granted."

"We'd better get out there and do some leafleting for you," said Nancy.

"It would be ironic if we were both to find ourselves back in LSE, where we first met – when was it? Must have been the end of '37," said Daniel.

"I don't think that's going to happen," said Rebecca. "I'm sure Arthur's going to win the seat. The people I talk to at the World Service can't believe that this country's ready to do an about turn, whatever the right-wing commentators may be trying to persuade us. I think we ought to start planning a joint celebration for the beginning of April – Arthur back in the House with a job in Government and Ruth's new book heading straight for the list of best-sellers."

"Rebecca is an irrepressible optimist," said Roddy, smiling and stretching out to take hold of her hand.

"I have had to be," said Rebecca.

When the telephone rang just before one o'clock Margarita jumped up and exclaimed, "That will be Arthur, to let me know it's time to go to the Count. Bill Coverdale's son, Wilfred, is coming to pick me up in a car. I hope the news is good."

As she left the room to answer the telephone in the hall Daniel switched off the wireless, interrupting in mid-sentence the announcement that Labour had held another seat in Lancashire with a reduced majority. He and Ruth were baby-sitting so that Margarita could be with her husband when the returning officer announced the result in his constituency.

"The Tories winning Wembley North isn't a good omen," said Ruth. "It's too close to here for comfort. But at least Labour are still well ahead on the seats that have been counted."

"But they were bound to be," said Daniel. "So far they've nearly all been inner-city constituencies. It's places like Wembley North that are more likely to swing. I should think it will be five or six o'clock before we know what the overall trend is. But Arthur's fate will have been decided long before that."

When Margarita returned to the room, buttoning her winter coat, she said, "Arthur thinks it looks too close to call. There's been quite a big turnout and up till now the count is looking very even. He thinks they should be finished in about half-an-hour. Wilfred is on his way to pick me up."

"We'll keep our fingers crossed for you," said Daniel, "and with any luck we'll hear the result on the wireless soon after it's announced."

"I'll leave the sitting-room door open so that you can hear Dan if he should wake up, but he seems to be sleeping soundly. Vera hardly ever wakes up now," said Margarita.

Daniel got up to accompany her to the front door as they heard a car drawing up at the garden gate.

"I love your coat. That colour really suits you," said Ruth.

"Arthur came with me to buy it at Marshall and Snelgrove in the January sale. He has very good taste."

"Don't forget your umbrella. I think it's still raining," said Ruth. "Somebody said on the Nine O'Clock News that this has been one of the wettest Februarys for years."

When Margarita had gone Daniel switched on the wireless again, and nothing very much seemed to have changed in the 'State of the Parties'. Ruth snuggled up to him on the sofa and he said, "We must be careful not to fall asleep in case one of the kids wakes up."

"Why don't I make a cup of tea?" she suggested. "Even if the result is announced straight away Arthur will have a lot of hand-shaking to do, and they're not likely to be back in under an hour."

"That's a good idea. But let's hope it will be congratulations, and not commiseration. I'm sure he's due for a job in government, now that he's served his apprenticeship in the House. He must be a brilliant administrator, when you think of the work he did during the War."

"I'm not sure if his heart is really in politics," said Ruth. "Margarita tells me that he gets very fed up with all the in-fighting in the Labour Party. He says a lot of it is more personal than ideological."

"That could be one of the reasons why he hasn't yet been picked for a government job. If you don't line up with one of the factions you probably don't get noticed. He's also a very honest bloke, and that must be a bit of a handicap in politics," Daniel observed.

"You're right," said Ruth. "That just reminded me of something that happened when we were first getting to know each other. Arthur took me to a Test Match at the Oval – and it was that day when Hutton hit three hundred and sixty-something. We were coming back on a bus and the conductor didn't get round to collecting the fares. Before we got off Arthur insisted on going up to him with the money. I think it was only about fourpence each."

"I remember you mentioning that match," said Daniel. "It bothered me, because I was afraid I was going to lose you to Arthur."

"And I wasn't sure whether you really wanted me," said Ruth, kissing his cheek. "But in those days we seemed to have all the time in the world to find out." She realized that what she had said wasn't strictly true. It was she who had actually been wondering which of the two men she really wanted; and it had been Arthur who had made the decision for her, when Margarita had appeared and – unwittingly, no doubt – swept him off his impressively solid feet. But no good purpose could be served by confessing that to Daniel. Much better that he should be happy in the belief that he had always been her first choice.

She kissed him again and said, "I'll go and make some tea. It will help to keep us awake."

When she returned from the kitchen with two mugs on a tray Daniel looked anxious. "It's just been announced that they're having a recount in Arthur's constituency. The voting must be very close," he said. "I should think it'll take them at least an hour to get the new result – maybe two."

"I hope it will be the right one," said Ruth, handing him his tea. "How are things going in the country?"

"The Government is still holding its own, but most of their majorities are down quite dramatically. The Radio Doctor – Hill, I think is his name – has won the seat he stood for in Luton. I expect doing the election broadcast gave him an edge. People at least knew who he was."

They sipped their tea. "It must be worrying for Arthur to think that he might be out of a job tomorrow," said Ruth. "With two kids to look after I should think he'll want to get back pretty quickly to having a salary, and it mightn't be easy to find the kind of job he'll enjoy doing. Margarita says he can sometimes be moody if he doesn't have a lot to keep him busy. He starts remembering things like that awful day he went to the Belsen camp."

"We all have memories we don't want to revive," said Daniel, gazing at the surface of his cup of tea as though it were a crystal ball. "I suppose I ought to start looking actively for a job, now the CO has indicated that I should be able to take my discharge in the Autumn. I ought to find out if any of my former mentors are still at the LSE."

"Can we also start looking for somewhere permanent to live?" Ruth asked.

"I'd like to; but supposing I'm not able to find work in London – we might be wasting our time."

"We could still have a preliminary look around," said Ruth, setting down her empty mug and snuggling up to him. "Is there any area you'd particularly like to live in?"

"I quite fancy Bloomsbury. It would be good to be able to walk to so many theatres and galleries and museums. And if I do manage to get a research job it will probably be in one of the colleges that aren't very far from there. And, of course, your publishers' office is just off Bedford Square, isn't it?"

"Yes, I must remember to go there tomorrow, if I can stay awake. I've also been meaning to visit the UNA office. I feel I owe Mr Judd a report back on my impressions of the American branch. I'm sure he has lots of official contacts with them, but he might just be interested in the sort of attitudes I discovered at the grassroots."

"I'd be interested to know how UNA has been progressing over here," said Daniel. "We must get involved with them once we're settled. I hope they've managed to get rid of the lack of realism that handicapped the League of Nations Union."

"I'm sure the London branch would love to hear about your experiences at Lake Success – or as much as you'd be allowed to tell them," said Ruth.

"That wouldn't be a great deal, I'm afraid, and they could read most of it in the records. The really interesting stuff happened before we got to the committee rooms, and talking about it is much better left to the historians. There's still a lot of work in progress."

"So maybe I shouldn't suggest your name as a speaker?" she asked, yawning.

"Maybe not."

As several results from Scotland were announced, each concluding with 'No change', she felt herself drifting off, held snugly in the crook of Daniel's arm. The voices on the wireless became a kind of aural wallpaper as she relaxed into a doze.

A gentle shake from Daniel brought her back to full consciousness in time to hear the commentator saying "So Arthur Leyland has won the new constituency for Labour with a wafer-thin majority of eighty-seven votes."

"He won it!" she exclaimed, jumping to her feet. "Oh, isn't that just wonderful? That recount made me so afraid he wasn't going to make it. I bet there's great excitement at the town hall."

"Now we have to wait and see if the Government is going to get back," said Daniel.

"They were still ahead last time I heard an update on the State of the Parties," said Ruth. "Was there another one while I was dozing?"

"No, but we're due for another one soon."

Not long afterwards an excited commentator reported that the Conservatives had now won an equal number of seats to Labour; and a few minutes later each party added two more seats to its total. "It's too soon to draw any conclusions – except that Labour isn't going to have that huge majority again," said Daniel. "There must be at least three hundred constituencies still to come, and a lot of them won't be counted till tomorrow. But if I was Mr Attlee I think I'd be a little bit anxious."

About ten more minutes had passed when they heard Arthur's key turning the lock of the front door, and as they got up to go and welcome him a tired voice on the wireless informed them that once again Labour was ahead in the number of constituencies won.

Margarita and Arthur showed no sign of tiredness as they received congratulations with beaming faces. "It was pretty tense all through the count, but Bill Coverdale was confident we were going to win and he was right," said Arthur. "I'm just not so sure about the overall result. We've lost a lot of seats that we needed to win."

"Well, we're not going to hear much more about that tonight; so we'll just have to wait and see what happens in the morning," said Margarita. "Now I think we should all get a few hours' sleep before breakfast. I've made up the bed for you in the spare room but you'd better have a hot water bottle. I'll put the kettle on."

Ruth thanked her, smiling and thinking how very English Margarita had become in just ten years.

At breakfast time there wasn't a great deal of change in the news, since constituencies which had not produced declarations during the night hadn't yet begun to count. When Ruth and Daniel entered the kitchen Arthur was sitting at the table with a copy of *The Times*. "The pundits don't seem at all certain what's going to happen," he said. "Morgan Phillips is confident we'll have a comfortable majority, but as Party Secretary he would have to say that at this stage in the proceedings. The PM, in his usual phlegmatic way, just says that the situation 'looks very hopeful'. But five ministers have lost their seats. Frank Soskice lost by over three thousand votes. I think anything is possible."

"With all those vacancies on the front benches I think a job in the Government for you might be possible," said Ruth, helping herself to some Kellogg's cornflakes.

"I'm not sure it wouldn't be better for the Party if we lost this election," said Arthur. "Let the Tories have a go at deciding where to make the next cuts in expenditure and which groups to infuriate by not being able to do all the things that need to be done. If they were only a handful of seats ahead of us they wouldn't last for more than a year; and next time it would be them that the voters would be fed up with. It would be good, too, for our Front Bench to have a break and some time to think quietly about where they want to go next."

"I'm sure some of the ministers could be doing with a rest," said Daniel. "People forget that Attlee and Bevin and Morrison have been working in Cabinet continuously since 1940, in about the most demanding decade in the whole of our history. They must be starting to fray around the edges."

"Attlee, as you know, is a public school man who keeps a stiff upper lip at all times and you can never tell what he's really thinking, but some of the others are starting to look a great deal older than they did when I first saw them in the Commons," said Arthur. "Poor old Ernie Bevin in particular – he's always having to fight off our own backbenchers as well as coping with the Israelis and the Arabs and the Russians and the Greeks, and just about everyone else. I'm sure he could do with a break. Meanwhile Churchill and Eden and Butler have been able to sit back and put their feet up for five years."

"And yet I'm sure the chaps who hold the levers of power are just as keen to hang on to them now as their opponents are to get their hands on them," said Ruth.

"Will you have a boiled egg?" asked Margarita; and thereafter attention was concentrated on the preparation and eating of breakfast, with Arthur being told firmly by Margarita to put aside his newspaper. The political situation was going to remain uncertain for a few more hours.

Ruth had just left the office of her publishers when she saw the election result on a news vendor's placard. *Attlee back in No 10* it said. She bought a copy of the newspaper and read its political editor's prediction that Labour was likely to have a final overall majority of as little as five or six when the last results came in. The Whips Office was going to be very important for the Government in the new Parliament, the writer observed. She wondered if Arthur's military background might qualify him for a job there, even though his personality was certainly not authoritarian.

There might be a lot of changes ahead, Ruth reflected, but for her, personally, most of them were going to be for the better. Nestling at the top of her overnight bag was the proof copy of her novel. She didn't expect it to be a best seller, but she knew how delighted her parents were going to be that evening, when she showed it to them. And next week she and Daniel would be starting to look at unfurnished flats; and after that there would be the excitement of choosing new furniture and fittings. But she mustn't allow herself to become too self-indulgent. There might be some work she could do for UNA; and already an idea for her next book was beginning to germinate.

Over the skyscraper summit of Senate House the sky appeared to be lightening as she put the newspaper into her bag and strode out cheerfully towards the Tube station at Tottenham Court Road.

CHAPTER NINETEEN: 14ᵗʰ April, 1950 - DANIEL

As the elderly waiter placed the first course – a small dish containing segments of grapefruit with a cherry on top – before each diner Daniel looked along the table and felt happy to be with his closest friends in a celebratory mood. The subdued grandeur of a House of Commons dining-room seemed an appropriate setting for what Arthur, their host, had declared to be a 'quintuple celebration'. The five causes for rejoicing were: Arthur's re-election as an MP; the publication of Ruth's novel; the forthcoming marriage of Roddy and Rebecca; Nancy's recent election to the chair of her local branch of the United Nations Association; and Daniel's impending return to civilian life.

"Shouldn't we really be calling this a sextuple celebration?" Ruth asked. "Margarita tells me you've just been appointed a member of the Commons Estimates Committee."

"I'm not sure if that's a cause for celebration," Arthur replied, "but I suppose it shows that the top brass think I'm up to doing a difficult job – and it's going to be difficult in the present circumstances."

"I hadn't heard of the Estimates Committee," said Roddy. "What exactly does it involve?"

"It's job is to examine estimates of expenditure that the government brings to the House and to report if it thinks the policies involved could be carried out more economically. Needless to say, the people in every government department think that other departments are being spendthrift, whereas their own department couldn't possibly manage with anything less. So I expect the members of the Estimates Committee can earn themselves a lot of unpopularity if they do their job properly."

"On the other hand," said Daniel, "I would guess that someone who does the job conscientiously might be a strong candidate for a difficult ministerial post if one happened to become vacant."

"The Public Accounts Committee tends to attract more attention," said Arthur. "It's the one that looks at how the money has actually been spent. However, at the present time, when funding is in desperately short supply, Estimates may well attract a lot of notice – that's assuming my more experienced colleagues are prepared to be honest about what they find. There's going to be a lot of wheeling and dealing going on, now that we have such a wafer-thin majority. I should think the Easter recess will have given people time to work out their devious schemes, and once we're back in session next week you'll see conspiratorial huddles all over this building."

"Were you happy with the turn-out at the book launch this afternoon?" Nancy enquired of Ruth.

"It wasn't brilliant, but the publishers seemed to think it was better than average for that kind of event. The journalists who turned up were a pretty odd mixture. The only dailies were the *News Chronicle*, and the *Daily Worker*. The *Chronicle* man said he was sure they would do a review, but the man from the *Worker* just seemed to want to get me to say something nasty about Adenauer. Oh, and I think the woman who came from the *Church Times* might be going to write a piece. She perked up when she found out that my father is a rector."

"That reminds me of something that happened just before Easter," said Arthur. "One of the new intake, a Conservative with a rather plummy voice, asked me the way to the library, and as I was going in that direction myself we got talking. I discovered he'd been in the Artillery during the War and we'd both been in Normandy at the same time; and we'd both been demobbed in the rank of lieutenant-colonel. When I asked what he'd been doing since the War he mentioned a number of different jobs and, to my surprise, one of them was News Editor of the *Church Times*. He seemed to be quite a decent chap, and I'd guess he's very ambitious. He had that air of a man in a hurry to find out as much as he possibly could about whatever was going to be useful to him."

"What was his name?" asked Nancy.

"Heath. I think his first name is Edward. Bexley is his constituency. But I've been digressing. If he'd still been at the *Church Times* he might have been useful to you, but he isn't. Did any of the others show interest in the book?"

"I'm doing an interview with Ruth about it for the German Service on Wednesday," said Rebecca. "I hope that will stir up some interest."

"A chap from the *British Weekly* said he was pretty sure they would be able to do a review, but that was the only other positive comment that we had," said Ruth. "Now we'll just have to wait and see."

The soup arrived. It was Brown Windsor and Daniel was instantly reminded of meals eaten at long tables, surrounded by the chattering faces of fellow-undergraduates. And the steaming liquid was no more palatable now than it had been then.

"When is the Commons going to get back into its old home?" he asked Arthur.

"The latest news is that we'll be back there by the end of October. I'm quite looking forward to it. I'd been afraid that I might have served my time as an MP and yet never be able to say that I'd sat in the place where Gladstone and Lloyd George and Keir Hardie had uttered their immortal words – though, of course, I'd be able to tell my grandchildren that I'd sat in the House of Lords."

"Has the chamber been restored to exactly how it was before the bomb hit it? The work seems to have taken a very long time," Rebecca asked.

"Yes, it has," said Arthur. "Apparently Churchill was very insistent that they should keep the number of seats at less than the number of MPs, so that there would always be a sense of drama on important occasions, when everyone crowds into the House and some members have to stand."

"I'd really like to listen to a debate one day when you're back in your own chamber," said Ruth.

"I'd be very happy to arrange that," said Arthur.

"Maybe if the time is suitable I could too," said Nancy.

"I'm sure we could work that out. We'll have plenty of time to plan it in advance," said Ruth.

"Talking of planning in advance," said Arthur, "I've managed to get tickets for the Halle's visit to London towards the end of May. I used to attend nearly all their concerts when I was a student in Manchester. And Sir John is still going strong."

"What are they going to be performing?" Rebecca asked.

"It will be a good mixture – Beethoven, Debussy, Vaughan Williams and Tchaikovsky," Margarita replied. "I am really looking forward to it because I have never heard that orchestra and Arthur has told me how good they are."

"Now that you and Ruth are going to be permanently in London you'll be able to enjoy the winter theatre season," said Roddy. "I hope it will be as good as the one that's just ending."

"We're looking forward to that," said Ruth. "Actually, we're seeing the Tennessee Williams play at the Aldwych tomorrow evening."

"Vivian Leigh is brilliant in that one," said Roddy.

"Do you miss very much being on the stage?" Ruth asked.

"Occasional hankering after the roar of the greasepaint and the smell of the crowd, but really not very much. I don't think I would ever have made it to the top; and I met a lot of people on the way down who had become self-deluding about their own abilities. I didn't want to become like that. The BBC is a great place to work, if you're prepared to accept the discipline you need to provide that kind of round-the-clock service."

"It's been a good place for me, too," said Rebecca. "Being involved with the international side of it, I can sometimes start believing that the world really is getting away from the nationalistic delusions that have done so much damage."

"Do you really think so?" asked Nancy. "I hope you're right. I sometimes wonder if I'm being too optimistic because I spend so much of my time with people in the PPU and UNA. Do you really think the average man in the street is any more international in his outlook than he was in 1939?"

"I think he probably is, because he's known what it's like to have the outside world come and knock his door down," said Arthur. "I'm not so sure if his sons and daughters are going to have the same awareness when they grow up. There seems to be a tendency – understandable, of course – to want to forget about the past, but that could have the effect of not helping children to realize what the real priorities are in life. I began to have that feeling during the Election. A lot of people didn't want to talk about anything but the price of beer, or why the trains are so dirty."

"But I'm sure the vast majority of people believe that having peace is more important than anything else, even though they don't talk about it," said Nancy.

"Wasn't that how it was after the First War, too, but people over here didn't realize that in other parts of the world there were people who had very different priorities?" Rebecca observed. "I agree with you, Arthur, that young people need to be told how things went wrong in the past, so that they don't repeat the same mistakes in the future."

The elderly waiter reappeared and cleared away the soup plates. While the main course – somewhat sparse portions of roast beef, with Yorkshire pudding and vegetables – was being served Ruth, Arthur and Margarita enthusiastically discussed the new Orson Welles film, *The Third Man*, while Roddy, Rebecca and Nancy disagreed about the fate of the two translators in Czechoslovakia who had just been sentenced to eighteen years' hard labour for 'insulting the Soviet Union'. (Nancy thought that Czech gratitude for liberation by the Russians explained, even though it didn't justify, the harshness of the sentence.) Daniel tried to listen to both conversations at the same time and realized he was missing an important ingredient in each of them.

For a few minutes eating took the place of talking; and then Nancy asked, "Has anyone read the review in today's *Times* of the new musical play at the Theatre Royal, Stratford, called *Lili Marlene?*"

"I haven't seen that one," said Roddy. "Is it a play about the wartime song?"

"From the reviewer's description it seems to have been inspired by the song, but it's actually about a German girl who, before the War, is loved by an English student and a German student, and can't make up her mind which to choose. The second act is set after the War and only the Englishman has survived; so finally she doesn't have to make a choice. It sounds a bit banal, but the review said the music is catchy," Nancy replied.

"I think I'd quite like to see it," said Rebecca, "but I didn't know there was a second theatre in Stratford."

"It's Stratford in East London, not Stratford-upon-Avon," said Roddy. "I think the theatre opens only occasionally, when there's a company needing somewhere to perform. It must be very run-down."

"I've been here for twelve years but I still learn something new about English geography every day," said Rebecca.

"I hear that the BBC Symphony Orchestra is going to have a new conductor," said Ruth.

"Yes – Malcolm Sargent. He's been chief conductor of the Proms for the past couple of years; so it was no great surprise," said Arthur.

"They say he's very popular with the ladies but not so well loved by the musicians," said Roddy. "Apparently his nickname is 'Flash Harry'; and somebody in the News Room was saying that Edwina Mountbatten had been one of his conquests."

"I hadn't heard the gossip," said Arthur, "But I know that he and Beecham set up the London Philharmonic, and he's been particularly good as a choral conductor. I have gramophone records of him conducting the D'Oyly Carte in *HMS Pinafore* and *Ruddigore*."

"I haven't been to a Proms concert since before the War," said Daniel. Glancing at Ruth he added, "We must try to get to a few of them this year."

"In that case I'd better keep a look-out for the date when they start booking tickets. They're always incredibly popular," said Ruth.

As the plates were being cleared away Nancy looked at the menu card and asked, "What is this 'Baked Alaska' that we're about to have? I'm afraid I've never heard of it."

"I think it originated in America," said Margarita. "The first time – I think the only time – I've eaten it was when I was a student in Boston. It's reputed to be named in honour of the time when the Americans bought Alaska from the Russians."

"I remember reading that when Secretary of State Seward made the deal with the Russians back in eighteen-sixty-something the political wiseacres of the time called it 'Seward's Folly'. It's amazing just how wrong the 'experts' can be," said Daniel.

"What does the dish consist of?" Nancy asked.

"It's a mystery – a surprise," said Margarita. "The outside is the opposite of the inside."

"That sounds a very appropriate dish for the Palace of Westminster," said Roddy.

"Since we're thinking about a piece of Russia in America it reminds me disturbingly of the speeches that Russian representatives make in New York when they come to the United Nations," said Daniel. "But I don't want to think about that now, because I'm on leave today. Nancy, I hope you will like this 'riddle wrapped in a mystery inside an engima' – as Churchill once described Russian foreign policy."

The elderly waiter entered bearing before him a large plate in the centre of which sat the Baked Alaska.

CHAPTER TWENTY: 18ᵗʰ May, 1950 - RUTH

In the centre of the painting a young woman in a black dress and a white bonnet was sitting on the grass underneath a gnarled old lilac tree, intent on a piece of embroidery, or maybe it was crochet work. Snuggling up to her, a dark-haired little girl stared intently at her busy hands, and nearby a younger, blonde infant in a white smock balanced unsteadily on tiny legs. Above their heads the lilac blossoms were suggested by daubs of paint that Ruth felt did little justice to the Springtime splendour of one of her favourite flowers, even though the picture was entitled 'The Lilacs at Maurecourt.'

"It's actually a painting of a mother and her children, and it captures the relationship very effectively," she remarked.

"According to the catalogue the woman is Berthe's sister, Edna," said Rebecca, who had suggested their visit to the Arts Council-sponsored exhibition of paintings and drawings by the French Impressionist, Berthe Morisot. "I think it shows the influence that Manet was having on her at that time. It was painted in the year when she married his brother, Eugène."

"I'd never heard of Morisot before this exhibition," said Ruth. "I'm glad you saw that it was on."

"In my opinion women artists have really been neglected by the art historians," said Rebecca. "I suppose their excuse is that if the women are not well known people won't read books or come to exhibitions about them. So then people never get to hear about them and nobody wants to exhibit their work. It's a vicious circle of neglect."

"Do you know that wonderful little picture of the head of a sheepdog, called 'Brisot', in the Wallace Collection?" Ruth asked. "It's by a French artist called Rosa Bonheur. I'd love to see an exhibition of some of her paintings."

"Yes, she was really outstanding with animals – just as good as Landseer. But I think nearly all her work must be in France. I've only seen reproductions in books. I read somewhere that she was so good she was made an Officer of the *Légion d'Honneur*, and Queen Victoria admired her work. I would also like to see an exhibition – maybe they'll have one in Paris and we could have a little expedition to see it."

They moved to a portrait of a young woman in a straw hat with long red hair tumbling down over her arms as she sat, a little stiffly, on a garden bench.

"Angelica Kauffmann is another painter whose work I'd like to see more of," said Rebecca. "I think she was quite prolific, probably because she had to paint to earn her living."

"That's always a strong incentive to be industrious. Daniel will be sorry to have missed this exhibition," Ruth went on. "I expect he's having a pretty boring time shuffling papers at Lancaster House. But at least he ought to be seeing the final result of his work over the past few months, if the Atlantic Council adopts the plans that he and his colleagues have been toiling over. He says it'll make him feel that he's completed at least one important job before he leaves the Army."

"Has he found a new job yet?"

"He's been talking to people at King's College, in their War Studies department, about a possible research project on the development of strategy in alliances. He says they seem very interested but they still have to find the funding."

"And what about your next book?" Rebecca asked, as they came to the end of the exhibition. "Have you started work on it yet?"

"I'm still doing the research. I've just joined the London Library, which I think is going to be a big help. I'm thinking about a story of love and politics set mainly in Germany, in 1848."

"Oh yes – the false dawn of democracy in Europe, and how it all went wrong? Something like that?" asked Rebecca.

"Yes, very like that," Ruth replied. "I thought I might have a young Englishwoman on a spa holiday in somewhere like Baden-Baden meeting an idealistic German student involved in the revolutionary movement and getting involved in his adventures. There would be plenty of opportunities for an exciting plot, but I'd need to get the period details right, of course."

"You could have a Caspar David Friedrich painting on the cover," said Rebecca, as they stepped out of the gallery into New Bond Street.

"That sounds like a very good idea, if the publishers don't mind paying the copyright holder. But I haven't even started the research yet."

Rebecca laughed. "Well, you'd better get a move on, then. I want to do another interview with you a year from now. By the way, have you had any luck with your flat-hunting yet?"

"Yes, we've found a place that we both think would be right for us. It's a bit grim on the outside but the flat itself is quite spacious and airy. It's in a five-storey block with a shop on the ground floor, in High Holborn, just a short distance from the Tube station at the intersection with Kingsway. The flat we want is on the second floor and there's an ancient lift with lots of gleaming brass-work that must be polished very diligently by the resident caretaker, who's a retired Free French sailor. He was very chatty and told us about the other residents. One of them is an Italian chef who works in a posh restaurant in Soho. I think it will suit us very well, especially if Daniel gets the job at King's, which is only a short walk away."

"You'd be very close to all the West End theatres, and also to Covent Garden market. If you got up early in the morning I expect you could buy some real bargains – fresh flowers and vegetables. And you'd be near to where I work. We have a good canteen – you could join me for lunch sometimes."

"I hope we'll be able to close the deal. It's a lease to rent for ten years. I think the agent was quite impressed by Daniel's rank. Shall we walk on down to Green Park? I'd like to see if the blossom is over yet. Some of the trees have been really good this year, especially in St James's Park."

When they had crossed over Piccadilly and gone into the Green Park Rebecca said, "Yesterday we heard the Royal Philharmonic performing Handel's *Solomon*. Roddy liked it, but I wasn't impressed. I saw it described by someone as 'Solomon the great lover rather than Solomon the wise ruler'; but it was the music that didn't do a great deal for me."

"That reminds me of something funny that happened on the day that the War began," said Ruth. "I probably remember it because it was in a context where everything else that was happening was far from being funny. It was actually the last job I did as a teacher. I had to escort three of the girls on the train to the place in Berkshire where our school had been evacuated. And I'd just said goodbye to Daniel, who'd been mobilized. He was in the Territorials.

"Anyhow, the train was held up en route to allow troop trains to go through, and the girls started singing to pass the time. They launched into a slightly ribald song – by the standards of the time – which they wouldn't have dared to voice if the Headmistress had been around. I think they might have been testing to see just how 'emancipated' I was. I can still remember the words.

King Solomon and David, they both led naughty lives,
Doing what they oughtn't to with other people's wives.
But when they got to feeling old they started having qualms,
So one wrote the Proverbs and the other wrote the Psalms."

"That's quite witty," said Rebecca, smiling. "But I can see that in those days making fun of the Bible, with a mention of sex for good measure, would not have been thought proper for young ladies. Did you allow yourself to laugh?"

"I think I did. There wasn't much else to laugh at on that particular day."

"Look – there are some late daffodils over there to the left, under the trees," said Rebecca. "I've just realized we're going to be passing opposite Lancaster House in a few minutes. What time do you think the NATO conference will end?"

Ruth laughed. "If you're thinking Daniel might suddenly be going to appear that's not likely to happen. I should think they'll go on talking for a few more hours. And he's told me that one of his jobs is to look carefully afterwards to make sure that nobody has left confidential papers lying about. I don't expect to see him until this evening."

When they drew level with the side entrance to the Lancaster House courtyard, where a solitary policeman stood gazing across the Park, Rebecca remarked, "It's a picturesque setting for an international conference. Do you think Daniel is going to miss meeting all these important people when he leaves the Army?"

"I suppose he might," Ruth replied. "But I hope he'll still meet a lot of interesting people if he gets the academic job."

"It's what makes life worth living, isn't it?" said Rebecca. "The people we meet – and the people we love."

"And the people who love us," Ruth added.

CHAPTER TWENTY ONE: 25th June, 1950 - ARTHUR

As they walked through the grandiose Jubilee Gates leading into Queen Mary's Gardens Arthur experienced an unexpected surge of happiness. Vera's tiny hand was clutching tightly to two of his fingers, and in front of him Dan was sitting contentedly in his pushchair, propelled by his mother. Margarita was wearing a new summer dress that she and Arthur had bought in Harvey Nichols last Saturday. He had gone shopping with her because he knew that on her own she wouldn't buy the dress she liked best if it cost more than something else that was available. The frugality she had learned in youth and maintained in wartime was hard to overcome.

The principal reason for his happiness was the memory evoked by walking through these gates towards the spot where, twelve years ago, a glimpse of Margarita's curves had made him decide that, although he had known her for little more than an hour, she was the woman he wanted to marry. He had, of course, told himself later it was ridiculous to choose a wife for the shape of her body, but very soon the sparkle of her personality had proved to be equally alluring, and he had never regretted his choice.

The sunshine and the scent of roses conspired with the laughter of his children to induce a feeling of utter contentment – an emotion he never experienced on a working day, even though he enjoyed his work in the House, in spite of the constant reminders, now, of how precarious his future there might be.

"Do you remember that day when we first met each other, right here in the Park?" he asked.

"I could never forget it," Margarita replied, her brown eyes sparkling as she turned her face towards him. "And if I hadn't been so desperately anxious to see a Shakespeare play at the Open Air Theatre you might never have asked me out."

"If you hadn't been so beautiful I might not have been interested in the play," he responded, surreptitiously patting her bottom.

"Look! There's Aunty Nancy and Leo," exclaimed Vera.

Arthur saw them approaching from the direction of the lake and guessed that they had, with Nancy's accustomed devotion to fresh air and exercise, walked all the way from home. As they came closer he saw that she had an anxious expression on her face.

"Have you heard the news? Isn't it terrible?" she asked as soon as they were within earshot.

"What news? We were so busy getting the children ready that we didn't switch on the wireless this morning," said Margarita.

"North Korea has invaded the South. It's a full-scale war."

Arthur found it difficult to believe what she was saying. "Are you sure?" he asked. "They're always having border incidents and uttering bellicose threats. Did the BBC say it was an actual invasion?"

"It said on the News that the North Koreans have actually declared war. And the Americans have called for a meeting of the UN Security Council; so they'll be wanting to drag everybody else into it," Nancy replied.

"You're talking about the Korean invasion?" said a voice behind him, and Arthur swung round to see that Daniel and Ruth had arrived.

"Yes, we hadn't listened to the News this morning, and Nancy's just told us about it," he said. "It's hard to believe they would mount a full-scale invasion without any kind of warning."

"I expect they thought it gives them their best chance of succeeding – and I should think it does," said Daniel. "The Americans pulled the last of their troops out of South Korea just about a year ago. My guess is the Communists think they'll be able to take over the country before anyone can get around to sending help to Syngman Rhee. And they've played the old trick of making their move at the weekend, when heads of government are away from their offices. But I hear the Americans have already asked for a meeting of the Security Council."

"Well, I hope the UN can prevent us from all getting involved in a war," said Nancy.

"I'm afraid we're already involved," said Daniel. "The war has started, and if we fulfil our obligations under the UN Charter we will be part of it until the aggressors have been driven out of South Korea. That's the primary function of the United Nations."

"No, it isn't," said Nancy. "Its primary function is to keep the peace. If it does that it mustn't get its members into a war."

"And how do you think the North Koreans are going to be persuaded to stop attacking the South?" asked Ruth.

"Maybe the Russians will persuade them to do that," Nancy replied. "I'm sure they don't want to have a war."

"Unless it's one that other people fight on their behalf," said Daniel. "All the guns and planes and bombs the North Koreans are using were given them by the Russians, and I'd be very surprised if they're being used without their permission – though it's possible that Stalin might not have been in on the exact timing of the attack."

"Why do you think that?" asked Roddy who, along with Rebecca, had just joined the group.

"Well, at this moment the Russians are boycotting the Security Council, over the issue of who occupies China's seat, and that means the Council might actually be able to make a clear decision about Korea. Otherwise the Russians would be able to veto any proposal that the UN should act to resist the North. So maybe there will be a chance to avoid the UN's built-in assumption that one member of the jury can also be a sponsor of the criminal on trial."

"I still think the UN's job is to stop the fighting," said Nancy. "If it goes on and the Americans get involved, and then the Russians, it could end up with atomic bombs being dropped, and it could even spread to Europe. I'm going to get our UNA branch to pass a resolution saying that the UN shouldn't get itself involved in any fighting – and Britain shouldn't either. If I thought there was any chance they'd publish it I'd write a letter to *The Times* as well."

"I'm pretty certain they would publish it if you signed it with your title, Nancy," said Daniel. "I can't see the Correspondence Editor spiking a letter signed 'Nancy, Dowager Viscountess Newingham', whatever its content might be."

"Do you really think so, Daniel? I never use the title of course, but maybe just this once I'll give it a try."

"The children are getting restless," said Margarita. "Shall we have a walk before lunch, like we agreed? If we go through the Rose Garden we could cross over to the Broad Walk and go underneath those wonderful elm trees."

"If it's not too far for the children we could go to that funny old drinking fountain, the one erected by the Parsee gentleman to show his gratitude for the protection the British gave to his fellow-Parsees in India," said Rebecca. "I think we could turn off there and come back to the Inner Circle and along to the restaurant."

"Let's do that," said Nancy; and they set off in a little straggling procession.

Arthur fell into step beside Daniel. "I'm surprised that you told Nancy how to get her letter published in *The Times*," he said. "What she's going to say in it will be the direct opposite of what you believe is right – as you well know."

"I do know that," Daniel replied, "but if we have to fight in Korea – and I'm pretty sure we will have to fight – we'll be fighting, ultimately, for Nancy's right to live in a country where she's able to have her opinion heard. Nancy may not want to believe that, but it's the truth; and that's why I felt the urge to help her. But I really hope there isn't going to be a surge of 'Don't get involved in Korea' sentiment in this country. If the UN doesn't act effectively now it might as well pack up and go home. What do you think? Will Attlee back the Americans?"

"I'm certain that he will," Arthur replied. "Unfortunately Ernie Bevin is still in hospital, and he could have been relied on to rally the Party behind a strong response. Of course the usual suspects will be saying that it's bound to be all the fault of the Americans, and the peace-loving North Koreans have been provoked into defending themselves. There are times when I despair of some of my colleagues – the ones who would like to be called 'comrades'."

Daniel nodded. "I don't envy Mr Attlee his job," he said.

"Arthur, do you think the West Indies are going to win this Test?" asked Roddy, who was walking behind them. "Did you get to Lord's yesterday?"

"Unfortunately I wasn't able to," he replied. "Apparently their batting wasn't all that impressive, but I think those two young bowlers, Ramadhin and Valentine, are capable of upsetting all the predictions. They're really good."

"We've got tickets for Wimbledon on Friday," said Rebecca. "Luckily we both have time off on the same day."

"I hope the weather will hold up for you," said Arthur.

As he closed the sitting-room door Arthur remarked, "I think Vera's getting to be a bit old for a seven-thirty bedtime. It took two Enid Blyton stories to get her off to sleep this evening."

"What about Dan?" Ruth asked.

"Oh, he goes to sleep as soon as his head touches the pillow. Long may it last."

"You must be glad that you'll be seeing more of them, now that Parliament has finished. You've had a lot of late nights there recently, haven't you?" said Rebecca.

"It's been a tough session, coping with the small majority," Arthur agreed. "That's one reason why we decided to have a celebratory dinner this evening, before we go off to Yorkshire at the end of the week."

"I read that the House was only being adjourned for this recess, instead of being prorogued until October. Does that mean you might be called back suddenly?" Ruth asked.

"It means that's a possibility. I think the PM decided he needed to keep the option open because of the situation in Korea. My guess is that it won't be necessary, because there was no serious opposition on Friday to his decision to send troops over there."

"I'm sure you'll all do better for having a rest," said Ruth. "It looks as if there'll be a lot of hard choices to be made when you come back in the Autumn."

"Seeing some cricket is what I'm mainly looking forward to," said Arthur. "I was sorry to have missed the Gentlemen and Players game at Lord's on Friday. Did you go?"

"No. I got involved with buying curtains for the new flat and it didn't seem worthwhile to go up later in the day. I see that Brown played a good innings; and they say he's going to captain the team in Australia this winter, even though he's nearly forty."

"Yes, I saw that. Batsmen seem to have advantage when it comes to age. If he'd been a fast bowler he'd have been played out by now."

"I hope you're not going to make Margarita a cricket widow, just when you've got some time now to be with her," said Rebecca, arching her eyebrows in mock severity.

"Don't worry: she's not going to let that happen," said Arthur, smiling. "Besides, the kids are still too young for cricket and I also want to be with them. I'll just be snatching a few hours now and again, provided the weather holds up. Tomorrow I'm taking Margarita to see Laurence Olivier in *Venus Observed*. Bill Coverdale's son, Wilfred, and his girlfriend are going to babysit for us."

"Last week we saw Danny Kaye in his new film, *The Inspector General*," said Rebecca. "It's very funny. But I don't like all the cigarette smoke you get in cinemas. It can spoil the evening's enjoyment if you have smokers just in front of you."

"What time do you expect Roddy to arrive?" Ruth asked.

"He should be here now. His shift ended about an hour ago."

"I thought Daniel would be here by now," said Ruth. "He doesn't usually have to work on Sundays, but of course today is different, with the Korean crisis going on. And he said he wanted to change out of his uniform before he came here."

"It won't be very long now before he's finished with the fancy dress," said Arthur. "I remember I couldn't wait to get out of my uniform in '45."

The doorbell rang. "I wonder which one that is," said Arthur as he stood up and made for the front door.

Roddy was the new arrival. He entered the room smiling broadly. "Arthur, just before I left the studio I was talking to one of our cricket chaps. He was in Sheffield yesterday and saw that brilliant innings Hutton played against the West Indies. I'm sure you would have enjoyed it."

"We were talking about cricket a few minutes ago," Arthur replied. "I hope I'll have a chance to see Yorkshire in action some time in the next fortnight, if they have any more home matches."

"You're going up to visit the family, then? Rebecca and I are planning a trip to Dublin at the end of August when, with any luck, the weather should be reasonable. She says she wants to see more of Ireland, in spite of all my efforts to discourage her," said Roddy.

The doorbell rang again, and this time it was Daniel. He was still in his uniform. "Sorry I hadn't time to change," he said as he came through the door, "but I didn't want to delay the dinner, and I'm sure Margarita has it timed to perfection, as usual."

"I take it you're having to get to grips with the implications of the Korean crisis at NATO," said Arthur, resuming his seat.

"Yes, we are; but from now on I'm not going to be involved in that." Daniel's expression was unusually serious as he moved across to where Ruth was sitting and stood beside her chair. She instantly had a sense of foreboding.

"I'm being sent to Japan, to do my old job of liaising with the Yanks," he continued.

Ruth tried to remain calm. "When will you have to leave?" she asked.

"On Tuesday. I'll be stopping off first in Washington and then flying on from there."

"Tuesday!" Rebecca exclaimed. "You'll scarcely have time to pack your kitbag."

Ruth was instantly overwhelmed by memories of standing outside Marylebone Station and waving goodbye to Daniel, wearing the uniform of a private in the Territorial Army, on the other side of the street. She found herself unable to speak, and reached out to touch Daniel's hand as he stood beside her.

"The situation's developing rapidly, and it isn't good," said Daniel. "There's no time to lose if we're going to be able to hold on to a chunk of South Korea to build up for a counter-offensive."

"But the Army could surely have found somebody else to do the job – like one of those military attachés who must at this moment be enjoying the high life in Washington," said Roddy. "You've done more than your share. A look at those ribbons on your chest could have told them that."

"We all did our share, in different ways. This is not about anybody's turn," Daniel replied. "It's about who's available with the right experience to do what needs to be done. I suppose I ought to feel privileged that they decided to pick me, though I have to confess it came as a nasty shock, just when I thought I'd finished my stint." Ruth felt his hand squeezing her shoulder.

"I admit my own first reaction was to think maybe it ought to be somebody else's turn," Daniel continued, "but then I realized that this is how it's always going to be if we want to make the world a safer place. Nobody else is going to do it for us. I've seen over the past few years that the big institutions the politicians talk so much about – like NATO and the UN – can't move forward a single inch without people like us being willing to move our feet on their behalf. So now I'm going to be part of something I never thought I'd live to see: a United Nations army fighting to protect a small country. I have to be glad I'm able to do that."

162

"And I have to be glad that you're willing to go, even though I don't want you to," said Ruth, looking up at his face and seeing the troubled look in his eyes. "It's not so long since we were saying that the best hope for peace would be a United Nations that really works," she went on. "Now that it *is* working we've got to do what we can to support it. I looked in at the UNA office on Friday and managed to persuade Audrey Davies to let me have a few minutes with Mr Judd. He showed me a stack of letters he's had about Korea. Quite a few of them were saying that the UN was supposed to be promoting peace and shouldn't get itself involved in a war; and several of the writers said they would resign from UNA if it didn't come out firmly against Britain sending troops to Korea. It made me wonder if they'd ever actually read the UN Charter."

"What's Mr Judd going to do about it?" Arthur enquired.

"He's strongly in support of the UN action and he's determined to rally UNA behind it. I volunteered to go in this week and help with a mailing he's planning to send out to the branches."

"I'm pleased to hear that," said Arthur. "If UNA doesn't back this stand against aggression it will very soon cease to have any purpose. Do you remember the split there was in the League of Nations Union when we were organizing the Peace Ballot? I remember you were involved in that, Ruth. You told me about it the first time we met, at that Left Book Club event in Notting Hill. The Ballot was supposed to demonstrate support for collective security but the LNU had to include a question that allowed pacifist-minded respondents to opt out of support for military action. That compromise totally confused the issue and made a lot of people – including Hitler – think it was a vote against resisting Nazi aggression. I'm glad Mr Judd is taking a firm line."

"Nancy won't agree with him, will she?" asked Rebecca.

"I'm afraid not," said Ruth. "She put her point of view very clearly in that letter she wrote to *The Times*. I think she feels very strongly that she must be faithful to the principles that she shared with Freddie."

"I wonder if young Leo will carry those principles forward into the next generation," said Rebecca.

"If he has inherited his father's determination not to be told what to believe by people who have authority over him he'll probably end up by joining the Parachute Regiment," said Ruth. "Nancy is so determined to bring him up as a perfect pacifist that I'm afraid she may overdo it."

"She was going to be here this evening but she rang up to say she wanted to go to Kingsway Hall to hear what Doctor Soper had to say in his sermon about the Korean crisis," said Arthur.

"I can understand her emotional reaction when you think about what must be happening to people out there," said Rebecca. "It isn't easy to move on to the next stage and think rationally about what needs to be done to achieve the least bad outcome for them. I remember once being so horrified by a story I heard back in '45, when I was helping to re-settle displaced people, that it took me a long time to come to terms with what I believed – politically, I mean."

"Was that something about the Nazi death camps?" Ruth asked.

"No; it was about the Russian advance into Germany. The story was told me by a young Polish lad – not Jewish – who'd been so shocked by what he'd seen that he needed to talk to somebody about it. The Nazis had sent him to East Prussia as a slave labourer to work in a factory, but the factory closed down for lack of raw materials and he was assigned to an elderly German couple to help on their farm. They were actually quite kind to him, and when the Russian Army was approaching he helped them to flee in a horse-drawn wagon, heading for Pillau, where they hoped to find a ship to take them to somewhere like Lübeck.

"As it happened, before very long they realized that the Russians had already passed through that stretch of country. The roads were all churned up and the fences were flattened. But the German farmer was an old soldier and guessed the Russians must be heading for the north of Königsberg, to surround it, and so he decided to press on. The area was completely deserted, but then they came to the outskirts of a village. Jan – that was the boy's name – said there was a large farm building at the side of the road and he climbed down from the wagon to see if there was anyone there. What he saw was four naked women nailed by their hands to the sides of cart. They were dead. And when he ran to the door of the house to look inside he saw it was full of dead bodies, women and children. He saw two babies with their heads smashed open. So he ran back and told the farmer to move on and get away from the place. They were lucky and they did eventually get to Pillau and find a ship that took them to Lübeck. But nine months later he was still having nightmares about what he'd seen."

"Did he get back to Poland?" Ruth asked.

"No, he didn't want to go back when he heard that the Russians had taken over there. Luckily we found out that an uncle he had who was in the Polish First Corps had been allowed to stay in Britain, and he was able to get permission to join him. We lost touch, but I hope Jan did eventually get rid of his nightmares."

"It makes you wonder what may be going on in Korea at this very moment," said Roddy.

Ruth glanced around the circle of solemn faces, all momentarily silent. Then, trying to sound light-hearted, she said to Daniel, "I hope this time you'll resist any temptation to volunteer for the front line, like you did at Monte Cassino."

"Don't worry," he replied, hugging her tightly around her shoulders. "I've been out of touch far too long for anyone to think of letting me get close to a gun. My job will be to help make sure that the lads are in the right place at the right time, with the right kind of back-up."

The door opened and Margarita came in, still wearing her apron. "The soup is on the table," she announced. "I hope I've timed it right so that we'll be ready to have our coffee in here at 9.15, when Mr Attlee is going to talk to us on the wireless."

They had just settled down with their coffee when Arthur turned the switch on the sleekly contoured Bakelite wireless set and a solemn voice introduced the Prime Minister.

I want to talk to you tonight about the world situation. I am sure that if I were to ask each of you to tell me what you most desired the preservation of peace would stand high on your list.

Mr Attlee's precise, emotionless voice put Ruth in mind of a headmaster addressing morning assembly. But she immediately engaged with what he was saying as he went on to talk about the shared memories of war and the post-war realization that the only way to ensure peace was to stop aggression in its early stages.

Between the wars aggression first started with an attack on China by Japan. It was not checked and aggression succeeded. That attack led to other acts of violence in other parts of the world, and eventually the Second World War started. That should have taught us the lesson that failure to take up a disagreeable but necessary duty only postpones the evil day and brings greater trouble upon us.

The evil forces now attacking South Korea were part of a world-wide conspiracy against the free democracies, he continued; but there were well-meaning people who were taken in by the sham peace propaganda of the Communists. It was tragic that resources now being devoted to raising standards of living in the less-developed parts of the world would now have to be diverted to strengthening our defences, but we had no option. In the United Nations the Russians had effectively frustrated every effort to achieve disarmament.

In solemn tones he warned: *This new effort will mean sacrifices. I ask all of you to do your part.* And as he went on to itemize the ways in which individuals could become involved Ruth looked up and saw the sadness in her husband's face.

The Prime Minister's tone changed and she could sense that he was moving into his peroration.

Finally I would ask you all to keep ever in mind the value of the things for which we stand – freedom, democracy, justice and the supremacy of the moral law. All over the world we are face to face with fanatics who believe in their creed. I think it is an evil creed, but there is no doubt that there are those who find it an inspiration, just as did the Nazis and Fascists in their creed. All of them deny the whole moral basis on which civilization has been built up.

Our fight is not only against physical but against spiritual forces. In Britain and the Commonwealth and in the democracies there are diverse creeds, but their adherents all believe in the supremacy of a moral law. Let us, then, arm ourselves against evil with an equal enthusiasm to preserve and protect the higher creeds in which we believe.

Arthur stood up and reached over to turn off the wireless. "Clem's style may not be Churchillian but his content certainly was," he remarked.

"If we didn't already know it we know now why we ought to be grateful to you, Daniel," said Rebecca.

Daniel smiled and looked at Ruth. "I think we ought to be making for home now," he said. "There's going to be a lot to do in the next forty-eight hours. When I get back – and I hope it won't be too many months before that happens – we'll invite you all to a celebration dinner at our new flat in Holborn. I really hope Nancy will want to come too, because we'll be celebrating preserving the peace – or at least as much of a peace as we're likely to see in our lifetime."

"I hope it won't be very long before we have that dinner," said Margarita. "In the meantime you can be sure we will do everything we can to help Ruth get the new flat ready for the celebration."

Ruth stood up and took her husband's hand. "I've just remembered something Daniel said to me, standing outside Marylebone

Station on the day that war was declared," she said. "He quoted those lines from *Hamlet*,

The time is out of joint – O cursed spite
That ever we were born to set it right!

It's still true, unfortunately. Maybe it always will be."

Turning his head to look into her eyes, Daniel said, "I hope for all our sakes that this is – to borrow the phrase that Churchill used after Alamein – not the beginning of the end but the end of the beginning."

The principal characters in **_Don't lose it again_** made their first
appearance in a novel entitled

Sleep quietly in your beds

(Available from www.lulu.com and www.amazon.co.uk
ISBN 978-0-9561569-1-4)

Following is an extract from the opening chapter:

"That young Methodist minister was terrific, wasn't he? Do you think he
was right when he said Europe is 'on the verge of a pacifist landslide'?"
Ruth asked her friend, Nancy, as together they walked downstairs from
the gallery of Westminster Central Hall in the midst of an elated throng of
young Peace Pledge Union members. The Armistice Night meeting had
been a rousing success and the speeches by the movement's famous
leaders, some of whom she'd never actually seen before, were still
reverberating in her head.

"He must have had some reason for thinking so. That German
Roman Catholic, Solzbacher, seemed to think a lot of people in his church
were coming round to the idea. Is that the first time you've heard Dr
Soper? He is terrific, isn't he?" Nancy replied.

"Yes, he is. I wish I could go with you to one of his meetings on
Tower Hill, but I'm always on duty at school on Wednesday lunchtimes.
You're lucky that your office is so close"

They had reached the foyer and were preparing to go out into the
November night when Ruth realized that her long, red woollen scarf was
no longer in the pocket of her mackintosh. "Oh, crikey! I must have
dropped my scarf. I'll have to fight my way back upstairs and see if I can
find it."

"What rotten luck. I hope the mob haven't trampled it under
foot," said Nancy. "I'll come and help you search for it."

They turned around and began to struggle upward against the
descending flow of bodies. At the first landing Ruth suddenly caught a
glimpse of the red scarf being waved above heads to attract her attention,
and a young man of about average height, wearing a grey trilby, edged his
way through the flow towards her. "I saw it fall out of your pocket but I
couldn't get to you because of all the people," he said, speaking with a
slight, unfamiliar accent. "I was sure you'd notice it had gone once you
got to the street."

"Thanks ever so much for taking the trouble," said Ruth, draping the scarf around her neck. "I'd really have missed it in this weather. It's a real life-saver in those awful fogs."

They began descending the stairs again, in company with Nancy, who had rewarded the young man with a broad smile when she joined them. By now the crowd was beginning to thin and they were able to walk three abreast.

"Did you enjoy the meeting?" Nancy asked the young man.

"Yes, there was a very positive atmosphere, wasn't there? I hope Dr Soper is right about the prospects for a 'pacifist landslide'. Mr Lansbury didn't sound so confident when he was appealing for 'a great crusade for a fresh outlook.'"

"Maybe he's been hearing about things that haven't got into the newspapers – Dr Soper, I mean," said Ruth.

They had reached the entrance again and the young man moved forward quickly to hold open the heavy swing door for them. "It's possible that he has," he said, as he rejoined them on the pavement. "I hear him speaking quite often, actually, because I go to his church – Kingsway Hall."

"I listen to him on Wednesdays when he speaks from the wall at Tower Hill," said Nancy. "I work in the City."

Ruth experienced an unaccountable irritation that her friend should have taken over the conversation. "Are you a Methodist, then?" she asked.

"Yes. It's how I was brought up. But Soper's not a typical Methodist. I think that's why I decided to attend Kingsway when I came to London."

She noticed that he was wearing his hat at an angle which might be described as 'jaunty', and that his eyes were blue and humorous. "Have you been here long?" she asked, still unable to place his slight accent.

"Only since September. I'm at the LSE, doing a master's degree. I've only just begun to settle in. Are you a Londoner?"

"No. I've been here about the same length of time. I've just started my first job, teaching German and French in a girls' school."

"I've been here a lot longer," said Nancy. "It must be more than two years now. Yes, I started my job in October '35. By the way, my name is Nancy – Nancy Barnett."

"And I'm Ruth Paynter."

The young man raised his hat with a gesture that could have been interpreted as ironic, Ruth thought; but maybe it was just straightforward good manners. "Delighted to make your acquaintance. I'm Daniel Hardstaff. In which direction are you going?"

"Shall we walk to St James's Park and take the Circle round to Notting Hill?" Nancy asked and Ruth assented.

"May I walk with you to the station? I'll get a bus from Victoria Street."

"Of course," said Nancy. "Shall we go round by Birdcage Walk? I know it's a longer way, but with the park on one side it's nicer than gloomy old Tothill Street."

"Lead on," said Daniel, and as they set off along Storey's Gate towards the corner of St James's Park Nancy moved round to his right side, leaving Ruth on his left.

"Are you a member of the PPU?" asked Ruth.

"No, I haven't joined up yet. I didn't really know much about it till I came over here, but I felt that I wanted to do something about the international situation and I heard Dr Soper talking about it."

"'Came over here'?" Nancy queried. "Where have you come from?"

"I'm from Northern Ireland, but I've spent the last three years at university in Dublin. Trinity College was my headmaster's old university and he persuaded me to go there. I enjoyed it, but it's a bit of a Shangri-La. When you're there the world beyond its walls hardly seems to exist. That's what I like about the LSE – it's right at the heart of what's happening."

"Dr Soper did his PhD at the LSE," said Nancy, "but it was something about Church history – Ultra-Montanism, I think he said."

Daniel laughed. "That must have been tricky. I'm pretty sure we don't have a theology department."

"Now I know why I couldn't place your accent," said Ruth. "I don't think I've ever met anyone from Northern Ireland before. I thought it might be Scottish or maybe Canadian."

"I've found that people often do have difficulty in identifying it," he replied. "I suppose it's been worn away a bit with living for three years in a foreign country. What part of England do you come from?"

"I grew up on the western edge of Surrey, near Farnham," Ruth replied, "but I've spent the last three years at Oxford – Somerville

170

College. I've tried not to let it affect the way I talk, but I'm not sure if I've succeeded."

"My father wouldn't let me go to university. He said it was a waste of money for girls," said Nancy, with a hint of bitterness in her voice. "My brother's going next year, to Imperial College, he hopes. He wants to join the University Air Corps – of all the stupid ideas. All I got was secretarial college. My family live near Sudbury, in Suffolk – a real dead end if ever there was one."

"I happened by accident to see the opening of the new London University senate house building yesterday," said Daniel. "I'd been in the Reading Room at the British Museum and afterwards I had a snack in a little café near Russell Square station. When I'd finished I walked across the square and saw all the crowds and policemen everywhere, and the tower was floodlit. It was like a New York skyscraper dropped into the middle of London. And then the King and Queen arrived."

"I read that they gave the Queen a degree," said Nancy.

"Well, she's a clever woman, I'm sure," said Daniel. "Though it may not be the kind of cleverness that gets you into university."

As they turned left into Birdcage Walk, which was totally empty of traffic and had only one pedestrian in sight, the subdued lamplight glowing against the shadowy arboreal outlines of the park gave Ruth a feeling of tranquillity. "Shall we cross over to the park side," she said. "It's so peaceful there."

"Did you see that the Cenotaph service today was going to be put on television?" asked Nancy. "I wonder if it worked out all right. I don't know anyone who has a television receiver. Do you?"

"I don't move in those circles," Daniel replied. "I wonder how much it costs per viewer to make a programme like that – just so that a few rich people can peer at it through a tiny little window in a box."

"But it is remarkable when you think about it – living images being transmitted through the air for miles and miles. After all, it's only a year since the BBC started doing it," said Ruth. "Before long it's bound to get better, and cheaper, like the wireless has. Did you know they're actually showing a whole play tonight – *Journey's End*, the one about the Great War?"

"I'd like to have seen that. I've heard it's the best play that's ever been written about the war," said Daniel.

Other novels by Derek Walker

(distribution at www.lulu.com and www.amazon.co.uk)

SENSE AND SENSUALITY

When Fatima, an asylum-seeker from Kazakhstan, meets Duncan Crauford she asks him to give her a bird's eye view of the history of Western civilization, to help her become British. Their quest takes them to the British Museum, the National Gallery and other sources of 'visual aids' in London. Meanwhile, Duncan, who is secretary-general of an international think-tank, is working with Paula, a Ugandan academic, on an analysis of the UN's failure to prevent genocide in Darfur. And his erotic friendship with Helen, a sensual university lecturer, is continuing even though she has decided to look for a husband, and thinks he isn't husband material. Her rejection makes him realize that he, too, is urgently in need of someone to share his bed; but he wonders what kind of woman could possibly be interested in a battle-scarred veteran like himself.

FOND DELUSIONS

In his final year at grammar school in Northern Ireland David Hunter's ambition is to work for peace in a world where the hydrogen bomb has just been invented. He wins a scholarship to the London School of Economics, and falls in love with a beautiful classmate. But when his love affair fails he joins the Foreign Legion, and takes part in the invasion of Suez. Returning injured to London he has an unexpected encounter that gives him new hope and a better understanding of the past.

MISRULE BRITANNIA

A journalist sent to cover a civil war in a former colony is plunged into the conflicts and corruption of an underdeveloped country. While the war escalates he falls in love with the woman of mixed race assigned to be his photographer. And when he gets close to the charismatic rebel leader he sees how personality can influence politics. The story sounds familiar, but the ex-colony is Britain and the journalist is Japanese – in an 'alternative history' scenario where eastern Asia takes on the historical role of western Europe. Looking at a world stage on which the actors have changed costumes may give the reader a new perspective on real events in recent decades. The pains and pleasures of the individual characters, however, could happen at any time, in any place.

A CASUAL CONQUEST

A young man from Japan starts his first job with the Honourable West Europa Company in Antwerp – in an 'alternative history' scenario in which Eighteenth Century Europe is reminiscent of South Asia in the dying years of the Mughal Empire. Before long he is listening to the Mozart Minstrels and is seduced by the Duchess of Holstein (who in 'real time' would have been Catherine the Great). Visiting Britain he sees a new altarpiece painted by Gainsborough and helps a young nun to escape to Antwerp. His bosses debate whether a trading company should take responsibility for governing failed states, and send him to observe a war between ambitious local rulers. He meets a famous native philosopher, and wonders if the British girl he left behind in Antwerp will welcome his return.

FAKING NEWS

When a minor news item on Radio 4 prompts Adam Turnbull to phone a friend he unwittingly takes the first step towards involvement in an international crisis. The action takes place a few years into the future, but underlying trends in politics and the media show few signs of change. Adam, an academic specialist in Balkan Studies, is sucked into ethnic cleansing, kidnapping and diplomatic deception, and he witnesses ways in which political, religious and NGO groups manipulate the media and are manipulated by them. His unwitting involvement in public events also brings him into intimate contact with two attractive women.